The Return of Simple

ALSO BY LANGSTON HUGHES

The Weary Blues
Not Without Laughter
The Ways of White Folks
The Big Sea
Simple Speaks His Mind
Laughing to Keep from Crying
Simple Takes a Wife
I Wonder as I Wander
Simple Stakes a Claim
Tambourines to Glory
The Best of Simple
Something in Common and Other Stories
Simple's Uncle Sam

Langston Hughes

The Return of Simple

Edited by AKIBA SULLIVAN HARPER

Introduction by ARNOLD RAMPERSAD

HILL AND WANG
A division of Farrar, Straus and Giroux
New York

Printed in the United States of America

FIRST PAPERBACK EDITION, 1995

Third printing, 2000

LIBRARY OF CONGRESS CATALOGING-IN-PUBLICATION DATA
Hughes, Langston, 1902–1967.
The return of Simple / by Langston Hughes; edited by Akiba
Sullivan Harper; introduction by Arnold Rampersad.—1st ed.
p. cm.
1. Simple (Fictitious character)—Fiction. 2. Afro-American men—
Fiction. 3. Afro-Americans—Fiction. I. Harper, Donna Sullivan.
II. Title.
PS3515.U274A6 1994 813'.52—dc20 93-45373 CIP

ISBN 0-8090-1582-X

FOR THE MEMORY OF

Richard Barksdale

and

Griffith J. Davis

A.S.H.

Acknowledgments

THE idea for this new collection originated with Arthur W. Wang, who had worked with Langston Hughes to publish both *The Best of Simple* and *Simple's Uncle Sam*. My involvement with the project resulted from the hearty recommendations of Arnold Rampersad. To them both I owe my deepest gratitude.

To obtain previously uncollected Simple stories for this volume, the editor gratefully acknowledges the helpful and efficient staff at the Beinecke, a special-collections library at Yale University. In 1941, Carl Van Vechten persuaded Langston Hughes to donate most of his correspondence and manuscripts to the James Weldon Johnson Collection, which Van Vechten had founded. This rich repository contains four card catalogue drawers devoted to Langston Hughes's manuscripts. What's more, each card can represent an incredible volume of material. For example, card no. 788 covers "NEWSPAPER COLUMNS: CHICAGO DEFENDER, 1942–1966" and represents thirteen boxes of manuscripts arranged chronologically by publication date. Apart from the card catalogues, a separate three-ring binder lists correspondence to and from Langston Hughes. Therefore, I needed to ask for box after box of material at the Beinecke. Fortunately, the staff are delightfully efficient in providing assistance.

Other copies of Simple stories came from the Schomburg Center for Research in Black Culture (New York City), the Atlanta University Library microfilms (including the Columbia University microfilms borrowed through interlibrary loan care of Atlanta University), and the University of Georgia microfilms. While my visits there were briefer, the staff members proved equally patient with my endless questions and with my technical difficulties in operating microfilm readers. To these staff members, many thanks.

For contributing the title of this volume, I thank Spelman College biology major Latasha Burgess. For volunteering her assistance in helping to prepare the final draft, I thank Spelman College English major Jennifer McZier. My colleagues and my students at Spelman College have offered support and enthusiasm for this project and have made my life generally richer and more pleasant. For their contributions, I am grateful.

All gifts and talents come from God, to Whom I give the glory for this work.

Editor's Preface

For *The Return of Simple*, I have grouped the stories into four sections, three of which are thematically linked: (1) women; (2) race, riots, police, prices, and politics (which Simple connects nicely); and (3) Africa and black pride. The fourth section is a bit eclectic, but I call it "Parting Lines" because several of the episodes have memorable final lines and because it includes the last Simple story, "Hail and Farewell," after which Simple truly departs.

The chronology of Simple's life is preserved within each section, and characters are introduced logically. However, as the reader moves from Part One to Part Two, the reader reenters the past. Simple starts off "courting" Joyce in each section and ends up married to her. Since we are capturing some of Simple's most memorable moments, we naturally must include some before and others after his marriage to Joyce.

Readers who know the five published volumes will be surprised by the previously uncollected episodes, which are sprinkled throughout the four sections. We find that Simple becomes a bit more raunchy than usual; Joyce is marvelously Pan-African; and Simple expresses concern for animal rights.

Readers who know Simple only through *The Best of Simple* will find this volume a revelation. The section on women reveals a level of sensitivity no one might ever have linked with Jesse B. Semple. Part Two involves a thought-provoking and surprisingly present-day interpretation of the rights and responses of oppressed people. Part Three reveals that Simple definitely links his racial pride to Africa. Part Four, once tentatively entitled "Jesse B. Kind," shares with the reader some remarkable moments, including Simple's "Hail and Farewell" to Harlem.

This volume includes some stories published previously in the earlier collections *Simple Speaks His Mind* (1950), *Simple Takes a Wife* (1953), *Simple Stakes a Claim* (1957), or *Simple's Uncle Sam* (1965)—but *not* in *The Best of Simple* (1961). Other stories in *The Return of Simple* first appeared in the weekly columns that Langston Hughes wrote for the *Chicago Defender* or the *New York Post*—some of which were syndicated and appeared in the *Pittsburgh Courier*, the *Norfolk Journal and Guide*, or *Muhammad Speaks*. Langston Hughes typically revised his newspaper columns for publication in a book-length collection. Thus, whenever I could find the revised versions in the manuscript collection at Yale University's James Weldon Johnson Collection, I used them. Otherwise, when no revised manuscripts could be found, I included the stories as they appeared in the newspaper columns. For the sake of consistency, with the early (1940s) unrevised newspaper episodes, I edited the terminology to bring those stories into line with the established "Simple" standards. These changes are not noted within the text, so that the reader may enjoy the episodes without being troubled by footnotes, brackets, and "[*sic*]'s." "Sources of Stories" at the end of the book will reveal the source of each episode.

Contents

Introduction xv

PART ONE: WOMEN IN SIMPLE'S LIFE
Remembrances 3
Wigs, Women, and Falsies 7
On Women Who Drink You Up 9
Better than a Pillow 11
Explain That to Me 17
Baltimore Womens 22
Less than a Damn 27
Never No More 31
Simply Heavenly 34
Staggering Figures 38
The Moon 40
Domesticated 42
Hairdos 44
Cousin Minnie Wins 47
Self-protection 51
Ladyhood 53
Lynn Clarisse 57
Riddles 60

PART TWO: RACE, RIOTS, POLICE, PRICES, AND POLITICS
Ways and Means 67
The Law 72
American Dilemma 74
Color of the Law 76
After Hours 78
When a Man Sees Red 83
Simple and the High Prices 86

Nickel for the Phone 88
Possum, Race, and Face 91
Everybody's Difference 98
Coffee Break 102
Intermarriage 104
Joyce Objects 106
Liberals Need a Mascot 110
Serious Talk about the Atom Bomb 112
Adventure 115
Brainwashed 117
Wigs for Freedom 119
Help, Mayor, Help! 124
Soul Food 127
Little Klanny 134
Simple's Psychosis 137

PART THREE: AFRICA AND BLACK PRIDE
The Necessaries 143
That Word *Black* 146
Colleges and Color 148
Whiter than Snow 151
Big Round World 155
Roots and Trees 159
Pictures 163
Simple Arithmetic 166
Africa's Daughters 168
African Names 170
Harems and Robes 172

PART FOUR: PARTING LINES
Nothing but Roomers 179
Simple Santa 184
Empty Houses 188
God's Other Side 192
Dog Days 195
Weight in Gold 198
Sympathy 201

Money and Mice 204
Population Explosion 208
Youthhood 210
Hail and Farewell 212

Sources of Stories 217

Introduction

On February 13, 1943, in the black-owned *Chicago Defender* newspaper, Langston Hughes introduced to the readers of his weekly column there one of the most memorable and winning characters in the annals of American literature—Jesse B. Semple, or Simple. Today, some fifty years later, Simple is still alive, still justly regarded as one of the most inspired creations in the rich writing career of Langston Hughes. This inspired new culling of material from the Simple archive by Akiba Sullivan Harper shows again why Hughes devoted so much of his creative energy to the development of Simple and his world, and why so many black Americans, and many whites as well, responded as enthusiastically as they did to his extraordinary saga as it unfolded over more than a generation of Hughes's newspaper writing.

In 1943, when Hughes introduced Simple to his readers, his career was at a crucial juncture. Born in 1902 in Joplin, Missouri, Hughes had grown up in Lawrence, Kansas, lived for a year in Lincoln, Illinois, then attended high school in Cleveland, Ohio. In the 1920s, he made his mark as a major star of the Harlem Renaissance with two volumes of verse and a novel that delved into African-American culture, most notably the blues. In the 1930s, and mainly in response to the Depression, Hughes turned radically to the left. He spent a year (1932–33) in the Soviet Union. Although in the 1930s he wrote several plays that betray no left-wing ideological bias, his poems sang most frequently of revolution and asserted Hughes's sense of himself as a radical artist (although he never joined the Communist Party). Around 1939, however, he began to be disillusioned by important aspects of Communism. With the entry of the United States into World War II, he turned back resolutely as a writer to earlier themes and forms, back—as he once put it—"to Negroes, nature, and love." His agreement in 1942 to write a column, "From Here to Yonder," for the *Defender* was a part of Hughes's political and cultural realignment. The creation of Simple in 1943 made this realignment complete.

Long before his death in 1967, Hughes came to be seen as the most representative of African-American writers and almost certainly the most original of black American poets. However, despite his successes in poetry, fiction, drama, and other fields, for many people the most inspired single creation in his considerable body of work was Jesse B. Semple. Not until 1965, when Simple's saga was being carried not only in the *Defender* but also in Hughes's column in the white-owned *New York Post*, did Hughes finally lay to rest his deceptively limited black Everyman—not in death but in a retirement that took Simple out of Harlem and into the suburbs, as seemed appropriate to a forward-looking African American in the dawn of the age of racial integration.

By Hughes's own admission, Simple came into the world casually, without any inkling that he would take hold of his readers, and his author, as compellingly as he did. As Hughes asserted, his main purpose in creating Simple was as a device to encourage African Americans to support the Allied cause during World War II. To the typical readers of the *Chicago Defender*, the arguments for supporting the national effort were by no means irresistible. Racism was still a raw fact of American life. Segregation, brutally enforced, still gripped the South and most of the North; the armed services themselves were segregated, and only a special Presidential order by Roosevelt opened defense jobs to blacks. Many blacks who understood the evil of Hitler's and Mussolini's regimes found it difficult, nevertheless, to see how their own lives in America could be much worse under Fascism. In addition, many blacks found it hard, in a land ruled by the law of white supremacy, to side with its government against the Japanese, the one colored nation that dared in modern times to lift its hand against the imperial rule of whites. The fact that the Japanese, too, were imperialistic meant little to many black Americans.

As a radical socialist in 1939, when the war started, Hughes himself had not rushed to sympathize with Great Britain in its confrontation of Nazi Germany. Only after the Nazi invasion of the Soviet Union in 1940 did Hughes and other radical socialists begin to call for a united front against Hitler and Mussolini. The Japanese attack on Pearl Harbor in December 1941 consolidated Hughes's support for the national effort. Moreover, as a traveler in Japan in 1933, he had encountered firsthand the militaristic and repressive nature of the Japanese authorities. He became an enthusiastic worker for the Allied cause. To propagandize the readers of the *Defender* about the need for unity in the face of an enemy worse than segregation, he hit upon the idea of Jesse B. Semple, or Simple.

Hughes later declared that the idea came to him early in 1943, after a man he knew mainly by sight in one of his favorite Harlem bars, Patsy's Bar and Grill, invited Langston to join him and his girl friend at a table in the rear of the establishment. What did the man do, Hughes asked. He helped to make cranks in a defense factory. What kind of cranks? Incredibly, the man didn't know. How could he not know what his cranks cranked, his girl friend inquired testily. The man became defensive. White folks, he protested, never tell black folks such things, and he knew better than to ask. "I don't crank with those cranks," he declared finally. "I just make 'em." "You sound," his girl friend responded, as Hughes listened, "right simple."

Perhaps this incident occurred; perhaps it never took place, and Hughes playfully made it up. Nevertheless, in it may be found the kernel of the Simple stories. The setting is a Harlem bar—although eventually that setting would give way to many other places in Harlem. The core relationship, captured in dialogue, is between Simple and a far more educated, poised, and yet conventional interlocutor, the writer of the column. At first this writer was clearly Langston Hughes, but gradually he became someone else, who nevertheless remained essentially defined by his difference from Simple, by his reticence, stiltedness, and apparent loneliness despite his "higher" station in life compared to that of Simple.

Almost as important is the relationship between the maker of cranks and his spunky girl friend, which anticipates Simple's own complex interaction with the various women in his life—his wife, from whom he is separated; his regular and highly respectable girl friend, Joyce, who hopes and expects to be his wife; his other woman friend, Zarita, far less respectable and far less inhibited than Joyce, whom he will never marry but to whom he is hopelessly drawn; and Simple's truculent landlady, who insists on referring to him mainly by the room he occupies in her house—"Third Floor Rear."

Significant, too, are the character and the language of the maker of cranks as they anticipate Simple's character and language. Both men are simple and yet complex. They are simple in their lack of education and the narrow boundaries of their vocabulary, as well as in their desires, which are for little more—at least, on the surface—than the basic comforts of women, beer, and a decent job paying a decent wage. Both men are aware of what they do not have in terms of education and money, and both men know why, essentially, they are deprived. They see the walls of racism and segregation clearly but have made peace with life on the dark side of those walls. However, their lives are not stamped with an uninflected stoicism or fatalism, a total acceptance of the force of racism. They have a philosophy and a language to match the repressive world in which they live, and they have a potent weapon as well. That weapon is humor, a native wit that from a conventional point of view seems twisted and yet also strengthened by that twisting, in a necessary response to the morally twisted world in which racism forces blacks to live.

Started as a wartime propagandistic device, which is clear in the first newspaper sketch and in several later columns, the saga of Simple proved instantly popular. Not only was Simple funny in his dealings with his women and other folks in the black community in which he lived, he also expressed defiantly and yet often comically his disgust at the white world (except for the saintly Mrs. Eleanor Roosevelt, whom he reveres). In so doing, he also expressed the disgust of the typical black readers of the *Chicago Defender* for the powers that barred them on virtually every side. Simple became by far the most creative and effective aspect of Hughes's weekly columns. Over the years, he appeared in about one-quarter of those columns.

Langston Hughes liked to pretend that there was no art involved in creating Simple—as if the notion of art was incompatible with the plain verities of Jesse B. Semple. Simple "simply started talking to me one day about the war, Hitler, the draft, Shakespeare, and getting up early in the morning, so I put down on paper exactly what he said." Nothing could be further from the truth. Hughes had devoted his life to creating a body of literary art that would reflect the realities of African-American culture and in the process also pay tribute to that culture for its humanity, dignity, creativity, and transcendence of the bitter conditions in which it was forced to exist. All of Hughes's life experiences as a black American, all his intimate knowledge of how blacks lived, and all his love of African Americans went into the Simple saga.

The deepest effects of the sketches were probably sounded in the relationship between Simple and the narrator. To the narrator's pale "standard" English and colorless logic, Simple responds in language garnished with both country folk tropes and the latest hip Harlem expressions. Behind Simple's amusing, vibrant front, one often glimpses the loneliness of the uprooted and the dispossessed. But although Simple sometimes edges toward despair, he is always saved in the end by his passion for life, laughter, and language. This conquest of loneliness and the dehumanization of racism is only frugally shared by the narrator. That man—Langston Hughes, "Boyd," or someone who is nameless in many instances—is informed, objective, but increasingly desolate. Unlike Simple, he appears to be bereft of family and friends. In an elemental way, he needs Simple, as black Americans need Simple, his defiance, vitality, and laughter.

Both the narrator and Simple are assuredly Langston Hughes, who once called Simple "really very simple. It is just myself talking to me. Or else me talking to myself. That has been going on for a number of years and, in my writing, has taken one form or another from poetry to prose, song lyrics to radio, newspaper columns to books." Simple and his narrator form a kind of colloquium of Hughes's conflicts of belief, as well as his deeper fears and desires. The uninspired narrator is Langston Hughes without love, laughter, and poetry—the man he might have been if he had not made his historic commitment to the life of the artist in service to black America. Simple personifies the saving graces of black America, the genius of black folk for self-redemption in the face of adversity.

Seven years after his "birth" in 1943 in the *Defender*, and after a difficult, failing effort by Hughes to gain the interest of publishers, who were afraid that white readers might not "get" Simple, or that they would reject any collection of Simple sketches as "a [political] tract," as one editor put it, Simon & Schuster published Hughes's *Simple Speaks His Mind* (1950). This book represented not a mere gathering of sketches but an extensive editing by Hughes of these pieces (guided by Maria Leiper, Hughes's editor at Simon & Schuster) to form a unified, consistent, and yet representatively diverse portrait of Simple in his Harlem setting. Leiper pressed Hughes, for example, to do more with the women in Simple's life, an idea to which Langston responded warmly. His labors paid off. *Simple Speaks His Mind* was perhaps the most enthusiastically received of all the books Hughes published to that time, in terms of both sales and the evaluation of reviewers. Hughes was able to tell his *Defender* readers that Simple, "this gentleman of color, who can't get a cup of coffee in a public place in the towns and cities where most of our American book reviewers live (unless it is a 'colored' place), is, nevertheless, being most warmly received by white critics from Texas to Maine."

Many reviewers echoed the words of Hughes's old friend Carl Van Vechten, who reviewed the book for *The New York Times*, that it was "better than a dozen vast and weighty and piously pompous studies in race relations." Writers also saw the connection between the creation of Simple and a grand tradition of humor in American writing, of which Hughes, who admired Mark Twain's work, was well aware. In particular, reference was often made to Finley Peter Dunne's classic Mr. Dooley, but links were also seen to nineteenth-century figures such as Artemus Ward, Petroleum V. Nasby, and Josh Billings. All of these writers and characters had in common a will to comment on the American scene, with its volatile mixture of ideals and corruptions, successes and tragedies, in terms of humor that was no less amusing for being so often caustic, and no less incisive for being amusing. All drew for their most powerful effects on the living, breathing American language as represented by one version or another of the American family of dialects. The American language had reached its most significant literary achievement in *The Adventures of Huckleberry Finn*, the book that revolutionized American writing by rendering the American experience, with its tragedy and comedy, lyricism and savagery, in the uneducated speech of a country boy. Simple, too, was a country boy at heart, pining for the Virginia woods and streams of his youth but aware that this simple life was lost forever to him and to America. He was proud of his origins and of his language, proud to be his African-American self speaking the truth as he saw it in the words he thought best.

Simple Speaks His Mind sold well but was not a bestseller, as such a book is defined by the publishing industry. Nevertheless, Hughes was able to publish four more volumes of Simple sketches: *Simple Takes a Wife* (1953), *Simple Stakes a Claim* (1957), *The Best of Simple* (1961), and *Simple's Uncle Sam* (1965). Through the newspaper sketches and these books, he reached thousands of readers, especially African-American readers, who had only a passing acquaintanceship with his poems, plays, and other work. In addition, his musical play *Simply Heavenly*, based on *Simple Takes a Wife*, was a hit, one modest but sustained, from its first off-Broadway production in 1957. To the end of his life, Hughes remained proud of his creation.

Now, with the appearance of *The Return of Simple,* readers have a fresh opportunity to appreciate the genius of Langston Hughes and the warmth and wisdom of Jesse B. Semple—Simple.

ARNOLD RAMPERSAD
PRINCETON UNIVERSITY

Part One
WOMEN IN SIMPLE'S LIFE

Remembrances

"THE first time I was in love," said Simple, "I was in love stone-dead-bad—because I had it, and it had me, and it was the most! Love! When I look back on it now, that girl couldn't have been good-looking. When I look back on it now, she couldn't have been straight. And when I look back on it now, I must have been simple—which I were. But then I did not know what I know today. At that time I had not been beat, betrayed, misled, and bled by womens. I thought then, if I just had that girl for mine and she had me for hers, heaven on earth would be."

"Why do you choose to recall all that tonight in this bar?" I asked.

"Because I am thinking on my youthhood," said Simple.

"How old exactly are you?"

"I am going into my something-or-other year," said Simple. "To-night is nearly my birthday, and if you are my friend, you will buy me a drink."

"I have bought you so many drinks on nights which were not your birthday before! Anyhow, what'll it be—beer?"

"Same old thing," said Simple. "I do not want to go home to Joyce with whiskey on my breath. Gimme beer. Joyce is my wife, my life, my one and all, my first to last, and the last woman I intend to clasp! But sometimes I still think about that first little old girl I were really in love with down in Virginia when I were nothing but a boy. She were older than me, that girl, but only by a year. She were darker than me, too, if that be possible. And she were sweeter than a berry on the vine. My Aunt Lucy did not approve of her because her mama had been put out of church on account of sin. But I loved that girl! I'll tell the world I did!"

"I gather your romance came to naught," I said.

"Our romance came to naught, but she weights two hundred and ten pounds now, so I have heard, and has been married twice," said Simple. "But she were the first person except Aunt Lucy who made me feel like somebody wanted me in this world, relatives included. Everybody else was always telling me, 'I am your mother, but your father went off and left you on my hands!' Or else, 'I am your father, but your mother ain't no good!' Or, 'Your poor old aunt loves you, Jesse, but your papa nor mama ain't sent a dime here to feed you since last March.'

"But this girl ain't never said nothing like that. She just said, 'Jesse B., you was meant for me.'

"I said, 'Baby, let's get with it.' And we did, until the old folks broke it up.

"I had nothing, neither did she. So her mama said, 'Let my daughter be.'

"My Aunt Lucy allowed as how I were too young to be going steady, anyhow—that I must be getting too big for my britches, telling her I knew my own mind. About that time they sent me to stay with Uncle Tige out in the country, so I did not see Lorna Jean any more, until I were passing through Richmond on my way North, running away from where I ain't been back since. At which time, I were only interested in getting North. Now here I is this evening, tonight on my birthday eve, remembering a girl I have not seen in twenty-five years, but who were once my sputnik. I wonder do Lorna Jean ever think of me as I think of her, and do she have remembrances?

"Whilst I were living with Uncle Tige, I met another girl named Elroyce. I did not fall in love with her—just sort of liked her a little bit. She were fun to go around with. Once I took her to a dance, and when I took her home, her door were locked. In that day and time down in Virginia, nobody locked doors, there being no robbers then. But her mama had locked her door, lights out, house dark. It looked like nobody lived there, house empty, as if she did not have a daughter who had gone to a dance. It were embarrassing to that young girl to have to wake up them old folks to get in. Besides, it was not *that* late. That young girl's parents told her to be home at midnight. It were only just a little after one o'clock when we got there. That music was so good we forgot about time.

"It might maybe have been my fault we was late, because her mama told me I could take that girl out, but she said, 'Boy, you get my chile back home here by twelve o'clock. If you don't, it will be you and me!' The way things turned out, it were me and her. That old lady tried to ruin my life."

"The night of the dance?" I asked.

"No, not the night of the dance," said Simple; "nine months later."

"Oh!" I said.

"It were worse than 'oh,' " said Simple, "because I had not touched that girl. I were just a young teen-age boy myself. All I did was kiss Elroyce once or twice on the way home from that dance, from which we walked in the night in the springtime in the sweet and scented air. But the next week, I fell for another girl—you know how young folks is. Yet come that following fall, Elroyce's mama sent for me.

" 'Is you the father of her chile?'

" 'What child?'

" 'You see my daughter, don't you? Her chile.'

" 'No, ma'am.'

" 'Don't lie,' says Mama. 'Don't you lie to me about Elroyce!'

"I do not know why they always assumes the man is lying. It turned out that girl were secretly in love with me, so Elroyce told her mama I were the father of her child. Before God, I swear to this day I were not. It could not be. I had not touched her. But I left town. That is when I come North to Baltimore. It were not my offspring."

"Why bring up such unpleasant memories tonight?"

"Because her child would be twenty-five years old this year, and I wonder what he looks like."

"How do you know it was a boy?" I asked.

"It would have been a boy if I was its father," said Simple. "I would not know what to do with a girl—daughter—was I to have a girl—when she got teen-age. I would be afraid of springtime and dances and being out late for her, too, like that girl's parents was, if I was a father. But I would not never lock my door on no child of mine, no matter how late they come home. The *home* door, the door of home, should always be open always—else do not call it home. Rich folks' doors is locked. White folks' doors is locked. But the door to home should never be. If I had a child that stayed out all night and all day and the next day and all week, I would not lock my door against her—or him—be he boy or girl, I would not lock the door."

"Since you are not a parent, you are just theorizing," I said. "The hard realities of how to control teen-age children in this day and age baffle most people. I am sure they would baffle you."

"I baffles not easy," said Simple. "I remember how when I were in my teens, my folks did not so much lock their doors at night, but they locked their hearts. They did not try to understand me. Old folks in them days was a thousand miles and a thousand years away from their children, anyhow. I lived in the same house—but not *with* them, if you get what I mean. I do not believe, in this day and time, there is such a high wall between old and young. Do you think so?"

"Yes," I said, "I think there is—and always will be. Unfortunately, the gulf between the generations is a perennial one. Take rock and roll: the old folks hate it, the young folks love it."

"I must not be very old, then," said Simple. "I like rock and roll myself."

"Perhaps you are just retarded," I said.

"Which is better," said Simple, "than being discarded. I wish me and my wife had seven children."

"Why?" I said.

"So we could always keep an open door," said Simple.

Wigs, Women, and Falsies

"I WONDER why peoples, when they have their pictures taken, always take their face? Some womens," said Simple, "have much better-looking parts elsewhere."

"You can pose the doggonedest questions," I said.

"Another thing I would like to know is why people's eyebrows do not grow longer, like their hair?" asked Simple.

"I do not know," I answered.

"But, come to think of it," said Simple, "some people's hair on their heads don't grow no longer than their eyebrows. In fact, some women's hair won't hardly grow an inch. Yet most mens have to go to the barber shop every two or three weeks. It should be men's hair that won't grow, not the women's. Why is that?"

"I am not a student of human hair, man, so I cannot tell."

"I knowed a girl once who was too lazy to comb her head," said Simple, "so she bought herself a wig. But she was too lazy to comb that. She would just put it on her head like a hat, and go on down the street."

"You have certainly known some strange people," I said.

"I have, daddy-o, but I have never seen nothing worse than a wet wig," said Simple.

"A wet wig?" I asked. "Where on earth did you ever see a wet wig?"

"On the beach," said Simple. "I seed a girl lose her wig in the water out at Coney Island. That woman had no business diving under the waves when she were in swimming, but she did. And off come her wig, which started riding the waves its own self. That girl were so embarrassed that she would not come out of the water until a lifeguard rowed out in a boat and got her wig, which, by that time, were headed for the open sea. She slapped the wig on her head. But it were a sight, tangled up like a hurrah's nest, and dripping like a wet dishrag. I never did see that woman go in swimming no more. In fact, I never took her to the beach again."

"How did you ever happen to get mixed up with a woman with a wig?" I asked.

"There is no telling who a man might get mixed up with at times," said Simple, "because in them days I were young and simple myself. Besides, she did not call it a wig. She called it a 'transformation.' I do not know why they call wigs 'transformations,' because I have seen some womens put on a wig and they were not transformed at all. Now, what I would recommend to some womens is that they get wigs for their faces—which, in some cases, needs to be hidden more than their heads. Some womens is homely, Jack! So if they gonna transform themselves, they ought to start in front instead of in the back."

"Some do," I said, "with falsies."

"Don't mention falsies to me," said Simple. "It's getting so nobody can tell how a woman is shaped any more, because they takes their shapes off when they get home. All those New Forms and Maiden Bras and Foam Rubber Shillouettes! I think there ought to be a law!"

"That would be a bit drastic," I said. "Don't you believe women have the right to make themselves more attractive? A little artifice here and there—lipstick, rouge, transformations, and such."

"And such too much is what some of them does," said Simple. "A wigless woman without her lipstick, rouge, and falsies would be another person. Impersonating herself, that's what! If it is wrong for a Negro to pass for white, it ought also to be wrong for any woman to pass for what she is not. Am not I right?"

"Every woman wants to put her best face forward," I said, "especially when she's out in public. At home, that's another matter. And you don't go home with every woman you see."

"I might try if my jive works," said Simple.

"You'd let yourself in for some rude shocks," I said.

"A man takes a chance these days and times," said Simple. "But then, men was born to take chances."

On Women Who Drink You Up

"HELLO, stranger! Where have you been hiding?" I asked as Simple strolled into Paddy's Bar after a noticeable absence.

"I been busy resting," he said.

"In seclusion?" I asked.

"Naw," said Simple. "I just changed bars."

"What necessitated that change?" I asked.

"Because these women around here drink a man up," said Simple. "And after they have drunk you up, they will not act right."

"What do you mean by that?" I asked.

"You know what I mean," said Simple. "For instance, the other night I met an old girl in here, and she sat right there at that table and drunk six rum-colas—for which I paid. Also two beers for a friend of hers I had never seen before. Also a whiskey for a cousin who happened to pass by. You know, it being payday, I was free-hearted."

"Also high, I presume," I added.

"Not high," said Simple, "just feeling good. So when I walked that dame home, I said, 'Baby, lemme taste some lipstick.'

"She says, 'Oh, no! I do not kiss no strange men.'

"I said, 'What do you mean, *strange*—and I been knowing you since ten o'clock this evening?'

"She says, 'I knowed my husband six months before I kissed him.'

" 'Where is your husband now?' I said.

" 'In the army.'

" 'Do he come home often on furlough?' I inquired.

" 'He is in Texas,' she says, 'and that is too far.'

" 'Then lemme taste some lipstick,' I begged.

" 'I will not!' she hollers. 'How would you like it if you was in the army, and some wolf in sheep's clothing tried to lead your wife astray?'

" 'If my wife stayed out till three in the morning at a bar,' I says, 'I would think she wanted to be let astray. Also if she drunk six rum-colas, then asked for a zombie, I would know she wanted to be let astray.'

" 'You did not buy me the zombie,' she says.

" 'What is your name?' I asked her very quiet.

" 'Zarita,' she chirped. 'Why?'

" 'Because,' I said, 'if I ever hear anybody say "Zarita" again, I will run the other way—and I will not look back.'

" 'It do not matter to me,' she says, 'because I will be missing nothing.'

" 'You will never know what you missed, baby, till you miss me,' I said.

" 'If you are referring to them few drinks you bought,' she says, 'I thought you was just being a gentleman.'

" 'I was,' I said, 'but now I am being a man.'

" 'Excuse me,' she said. 'I do not like to be seen standing on the stoop talking to a strange man. Besides, it is chilly this evening.' And she went in and shut the door."

"I see! She left you standing in the cold," I said. "So you never did get to taste that lipstick?"

"I do not care nothing about that old broad," said Simple. "Nor any other old broad that drinks a man up that way."

"So that is why you changed bars?" I said. "Don't you realize there are women like that in every bar?"

"I do now," said Simple. "And I may buy one more drink for Zarita—but that is all."

"Leading army wives astray," I said, "is bad for morale."

"I reckon I am weak that way," said Simple. "Besides, if a woman wants to stray, I am here to help her. Look! Yonder comes Zarita now. Boy, lend me a couple of bucks till payday. You know, I'm kinder short."

"I thought you said you had turned away from women who drink a man dry. Haven't you learned your lesson yet?"

"I did not ask you for no sermon," said Simple. "I asked you for two bucks. It is a poor fool who cannot change his own mind . . . Take it easy, pal! . . . Good evening, Zarita!"

Better than a Pillow

"YOU remember I told you once about that fellow who roomed next to me in Baltimore?" Simple began to reminisce one evening.

"Jog my memory," I requested.

"He died," said Simple, "all alone, with nobody to claim his body, nobody to come and cry."

"His death made quite an impression on you, I presume."

"You presume right. After that man's dying I got to thinking about myself—suppose I was to die upstairs all alone *by myself* in a lonesome room! Man, I hustled up quick on a stick-close gal before the year was out. I had had three or four on-again-off-agains and plenty of fly-by-nights since I'd arrived in Baltimore City. But before I got married, this was the first woman I ever stayed with regular, the one I'm gonna tell you about. I lived with her so long she started to calling herself Mrs. Semple."

"You never told me about her," I said.

"I know I didn't. There are some things I have not told God—He has to find out for Himself. I am somewhatly ashamed, even now."

"I am not God, so I won't pass judgment," I said.

"Well, I will tell you. She was the first woman I ever went with steady. Also she was the first woman for which I ever kept a job. Yet and still, I did not love that woman, I don't believe. There was always other womens I had my eyes on, younger and sharper, like Marvalene, or that fly baby-faced chick named Cherie. And I did not have to give that woman I lived with my money. She did not ask for it—so I spent it on other womens. But I always went back to her. That woman was home to me.

"Now, that's funny, ain't it? I did not give her my money, yet for her sake I kept a job, respectable. Up to that time I had quit and rested any time I wanted to. She settled me down, in fact, almost got me housebroke. She were a good influence in my life. I wasn't but nineteen, twenty, something like that. We lived together going on two years. She didn't leave me. I left her. But I bet right now if I was to write that woman and ask her for something, she would send it to me.

"Do you want me to tell you what that woman was like? Boy, I don't know. She was like some kind of ocean, I guess, some kind of great big old sea, like the water at Coney Island on a real hot day, cool and warm all at once—and company like a big crowd of people—also like some woman you love to be alone with, if you dig my meaning. Yet and still, I wasn't *in love* with that woman. Explain me that, daddy-o."

"That's deep psychology," I said. "It'd probably take Freud to explain why you think of water when you think of that woman. I didn't get *that* far in college, so I can't explain it. You haven't told me anything about her, anyhow, except generalities. Who was she? Where did you meet her? Was she a rich widow, or what?"

"She were not rich," said Simple, "but she were settled. She worked out in service for wealthy folks and she got up early and come home late, and she did not have but two Thursday afternoons and every other Sunday off. Before she met me, she slept on the job. But after she met me, and we got acquainted, we taken a furnished room together. She was considerable older than I were."

"Now I begin to get a clearer picture of the liaison," I said.

"I didn't lay it on," said Simple. "It just kinder growed on both of us. I met her in a beer garden one Sunday night on the way to church and she asked me to go with her. It were a friendly Baptist church, so the next Sunday I met her in the bar again—and we went to church again. She asked me did I want to escort her home, so I rid way out in the suburbans on the streetcar with her to the white folks' mansion where she stayed. She kissed me good night. Then I rid way back downtown to my cubbyhole. She asked me did I want to come out some night to dinner, or else some Thursday afternoon when she was off. She said she would cook me a pot of greens. Well, you know I will ride a long, long ways for greens. So I went out, et, and kissed her good night. She was kind of settled for a young boy like I was then, but she had nice ways, no glamour ways, just nice ways. But I did not try to spend the night."

"What was her name?"

"Mabel," said Simple, "just plain old Mabel. One evening she told me, 'Honey, I might adopt you if I could get the consent of your parents.'

"I said, 'Baby, my parents don't even know where I am at. They ain't hardly kept track of me since they borned me.'

"Mabel said, 'You are a good-looking black boy, Jesse. I just like to set and look at you.'

"Sometimes she looked at me so hard I would turn my eyes away. Anyhow, we kept getting acquainted better and better. Mabel had some friends in town, so she took me around there to meet them, church people older than I were, nice married respectable folks who got high on just *one* quart of beer, all of them, including Grandma. It were at their house that it happened on a Sunday evening.

"They had a nice fire going in the base-burner and it were warm as toast and we had et a nice big Sunday dinner kind of late in the afternoon that Grandma had cooked. Long about dusk-dark it started snowing outside and kept on coming down. It were November. Mabel told her friends she did not have her overshoes with her, so she did not see how she could go with them tramping through the snow to evening services with nothing on but open-work sandals.

"So Wilbur said, 'Why don't you and Jess stay here and keep the fire burning while we run around to the church? Hattie Belle is on the Usher Board, so she has to go. And Grandma would die if she didn't get there to put in her Dollar Money, not having attended this morning.'

"So Wilbur and his wife put their two kids to bed, and they and her mother bundled up and went on through the snow to the church. Mabel and me was left setting in the parlor with the radio on when they departed. There wasn't but two lights in the room, and Mabel turned one of them out, which left just the red one—and the fire glowing through the cracks of the stove, friendly. We set on the davenport. By the time them folks got back from Zion Baptist Church we was the same as married in the sight of God.

"Wilbur's family was respectable folks, and, his wife being an usher in the church, Mabel did not want them to think nothing like that what had happened *had* happened whilst they was away. So, long before they got back, all the lights in the parlor was turned on again—including lights that hadn't even been burning when they left. We was listening to Walter Winchell.

"Wilbur's wife had brought some ice cream, so we all sat around the kitchen table and talked awhile. Then I spent Two Dollars and Fifteen Cents to take Mabel out to where she worked in a taxi and get myself back to the car line, whence I rid in to town.

"The next night I had a date with that young chick Cherie, but I did not go, being broke. I called up old Mabel instead and we talked a long time. I put three nickels in the phone before we got through. That coming Tuesday, I went out to see her, but I did not stay overnight. She would not let me.

"Mabel said, 'I am working for respectable people with children in the house, and I have never kept no Negro here with me overnight—not even a child.'

"She were digging me on account of my young age. I reckon she was about thirty-five. The next coming Thursday, when she were off, was the first time she had visited my little old beat-up furnished room.

"She said, 'I am going to make some curtains for you.'

"She did. She also made me a pair of pajamas with a monogram *J-S* on them and give them to me for Christmas, the first pajamas I ever had. They helped to keep me warm, for that were a hard winter in Baltimore. Most of the time it blowed and snowed and blowed. And I caught cold from going out to see Mabel so much. She gave me some hot lemonade with a shot of whiskey in it.

"Mabel says, 'Jess, I believe I ought to move in town so's I can look after you. I do not *have* to sleep on my job. I was just saving rent, beings as how I did not have nobody. Sometimes I get so lonesome I hold my own hand for company. Now that I have got someone, I do not like to be way out yonder in the suburbans amongst nothing but white folks on these cold nights. Let's me and you get ourselves a room next week.'

"That is how we shacked up. The day she moved, I moved. It was a good thing we was *together* in that big old furnished room, too, because it was so cold that winter we both would have friz if we had not kept each other warm. In fact, it was so cold we moved again. We found a house that at least had heat, if not much of anything else. There we settled down.

"I found out how much better it is to lay your head on somebody's arm than on a pillow. But womens are sensitive. They get shamefaced. Mabel would not go around to see Wilbur and his wife much no more, neither did she attend their church.

"She said, 'What will they think, especially Grandma, about me, a woman going on thirty-five years old living with a young man like you? That is why I don't want to go around to their house.'

"I said, 'I would not care what they think.'

"She said, 'You are a man. Wilbur is, too. But his wife is a woman. Maybe if I had not had such a hard road to go, and my first two husbands had not been so no-good, I wouldn't do this. It ain't respectable. But I work hard for a living, and I got a right to have somebody. You don't think I'm a bad woman, do you? Even if I am a fool, Jesse, honey, I love you.'

"Very often she would say she must be a fool at her age, liking a young boy like me. Then I would kiss her, and she would say, 'I love you.'

"I would lie like in a moving picture, 'I love you, too.'

" 'Two husbands,' she would say, 'and neither one of them as sweet as you, nowhere near. One dead, and left no insurance. The other one quit, and took my radio and my electric clock.'

"I natural-born felt sorry for that woman and I liked her, so I would say, 'Don't worry about it, Mabel. Don't talk about the past, baby.'

"And she would say, 'You're *my* baby to me. But I had a rocky road, Jess, a rocky road.'

"Afterwhile we would go to sleep and sleep till the alarm rung. Cold old dawning of another day."

"Mabel sounds like a pretty good old girl to me," I said. "You haven't mentioned any fights, quarrels, arguments, or anything like that, such as you went through later with your wife."

"We had none," said Simple, "until the last one—and that was terrible. Mabel and I did not fuss and fight, never. Maybe it was because she were not my wife, also she were older and wiser than Isabel. Mabel had a good heart and she talked soft. She just looked, and cried, when her feelings were hurt—not like that woman I married, who *hollered*."

"But didn't your wife have a good heart, too?"

"Isabel talked so fast and so loud I never found out about her heart. But Mabel was soft-spoken, like I just told you. If I even growled at her, she would hang her head. If I barked, she would cry. But if I barked at my wife, she would bark right back at me, also bite if she got close enough. Isabel were a hell on wheels. I have heard tell, from men who have had lots of womens, that a wife is always worse than your girl friend, and I believe that to be true. I never did argue with no woman as much as I did with the one I married."

"Mabel never suggested marriage?"

"Her second husband didn't leave her no divorce when he departed," said Simple, "and he were not dead. Anyhow, Mabel knowed she was too old for me, thirty-five, and me nineteen-like. She always said, 'Jess, honey, the time will come when I will be no good to you. Maybe that's why I just like to lay here now and look at you.'

"I'd say, 'You will always be good to me—and *for* me, too.'

"She would say, 'June-time is a good month, sugar, but it goes away and stays all winter. When it comes back in the spring, it don't always come back the same. And for some folks, June don't come back a-tall.'

"I would say, 'I'm no June-bug. Kiss me, baby.'

"Then Mabel would laugh and say, 'I'm no baby.'

"I would say, 'You're my baby to me.'

"Then she would laugh some more. And sometimes, when she was laughing, I thought she was crying. Afterwhile I would go to sleep with my head on her arm, which was better than a pillow. Maybe she was still looking at me. But before you knowed it, that old alarm clock would be ringing, and it seemed like the middle of the night. But it wasn't. It was morning."

Explain That to Me

"I LOVE to be woke up easy," continued Simple. "Maybe that is what I liked about Mabel. On them cold mornings after the alarm went off, if I turned over and snoozed a little while more, she would let me sleep until she got dressed, then wake me up gentle-like before she went to work, since she had to be on her job early. But I had time to make myself some coffee before I went out. Her white folks was crazy about Mabel because she never missed being at work in time to cook breakfast for their children and get them off to school. Then she got breakfast for the old man to get him down to the office. Then she made toast and coffee for the Madam about ten. By that time she had been at work a long time. And she worked hard.

"But I was ashamed of Mabel. Just as she didn't like to take me around to Wilbur's house any more, or to none of her church friends after we started to living together, because I was a young boy, so I didn't take her around to none of my friends or to the bar where they hung out, because she was a settled woman. She didn't know the jive and couldn't lindy-hop the first step. She were neat and clean, but not young and sharp. She were sweet but didn't have what the boys call *class*. You know what I mean, no glamour. You see them around Harlem by the thousands—nice respectable womens that don't have but one boy friend at a time—which may be the reason they're so nice. They don't have class. They look like women who keep house fine and cook good—but a cat can't show them off at the Shalimar, neither the Theresa Bar. At Sugar Ray's they would be out of place.

"As nice as Mabel was to me, I ought to've been ashamed to be ashamed of her. But a young man do not have much sense. So when I fell for that little teen-age, Cherie, I started not being home nights when Mabel would get home from work. I started coming in any old time, twelve, one, two o'clock in the morning, then eating what Mabel had brought me.

"All she would say was 'Baby, you won't get enough sleep to go to work in the morning.'

"I would say, 'Don't worry about me,' as I et from the thank-you pan.

"She would say, 'I does worry about you. I can't help it.'

"But she never did ask me where I had been—until one night I stayed out *all* night. Then she said, 'Jess, where did you stay?'

"When I said, 'None of your damn business,' Mabel cried.

"I thought I was supposed to be a man and ignore her. But I guess that were the beginning of the end. She did not get much sleep that winter whilst I was running around with Cherie, taking her to dances over in Washington, and staying out till all hours. Mabel got thin and dark circles came under her eyes. Sometimes she would leave a note in the empty bed if she left for work before I got home in the morning:

Baby, please wait for me this evening before you go out.

"I usually got home from work about six o'clock. Mabel didn't get home until maybe 9 or 10 p.m. after the white folks had been served their dinner. She wanted me to wait for her. But it was always the *very* day that she would leave a note that I would not wait. I reckon I wanted to show Mabel who was the man in the house, also that I were not a child she could tell when to come and go. But it was not until I stayed out three days straight one weekend which were her Sunday off, that she turned her back on me in the bed. I slept on my own arm that night. I did not hear her crying, but the next morning her pillow were wet.

"That were the weekend I spent in Washington with Cherie at the Whitelaw Hotel, and we had a high old time. But who should I run into on U Street in Washington on Saturday afternoon but Wilbur and his wife, Hattie Belle, who had come over to see the cherry blossoms which bloom in the spring! They went back to Baltimore Saturday night. And it were that Sunday morning, of all Sundays, that Mabel went to church. Being home by herself in that big old furnished room without me, she decided to go and worship.

"At church the first thing Wilbur's wife said was 'Mabel, we seen Jess in Washington yesterday with a pretty high-yellow, dressed back, hanging on to his arm.'

"When I returned from Washington about two o'clock Sunday night—or rather Monday morning—Mabel did not say a word, although her eyes were open when I turned on the light. She just looked at me while I took off my clothes. When I got in bed, she turned her back.

"I was tired, so I slept good, anyhow, not worried about a thing —too beat to worry. Had I been older, I might've been afraid Mabel would have killed me in my sleep. But when you are young, you don't have sense enough to be afraid of women nor beasts. I slept. The next morning when I just barely heard that old alarm go off, I didn't wake up enough to realize it was almost time to go to work. Mabel left me in bed and departed. When I did wake up, I saw where her pillow was wet. And that night she did not leave a note for me to wait.

"If I was quitting, I should have quit her then. But not knowing my own mind, I made it hard for Mabel, keeping late hours, igging her, and playing Cherie. Then, one day while Mabel was at work, I packed my clothes and left. But I did not do her like her second husband did—I did not take our clock nor her radio, just myself.

"I thought I was going to move right in with Cherie. But Cherie said, 'No, baby, I ain't situated right to have you living with me.' In fact, she acted real surprised. 'Honey, you are more serious than I took you to be. Besides, I thought I told you, I got a nice old married man who pays my rent. He wouldn't like me rooming with you.'

"Chump that I was, I kept on seeing her, though, taking her out, and giving her half my pay check each and every week. Cherie had class—and I paid to gaze upon it. The way the boys I worked with made admiration over her when we passed tickled me no end. She was a beautiful thing to have hanging around on your arm. Daddy-o, she *was* fine, and only eighteen. I was fascinated by that woman. I knowed she was nothing but a playgirl, like Zarita is now, but I didn't care. She was the first sure-enough glamour chick I ever had contact with and I felt like a solid ton.

"I put down Marvalene, who was an older kid about my own age of twenty or so that I kind of liked and used to meet sometimes in the candy store in the early evening. I put down all my other interests for Cherie. In fact, Cherie took so much of my dough that I had nothing left to spend on anybody else anyhow—except that I did manage to buy myself a fall suit on credit so I could look hep when I took Cherie out.

"I had on this new suit, draped down, reet-pleated, and pegged, the night Mabel no doubt must have saw me as I escorted Cherie down the avenue to the Morocco Bar. When I looked up from the booth we was snuggled in, Mabel were standing there looking me dead in the eyes.

"What did I say? Nothing. I were struck dumb. I was not scared. But it was like a wave had washed over me. I was confused.

"Cherie was not very comfortable herself. 'Do you know this woman, Jess?' Cherie asked me. 'What's she standing here looking at us for?'

"Mabel did not raise her hand nor her voice. She just stood and looked at Cherie, one of them long silent looks.

"All of a sudden Cherie screamed. People thought there was a fight in the bar. But there wasn't no fight. Mabel did not do a thing but stand like a statue just outside that booth and look at us.

"Cherie screamed again. She jumped up and scrambled out of the booth and ran past Mabel out of the bar. She ran out the side door, screaming all the time, although Mabel didn't do a thing but just look at her that long quiet look.

"When Cherie had gone, Mabel said, 'Jess, come home with me and talk.'

"Thinking I was due to be a man in front of all them big-time bar-friends of mine, I said, 'Woman, if you want to talk to *me*, talk here.'

"She said, 'I do not want to talk to you in this place.'

"I said, 'I'm through with you, anyhow.'

"She said, 'I am through with you, too. But I hate to get through like this.'

"I said, 'Like what?'

"She said, 'Like this.'

"I didn't answer. That was the longest minute I ever spent. She didn't say nothing, and I didn't say nothing. Then all of a sudden her eyes screamed. Not a sound came out of her mouth, but her eyes screamed.

"Mabel drew back and picked up a bottle on the bar and threw it at me. I ducked. Then she picked up Cherie's glass from the table and broke it into a thousand pieces on the wall behind me. Then she snatched another glass and it flew over my head. Then everything Mabel could lay her hands on made a bull's-eye out of each place from where I had just dodged. She not yet had said a word, nor cried the first cry—until the bartender grabbed her and put her out. Then Mabel cried.

"I was backed up in that booth, as pale as possible, wet and glass-splintered, but not hurt. Mabel could've cut me to death with all that glassware if her aim had been good. But she didn't even hit me—I was a dodging soul. My suit had to go to the cleaners, but not me.

" 'Why don't you slap her head off?' the barflies asked. 'Man, run and catch her and knock her block off before she gets to the corner.'

" 'Aw, let that woman go,' I kept saying to those guys at the bar. 'She don't mean nothing to me. That old has-been don't mean a thing. She's just my used-to-be. She don't mean nothing.'

"I went to the GENTS' room and bent down to wash my face. It seemed like the floor was slipping out from under me in there, like sand does at Coney Island, when a big old wave goes sucking itself backwards into the ocean, pulling out from under your feet, water and sand from under your feet. I was sick when I bent over that washbowl to run the water. Explain that to me, daddy-o. I was sick as hell."

Baltimore Womens

"MAYBE if Mabel had only hit me just once when she aimed at me, I could've felt *mad*—instead of just sick, sad, and bad. The reason I don't tell nobody about it hardly is because I hate to look back on it. The way I treated that woman, I can't hardly believe it myself.

But I did. Like when you look at somebody who has done something awful wrong, you say, 'I can't believe you did it!' But he did do it. But neither one wants to believe it, least of all the one who did it. That's how I hate to believe I ever treated Mabel the way I did. But I did. I did do it. Which is why I reckon I got sick.

"The next time I saw Cherie, Mabel had scared her so bad she started to run from *me*. That made me so mad I thought I might run after her and bop her one, but I didn't. I lost my admiration for that girl, so I put her down. Cherie never got another dime of mine, nor drunk another drink. That July-August I did not have no women to drop in on and visit, which is not good for a fellow. After he gets through working hard all day every man ought to have a little honey in the evening. But that summer, my honey had done turned to fly paper. I was stuck in bad luck.

"Then I met Isabel, coffee-brown, fine-hipped, young, and dizzy, with gold hoop earrings in her ears, sharp as a tack, jack! She were just my age. But I did not realize she were *twice* as old as me in the head. To look at that girl, I ought to have knowed she could outsmart me at every turn.

"Isabel worked nights just coining tips in a hot-dog stand. She knew all the big-time jokers in town. But I told her she hadn't met anybody until she met me! And don't you know, she fell for that jive. She could hardly make change for the customers when I was setting on one of her stools. At that time I wore my hair conked—shining like patent-leather. I looked like Kid Chocolate.

"After Cherie took off like a sprint-dasher, I had to taste some kind of lipstick once in a while. So every time I thought about a woman I bought a hot dog. And every time I bought a hot dog, I asked Isabel what time she got off from work so I could walk her home. At first she wouldn't give me any satisfaction.

"Finally she said, 'Ask me some Monday.'

"On Monday evening I was right there. I said, 'This is our night. What time do you check out, leave here, put it down?'

"She said, 'Twelve p.m.'

"I said, 'I'll be waiting right on this stool.'

"Isabel said, 'No, wait on the corner. I don't want nobody to see who I leave the job with.'

"It seems like she portioned each fellow a different night, she had so many. Mine was Monday for a time. But later on I got to know all her boy friends, including Walter, just by eating hot dogs and setting on her stools. When some fellow wouldn't show up at midnight to take Isabel home, there I would be. From then on, his night was mine. Man, I were a lover in those days—with a capital 'L.' Lover Man Semple, that was me.

"It were really Isabel's idea that we get married. So we did. And we might have made out right well in the beginning, had we had anything solid to build on—since we started with love. But I had not saved a penny in my whole life and neither had she. When I bought the license and paid for the wedding party—which were a supper with invited friends, since didn't neither one of us have any relatives in Baltimore at that time—I were cold in hand. So we spent our honeymoon in a hotel on Druid Hill and *took up residence*—as they say in the society columns—in a furnished room. Isabel had a lot of clothes. The closet were not big enough to hold her clothes and mine, too, so I hung my one suit on a hanger behind the door.

"Isabel dressed down, and was built, man, built! I loved to tell her, 'Baby, latch on my arm and let's walk down the street this evening.'

"So I made her quit her night job so she could be home when I come and we could go out sporting together. She started to work daytimes in a FISH RESTAURANT and every night she brought home the best old fish sandwiches for her daddy.

"Isabel were right sweet—until she asked me for that *first* fur coat, and I could not produce. The Depression were coming on, but I did not realize it. All I knowed was when I got out of work at the foundry, the next job I got as a porter in a dress shop paid less, and the job after that didn't hardly pay nothing at all. When that place closed down, I was broke, busted, and disgusted—with a wife on my hands who could make more money than me and eat where she worked, too. Some of her customers tipped her a dollar. Yet she would take *my* money to buy herself some jewelry. Isabel wore more bracelets on one arm than Sheba had on two.

"We was living when we first got married in a one-room kitchenette in a house full of chinches and Negroes. Negroes I love, but not bedbugs. One nice thing about Harlem is that it does not have as many bedbugs as Baltimore. Harlem has rats, roaches, winos, reefer-heads, and no-good womens, but Harlem does not have bedbugs—except in very dirty places.

"The further South you go, the more bedbugs you see. A friend boy of mine in Richmond took a girl to a hotel one night which he did not investigate. There were so many bedbugs in the room he could not sleep. So he got up and said to the chinches, 'See here, you-all, I rented this room.'

"A great big old bedbug looked up at him and said, 'You just rented this room for one night, buddy. We live here *all* the time.'

"Well, anyhow, to get back to Baltimore, me and Isabel did not wish to be disturbed by bedbugs, so as soon as we moved into that kitchenette, we started battling. First I went out and bought some spray—but the bedbugs stayed. Then we got some coal-oil and oiled the springs. Them bedbugs thought it was Coca-Cola and lapped it up. One night when I come home from work, I took the whole can of kerosene and poured it all over the bedsprings and set fire to it to smoke them out. A woman down the hall got scared and nearly jumped out the window. But it did not scare them bugs. The next night they was back stronger than ever.

"We put shoe-polish tops full of water under the bed legs, but they swum. Some climbed up on the ceiling and parachuted down. Every morning I was bit everywhere except under the soles of my feet, since I slept with socks on.

"The next Sunday after the kerosene burning, I told my old lady to take the bed down, scrub it, and put it in the back yard to air. Also the covers.

"Everything aired all day from our mattress to the Kewpie doll that Isabel set on the pillows when I were not home. No good. That night new chinches come out of the walls fresh and strong and hungry. I got so mad I heated six kettles of hot water and scalded a battalion. Then I set up in the chair the rest of the night. Isabel said nothing could drive her out of her bed, so she stayed put. But when she woke up she were evil.

"She said, 'I could have married Walter and not lived in no run-down place like this with you and all these chinches.'

"I said, 'Go marry Walter, then—but you will pay for your own divorce, if you ever get one. Just because Walter's got a car, you think his house don't have bedbugs?'

"She said, 'At least I could go out riding at night and get some fresh air.'

" 'You can go out walking and get some now.'

"And don't you know, Isabel left me that morning without cooking my breakfast! All because of them bedbugs. I started to burn the mattress up but I did not have the cash to buy another one. Besides, the whole house needed burning up. So I just went on out to work. But one of them bedbugs had the nerve to go to work with me! Along about half-past 10 a.m. he came crawling out of my coat and said, 'Good morning!'

"I said, 'If you say another word to me, I will bust you wide open!'

"That is what I started to do when that chinch hit the floor and run like mad. Amongst all them white folks I would be embarrassed to chase him, so I let that bedbug go. But when I got home, I took it out on his relatives.

"As soon as one of them housing projects opened up, me and Isabel moved in, fumigated all our clothes, bought new furniture on credit, and, thank God, never did see another bedbug the rest of our married life. It were not bedbugs that brought our happiness to an end. It were Isabel herself. Both womens and bedbugs can *really* bug a man. I don't know which I hate to remember worse, Baltimore womens or Baltimore bugs."

Less than a Damn

"AT any rate, it were not another woman that caused Isabel and me to break up," Simple continued. "It were Isabel. She was two women in one—one good, one bad. And the Depression added to that. The less I brought in, the more she got depressed, mad, and bad. She would rag and nag. I would cuss and fuss. She'd raise her voice and I'd raise mine, until finally it came to the point where I almost had to raise my hand. She dared me—and raised a flat-iron. So no blows passed. But my patience broke down completely."

"That is your side of the story," I said. "But no doubt she had some reason to condemn you."

"I'll be con-damned if she did," said Simple. "I tried to treat that woman right. It was not me brought on the Depression. How did I know when I got married that in a couple of years I wouldn't be making enough to keep a bird alive, let alone myself. But birds scramble for themselves. That my wife objected to.

"She said, 'You the man of the house. I did not marry you to work my fingers to the bone. I was doing right well when I met you, not begging anybody for my meals. Now, if I get something decent to eat I have to not only cook it, but *pay for it*, too. A wife ought to be able to set down at home, dress up when she goes out, and not worry about a thing. I worried more since I married you than I ever did in all these twenty-some-odd years I have lived before. Besides, my mama thinks I am a fool.'

" 'I did not marry your mama,' I said, 'so I give less than a small damn about her opinion. She's come up here to Baltimore from the Eastern Shore as soon as we got married, expecting to settle her big fat frame down on us. Just because this apartment is too small for even a dog, plus a couple, she gets sore and starts talking about why don't we get a big house and live like folks. We lucky to have this, Isabel, young as we is and just starting out in life. It will take us another two years to pay for these three rooms of furniture—so what would we put in a big house?'

" 'I knowed I should have married Walter all the time,' says Isabel.

"Walter were her Thursday night Negro when she was working at the hot-dog stand, her main dancing man. Walter bell-hopped and also wrote numbers, and sold as much of his *own* licker to the hotel guests as he toted from the bar. Walter were a slick hustler, with a Buick car and no morals. I told Isabel if she so much as said *Wal*, let alone *ter*, again, I would slap her down. Then it was when she raised the iron—after which she started sleeping on the davenport in the parlor."

"Did she ever take up with Walter again?"

"Not that I knows of. Walter had fifteen chicks and did not need Isabel."

"So you could not name Walter as a co-respondent if you were to cross-file your current divorce case?"

"Money were the correspondent," said Simple. "Walter did not enter into the picture, except on Isabel's tongue. Anyway, it were shortly after that that I left town—which is maybe why I drank so much when I first come to Harlem, trying to wear that woman off my mind. I had found out by then that she did not really care a thing about me, only what I had in my pocket."

"I think perhaps you exaggerate," I said. "She probably loved you, but naturally she wanted to be fed, too."

"Fed and furred both, you mean," said Simple. "She were always throwing it up to me that we had been married two years and I had not yet bought her that fur coat I promised."

"Did you make such a promise?"

"You know a man will promise anything when he is trying to make a point, and all I had to go on when I was courting Isabel was my mouth. I guess I have a way of talking real positive, because women seem to believe everything I say—even Joyce. Womens are simple when it comes to a man."

"And men are simple when it comes to women."

"You got something there, daddy-o. Joyce has been planning all winter to marry me in June and I was too simple to tell her I hadn't heard hair nor hide of my divorce since Isabel first wrote that it was started. Finally I got worried and wrote Isabel and Isabel writ back that the second and third payments was still missing. It were a sorry day last month when I broke that news to Joyce, which is why she ain't herself this spring. I wish it were not against the law to commit bigamy because Joyce had her mind set on a honeymoon this June. I reckon, just to remind me of it, last week she went and got a whole lot of vacation folders. She also purchased herself a pocket *Travel-guide* for our race, which is a very good book as to where Negroes can stop in different towns.

"I said, 'Joyce, them books is all very pretty, but you know we ain't ready to travel yet.'

"Joyce says, 'I reckon you will be ready perhaps maybe sometime before I die. So I can dream, can't I?'

"Which made me feel bad. And she didn't hardly say nothing to me the rest of the evening. But when her big old fat landlady came down the hall, Joyce asked her which place she thought was the best for honeymooning, the Grand Canyon or Niagara Falls.

"Old landlady said, 'It's all as to whether you prefer a dry climate or a wet one.'

"I said, 'It makes me no difference.' But Joyce did not even answer me."

"Were you ever at the Grand Canyon?" I asked Simple.

"I were," he replied.

"And were you ever at Niagara Falls?"

"I also were," he answered. "In fact, I was at Niagara Falls, and I were at the Grand Canyon."

"I do not wish to criticize your grammar nor change the subject, but listen, my friend, why do you sometimes say, 'I *were*,' and at other times, 'I *was*'?"

"Because sometimes I *were*, and sometimes I *was*," said Simple. "I *was* at Niagara Falls and I *were* at the Grand Canyon—since that were in the far distant past when I were a coach-boy on the Santa Fe in my teens running out of Chicago. I was more recently at Niagara Falls."

"I see," I said. "*Was* is more immediate. *Were* is way back yonder."

"Somewhatly right. But not being colleged like you, I do not always speak like I come from the North."

"Regional differences have nothing to do with it," I said. "Plenty of Southerners speak correct English. I am not trying to make a Harvard man out of you—I am only concerned about your verbs. It is *not* correct to say, 'I were.' "

"Not even when *I were*?" asked Simple.

"You never were 'I were,' " I said. "There is no 'I were.' In the past tense there is only 'I was.' The verb *to be* is declined 'I am, I was, I have been.' "

"Did you say, 'I have *bean*?' " asked Simple.

"I am not from Boston, so I did not say, 'I have *bean*.' A bean is a vegetable, not a verb. I said, 'I have been,' with a slight intonation."

"O.K.," said Simple, "I have bee-ee-een dry for the last half hour. Buy me a beer."

"Why should I buy you a beer?"

"Because I take for granted you are my friend."

"You take a great deal for granted when it comes to beers."

"What you do not take, you do not get," said Simple. "If you can afford it, I will take a bottle. If not, I will take a glass."

"You will accept a glass," I said. "Bartender, fill them up. Now, to get back to grammar. I often wonder why so many colored people say, 'I taken,' instead of, 'I took'?"

"Because they are taken, I reckon," said Simple. "Lord knows I have been taken in more ways than one—for a ride, for my week's salary, my good name, and everything else but undertaken. Someday I will be undertaken, too, and it will cost me Five Hundred Dollars. Funerals is high."

"Funerals *are* high," I said.

"Neither *is* or *are* reduces expenses," said Simple. "Funerals and formals is both high, so what difference do it make?"

"What difference *does* it make," I said. "Your verbs are frequently wrong, old man. I wish you would speak correct English."

"I am American, not English," said Simple, "so if I want to say, 'I were,' I will say, 'I were.' Likewise, 'It do.' Also, 'She ain't.' Now, don't tell me *ain't* ain't in the dictionary."

"It is in the dictionary, but only as a colloquialism. It's not Oxford or Boston or Washington English."

"I am glad it ain't Washington English, since I do not like that Jim Crow town. I do not know where Oxford is. And Boston, I have never *bean*. So about them, I give less than a damn. I ain't bothered."

"Didn't I just tell you 'ain't' isn't correct?"

"What if it aren't?" he said.

Never No More

"IF sin was free, this world would be ruint. Mens pay for sin just like everything else. You know, since I have been in Harlem, if I had back all the money I have spent on Zarita, I could buy me a house. I have swore off from that woman more times than once. But the thing about Zarita is she's so handy. All you have to do is turn around on your bar stool, and there she is. Even when a man is not idle, the Devil sends his wenches after you. Last night I did something I regrets now."

"Well, what did you do it for?"

"Because I am a rumble-seat lover from way back. And when that boy come by the bar with his Methusaleh of a car and asked me did I want to take a ride, I said, 'Yes.' "

"I haven't been in a rumble seat for so long, I thought they didn't make them any more."

"You are too old to get in a rumble seat," said Simple, "but not me. Me and Zarita was in one at this very time last night. I did not go riding alone."

"I thought, now that you are planning to get married, you would no longer associate with Zarita."

"A man cannot go riding in a rumble seat alone, I tell you. And Zarita were right there handy, so I just said, 'Come on.' That was all it took. Next thing I knew, me and Zarita, and Coleman and his girl, was heading across the George Washington Bridge to Jersey, and hair were blowing in my face."

"Stop lying," I said.

"I did not say *my* hair," said Simple. "It were Zarita's. She done bought herself one of them Josephine Baker horsetails. It is a good thing she had it, too, because even if it is spring, it were cold, so she finally wrapped it around her neck for a scarf. You know a lot of air blows in a rumble seat, and even if Zarita were in my arms, she were cold. I were cold myself, which is why I am sniffling today. And I reckon Zarita ended up with pneumonia because I do not see her here in the bar tonight. But I hope I never lay eyes on her again. Don't you know, she got in a roadhouse juke joint over there in Jersey and cut up like a clown.

"We hadn't even got there before Coleman's old roadster run out of gas, so I had to put in a dollar to buy some, which left me with nothing but small change. All I could offer Zarita on arrival were a beer. Well, some other cat what did not know how much Zarita can drink, and what had never laid eyes on her before, offered her a drink. Zarita ordered Scotch, thinking she should show him she were from New York. He must have been a numbers banker because she could not drink him out of money, and he could not drink her down. Meanwhile all I got is small beers, and all Coleman got is his girl in his arms, because we were both broke. Meanwhile them Jersey mosquitoes is having a meal on my ankles whilst Zarita is having a ball.

"About 3 a.m. I says, 'Zarita, babes, let's cut on back to Harlem.'

"Zarita says, 'Just because I come over here with you, Jesse B., is no sign I'm going back with you. You are just my play-cousin. After all, buses do run. I can get back to Harlem. Even maybe my friend here has a car.'

" 'I will drive you home,' says the old Scotch-buying Negro, which made my Indian blood rise.

"I says, 'Zarita, you come on here with me!'

"I grabs her. Knowing good Scotch when she drinks it, she pulls away. Whereupon, I grabs her again. And don't you know, that other Negro ups his dukes to me. I let Zarita go to paste him one. But before my left landed, his right had hit my chin—and I were flat on my back. He cold-cocked me for fair.

"When I come to, I were dumped in Coleman's rumble seat by myself and he was crossing the bridge to New York. It were the motor sputtering that woke me up and brung me to, because just about then that car broke down for good and would not run another inch, neither a foot, right there in the middle of the George Washington Bridge with the wind just a-blowing through my hair.

"By the time we got towed off that bridge by the police, it were 7 a.m. and time for me to be starting to work. I did not get there. I were chilled to the bone and had to go home and drink a hot toddy. Also my jaw hurt. So I not only lost my money last night, but I lost my time today, also my pay. And I have lost a friend, because I will not speak to Zarita again—except to tell her what I think of her, which I cannot say here. I swore to put Zarita down a long time ago, as you know. But I backslid. It is not bad to backslide, but to be knocked on your back, daddy-o, that is too much, especially over a chick that don't mean a thing. Also I never intends to get in Coleman's old broken-down car no more. From here on in, I stick to this bar stool."

"You had a real joyride last night," I said.

"Except that it were no joy."

Simply Heavenly

"ONCE, when I were a child, I were kicked by a small mule. Neither the mule nor I had any sense. I were trying to make the mule go one way, but the mule was trying to make me go another. I were for hitching the mule onto a plow. The mule were for nibbling grass. So, after that kicking, I learned right then and there to respect animals and peoples when they are not of the same mind as you are."

"What prompts you to make these remarks?" I asked.

"Joyce," said Simple.

"Why?"

"Because last night it were her determination to see Tyrone Power's picture at the Rex along with Tarzan, and it were my determination to see Ava Gardner at the Lincoln."

"I know you ended by seeing Tyrone Power."

"We did," said Simple. "Joyce can be stubborn as a small mule—although she has not kicked me yet. But sometimes she rubs me the wrong way. I said, 'Baby, they ain't neither one of them double features nothing but movies. Me, I had much rather set up in a bar and have a cold beer.'

" 'You never think of nothing but beer, Jess Semple,' Joyce says. 'You know I am a respectable girl and do not like to be seen setting up in no bar like Zarita. I pay my church dues regular, attend services every first Sunday, and would sing in the choir if I had not lost my voice in the flu. Neither beer, whiskey, gin, nor bars appeals to me.'

"I said, 'Joyce, that is one reason I like you because you are a good woman. But I don't believe a little beer ever hurt anyone.'

" 'You do not stop with a little,' says Joyce. 'You go the whole hog. When you was courting me, and I was weak for you and followed you around, I have seen you set up and drink as many as six bottles—after which you expected me to see you home, instead of *you* seeing me home like a gentleman should a lady. Alcohol gives you loose thoughts, which is no way for a man not divorced to behave. A good girl always has expectations, otherwise she is loose, too. Have you ever known me to be loose, Jess Semple?'

" 'I have not,' I says. 'You always have been a lady. In fact, at times you have been too much of a lady. But just as bar booths was made for kissing, you know me—I do not believe in going to a movie *just* to look at pictures. And in the dark, baby, I cannot always see you.'

" 'If you are referring to my complexion,' says Joyce, 'go get yourself one of them bleached blondes and see if I care. Just because I asked you to go to a show with me tonight, you must be trying to make an issue or something. I am going upstairs and dress.'

"And she went upstairs, leaving me sitting in the landlady's front room. Joyce knows I did not intend to mean to hurt her, but, after all, she hurted me."

"How?" I asked.

"By trying to make me out ignorant and a lickertarian. A woman thinks she knows everything, and Joyce is a woman. Sometimes she tries to be two women at once and outtalk herself. Me and her landlady began having a nice pleasant conversation—for a change —whilst I were waiting downstairs for Joyce to dress. But when she come down, she took it up. And she crossed me again."

"What was the subject of the conversation?" I asked.

"Marriage," said Simple. "Old landlady said she thought nobody had a right to get married less they owned their own house, could afford to set a woman down and not let her work, just let her keep house and get her husband's dinner. Too many colored womens, she said, had to work, keep house, *and get dinner, too.* Now, I agreed that that were not the best thing, but, I said, if every colored man waited until he owned a house to get married, most men would not get married at all. Also, if women waited for a man who made enough loot each and every week to say, 'Here, baby, take this money and set down—this will cover all expenses and leave you some spending change, too,' most colored womens could never get married. Black men ain't white men making One Hundred Dollars per week.

"Old landlady admitted I had a point. We was having a real pleasant time chewing the rag when Joyce come down the steps and heard the last words I said and from there on in, murder!

"Joyce said, 'Jess Semple, Simple ought to be your name, instead of your nickname. If you don't make money, you ought to. I don't call a man ambitious who can't take care of a wife without her going out and slaving every day. Besides, don't say 'most colored women' because I know plenty of women married to men who can take care of them—but good, too.'

" 'Baby,' I says, 'don't take it so serious. Me and your landlady were just discussing. I did not mean no harm. Don't you feel good?'

" 'I felt all right until just a few minutes ago,' says Joyce, 'but I hate to hear anybody talk ignorant. Also I believe in looking on the positive side. If you don't *have,* make an effort to get. You do not make an effort.'

" 'What do you call that which I make each and every day from 8 a.m. till the five o'clock bell rings?' I asked. 'Furthermore, how come you gets so personal, Joyce? Me and your house lady were talking theoretical—till here you come getting personal. Womens have to bring every conversation down to their own level—which is them.'

" 'Women want a decent home. We don't want to ride that crowded subway to work and back every day before we can enjoy home,' says Joyce. 'When working women get home at night we're too tired to take pleasure in it—and then have to clean up and cook for some great big old—'

" 'Don't say it,' I said. 'Don't call me no kind of name, not even a decent one! Joyce, do not call me a great big old nothing. I am not your husband—yet. And if I am going to have to earn One Thousand Dollars a week to be your husband, skippy! Shame on you! It will never be.'

"Now, that is what hurt her feelings. She thought I meant we would never get married. What I really meant was I would never make a Thousand Dollars a week. Hardly even a Hundred. But Joyce took it the wrong way like I was saying she were not worth a Thousand Dollars. Her feelings was bruised. But she had bruised mine, too. I felt hurted and she felt hurted. I got mad and she got mad.

"Her landlady just waddled on back to the kitchen and started singing 'Precious Lord, Take My Hand.' After a while, Joyce and me went down the street, but Joyce were still salty.

"She said, 'You don't need to spend nothing on me tonight. I got my own money.'

"I *was* kinder embarrassed in the pocket, so I said, 'Since you got money, lend me Five. I will spend it on *you*, but I'll give it back.'

"Just to prove she still loved me, I reckon, Joyce came through with the loan. She knowed I did not intend to mean to hurt her, also that I would buy her a house and a car, too, if I could.

" 'Let's go see Tyrone,' I says, as if she hadn't suggested it herself. I give in to Joyce on the picture—just as I give in down South to that little old small mule after I got kicked. A woman can always find words to get a man's goat, have her way, hurt his feelings, and make him do what she wants him to do.

"When we got to the movies, I said, 'Joyce, lay back in my arms and rest yourself and have a piece of gum.'

"But Joyce refused to lay back, so in no time I were asleep—the picture not being a Western nor Ava Gardner. When I woke up, instead of Joyce laying in my arms, I were laying in *hers*—which is just as good. And which proved there wasn't nobody really mad after all.

"I said, 'Joyce, is you feeling all O.K.?'

"She looked right into my eyes and whispered, 'Simply heavenly!'

"So I went back to sleep again."

Staggering Figures

"IF you had a Million Dollars and no poor relatives, what would you do with your money—buy a saloon?" I asked Simple.

"First I'd marry Joyce," said Simple. "And I would not buy no saloon, since I can come in here and drink. I would buy a house. After I bought the house, I would set Joyce up in business, so she would not always be around the house."

"That's a strange thing to say," I said. "Most men want their wives to stay home and keep house."

"I like to drop ashes on the floor sometimes," said Simple, "so I would want Joyce to be home in the daytime only to cook because, if I had a Million Dollars, I would be home all the time myself. I would not go out to work nowhere—I would just rest and get my strength back after all these years I been working. I could not rest with no woman around the house all day, not even Joyce. A woman is all the time saying, 'Do this' and 'Do that.' And 'Ain't you cut the grass yet?'

"I would say, 'No, I ain't, baby. Let it go till next week.'

"Then, if she's like the rest of the women, she would say, 'You don't take no pride in nothing. I have to do everything.' And she would go out and cut it herself, just to spite me.

"That is why, if I had a Million Dollars, first thing I would do if I was married would be to set my wife up in business so she wouldn't worry me. Womens like to be active. They *hate* to see a man set down. So I would give my wife some place else to be active other than around me."

"In other words, you would make your wife work," I said.

"I would rather make her work than to have her make *me* work. Of course, if she was the type that just liked to lounge around and eat chocolates, which I have never known no colored woman to do, that might be different. Colored women are so used to working that they can't stop when they get a chance to set down. And they hate to see a man do nothing. Why do you reckon this is?"

"You've supplied the answer yourself. Activity over a long period of time breeds intolerance to inactivity," I said. "One has to be accustomed to leisure to know how to enjoy it."

"I am not accustomed to it," said Simple, "but I really could enjoy it. Why, man, if I had a Million Dollars, I would not stir a peg nor lift a finger! Of course, I might tap my own beer keg. But I doubt if I would even do that. I would have a houseman to tap it for me. I would also have a butler serve it. And I would have a valet to press my clothes, so all I would have to do would be to get in my car and go downtown to see how my wife was running her business. If I found her with time on her hands, I might say, 'Baby, come on home and cook me some lunch.' "

"You certainly do have old-time ideas about women," I said.

"I cannot put them in force," said Simple. "Lend me a dime for that last beer so I can get home and see if F.D. is in the house. I am not only broke tonight but beat. Buddy, you are heaven-sent! Any man who will lend me a dime is O.K. by me any time. Money talks! Big money hollers! I couldn't hear my ears if I had a Million Dollars! I don't like noise—so gimme *just* a dime, and we'll have a drink."

"No! I've set you up twice already. I do not intend to break a dollar, not having a million."

"Loan your dollar to me and I will break it. Buddy, I am as free from money now as a Christian is from sin. Gimme the dollar. I will treat you."

"Calm down, calm down! What are you celebrating anyhow?"

"I'm celebrating just because it's Monday. Tuesday I'm always too broke to celebrate. Wednesday I'm too tired. Thursday I'm disgusted. Friday, exhausted. But Saturday, Sunday, and sometimes even Monday—whoopee! So let's have another one. If I go to sleep sober I might dream I'm handling money, and wake up screaming.

I don't trust myself. My left hand might short-change my right. Let's have one for the road. Go ahead and break your dollar. What difference do it make?"

"With my dollar intact," I said, "I'm only $999,999 away from having a million."

"Such figures staggers me," said Simple.

The Moon

"LOVE is a many-splintered thing," sang Simple, standing at the bar. "If my heart had rings in it like a tree log, you could tell how many loves I have had—I mean of the heart, not the body. I used to fall in love with movie stars when I were a young boy, and you know I could not get near no movie star, they being white and way up yonder on the screen and me in a Jim Crow balcony down in Virginia. When I come to Baltimore as a young man, setting in a Jim Crow theater on Pennsylvania Avenue, the first colored movie star I fell in love with was Nina Mae McKinney, who was showing herself off in a picture called *Hallelujah*, which were fine. Nina Mae were so beautiful she made my heart ache. Then I fell in love with Isabel, who became my first wife, and I forgot about movie stars. Isabel kept my nose to the grindstone, so I did not have neither time or money to go to movies.

"With Isabel it was always *buy* this, *buy* that, *buy* a icebox, *buy* a toaster, *buy* a washing machine which runs by electricity so I don't have to wash by hand, *buy* me a fur coat, *buy* me a boxer-dog. Isabel sure could want more things than you could shake a stick at. And when I was bought out, I was put out. Thank God, my present wife, Joyce, is not a *buy-me* girl, neither a *gimme* woman. Joyce works, too. We puts our money together, what she makes and what

I make, and run on a budget. It's me who has to say 'gimme' to my wife now to even get beer money from that budget. We are saving to buy a house. But Joyce wants to go to the suburbans. I wants to stay in Harlem. So there's a conflict."

"And who will win?" I inquired.

"My wife," said Simple, "but not without a struggle. I can see myself now shoveling snow and cutting lawns so far from Harlem I can't even smell a pig's foot. Me, I do not want to go to *no* suburbans, not even Brooklyn. But Joyce wants to integrate. She says America has got two cultures, which should not be divided as they now is, so let's leave Harlem."

"Don't you agree that Joyce is right?"

"*White is right,*" said Simple, "so I have always heard. But I never did believe it. White folks do so much wrong! Not only do they mistreat me, but they mistreats themselves. Right now, all they got their minds on is shooting off rockets and sending up atom bombs and poisoning the air and fighting wars and Jim Crowing the universe."

"Why do you say 'Jim Crowing the universe'?"

"Because I have not heard tell of no Negro astronaughts nowhere in space yet. This is serious, because if one of them white Southerners gets to the moon first, COLORED NOT ADMITTED signs will go up all over heaven as sure as God made little green apples, and Dixiecrats will be asking the man in the moon, 'Do you want your daughter to marry a Nigra?' Meanwhile, the N.A.A.C.P. will have to go to the Supreme Court, as usual, to get an edict for Negroes to even set foot on the moon. By that time, Roy Wilkins will be too old to make the trip, and me, too."

"But perhaps the Freedom Riders will go into orbit on their own," I said. "Or Harlem might vote Adam Powell into the Moon Congress."

"One thing I know," said Simple, "is that Martin Luther King will *pray* himself up there. The moon must be a halfway stop on the way to Glory, and King will probably be arrested. I wonder if them Southerners will take police dogs to the moon?"

"You are a great one for fantasy," I said, "maybe stemming from your movie-going days."

"Which is when I first discovered that love is a many-splintered thing," sighed Simple.

Domesticated

"My Cousin Minnie, beings as she is temporarily alone again, tells me she is looking for a boy friend these days who means business," said Simple. "And what Minnie means by *business* is when she asks a man, 'Baby, can you pay my rent? That kitchenette of mine costs me $155 a month, which is without gas—so he who lives there must share.' That's what Minnie says."

"Economics plays a large part in love in Harlem these days," I agreed. "He who would woo must shell out, too."

"Which is one reason I do not stray at all since I been married," said Simple. "I cannot afford it. My budget do not allow for me living with nobody but my wife, or drinking with nobody but myself, and playing more than one number a day, combinated. I am a man. Minnie is a lady. I takes care of myself. Minnie needs taking care of. I do not blame my boon cousin for asking what a man's finances are before she chooses a permanent friend. To get a good woman, any man must pay, and my Cousin Minnie is not to be sneezed at. Brains run in the Semple family."

"Your Cousin Minnie ought to make some man a good wife," I said.

"In the far distant future, when she gets tired of setting on bar stools," Simple replied. "Right now, let Minnie play the field. She's still young. If she picks a winning horse, she can always get hitched before the season ends. If the man is a sometimer, she can let him go and wipe the slate clean to chalk up new bets."

"It is too bad love and money have to be so mixed up," I said, "especially for a woman."

"Landlords are not interested in love—just money. They wants their rent each and every month," said Simple. "When a man and a woman are both working, they can share the rent. But Minnie is the type that likes to set down on a man. That is her way of 'making him a home,' as she puts it. She claims that if she goes out and works, too, the home is nothing but an empty shell. Minnie has got the same ideas as a rich white lady."

"I don't blame her," I said, "if she can get away with it. But most colored men hardly make enough to take care of themselves, let alone a family—which is one of the regrettable facts of Negro economics. Yet Minnie has the right idea. A woman should be a wife, not a work horse."

"She should have a man's dinner ready when he comes home," said Simple. "It is hard for a man to love a woman on an empty stomach."

"You are the old-fashioned type," I said. "You want your wife to work outside the home, and inside it, too."

"I wants my dinner at night."

"Then you ought to hire a cook."

"I married one," said Simple. "Joyce has to eat the same as me. Since women have to cook for themselves, they might as well cook for their man, too."

"Also, you expect your wife to keep the house clean?"

"Joyce swears she cannot live in filth, for which I am grateful," said Simple, "as I never was one for house cleaning, myself. I might sweep a little on Sunday. And lately Joyce has bulldozed me into scrubbing the linoleum. I also last week washed the front windows."

"Gradually getting domesticated," I said. "I am glad Joyce can get something out of you on Sundays, as late as you stay up sporting around on Saturday."

"Late?" said Simple. "I go home at closing time. I must love Joyce, as much as I have changed since I got married. Comes midnight, no matter where I am, I think about my wife."

"You are probably scared she is thinking about you," I said.

"How did you guess it?" asked Simple. "I am going home right now before Joyce gets ready to raise sand. If you see my Cousin Minnie, tell her Jess Semple has been here and gone. Good night!"

Hairdos

"WHY is it," asked Simple, "you always hope you have good relatives, but you usually don't?"

"Don't what?" I asked.

"Don't have good ones," said Simple.

"I can't say I agree with you," I said. "Some of my relatives are fine people."

"A few of mine are," said Simple, "but I've got enough bad relatives to make up the difference. Take Cousin Minnie. She not only drinks, but out-drinks me. Of the lady sex, too! And she makes no bones that her father, my uncle, were not married to my aunt, which makes her my cousin in name only. What you gonna do about relatives like that?"

"If she's a relative in name only, you certainly don't have to claim her."

"But she claims me," said Simple. "And she's as ugly as I are."

"In other words, you can spot the kinship."

"Spot it?" said Simple. "Minnie is not beautiful, I'm telling you. Minnie looks like me around the nose, but not around the head. These brownskin blondes and colored girls with yellow streaks through their hair, attracting attention to themselves with heads as God never gave them, look like nothing human to me, including Minnie."

"Some of them look very strange," I said.

"Have you seen them chicks whose hair is all black on top, but their ponytail is blond?" asked Simple. "That is the most. Then when they wear skin-tight toreador pants on the street to boot, and their behinds look like a beer barrel, I give up! At least my Cousin Minnie from Virginia does not wear no skin-tight pants in public."

"Has your Cousin Minnie got a yellow streak through her hair these days?"

"She has," said Simple, "which is one reason why I no longer speak to her when I see her in a bar. Cousin Minnie is too stout and too colored to be attracting attention to herself thataway. Everybody knows nature did not give Minnie no blond hair nowhere on her body. Yet she has done gone to the beauty parlor and had three inches of blondine put into her head. Do you think women are right bright?"

"They do strange things at times," I said. "Rings through their noses in India, saucers through their lips in Tanganyika, ivory splinters through their ears in Australia."

"And blond streaks in their heads in Harlem," said Simple. "You can never tell what a woman will think up. I said, 'Minnie, why did you do it?' "

"What did Cousin Minnie say?"

"Minnie said, 'I want to attract some attention to myself before I get too old to totter and dodder. I want the mens to notice me, that's why.' "

"I said, 'Girl, everybody has to turn around and look at you now, not once but twice. You look like nothing I ever saw in my natural life. You look like you belong in the sideshow at Coney Island.'

" 'If you was not my cousin by book, Jess Semple,' says Minnie, 'I would not take such remarks off you. You are trying to tell me I look like a freak?'

" 'I am,' I says, 'and you do! You was right nice-looking until you let them beauty-shop people put that yellow frizzle from your forehead down to the nape of your neck. Now you look like a stoplight before it changes to green—that in-between signal which is neither stop nor go. You don't look like a woman no more—and you don't look like nothing else either. Minnie, I will give you the money to go and have your hair put back like it was, if you will do so.'

" 'Gimme Five Dollars,' says Minnie, 'and I will think about it.'

" 'Oh, no,' I says, 'think about it is not what I meant. I do not want to see you again messed up like you is tonight. After all, we are related.'

" 'Didn't nobody else say they don't like my hair,' says Minnie. 'And this is the latest style.'

" 'I am glad your hair is not long enough for you to have a horsetail hanging down behind like Josephine Baker. If you did, I expect you would dye that yellow, too.'

" 'I am thinking of letting my hair grow long,' says Minnie.

" 'Baby, you would have to do some hard thinking,' I said without thinking. Knowing hair is a sensitive point with short-haired women, I did not mean to insult Minnie. But insulted she were.

" 'You do not need to hurt my feelings just because you do not like my new hairstyle. You have hurted me so bad now, being so critical, that I feel like crying. I am liable to break down right here on this bar stool if you do not buy me a Scotch and soda. Bartender, White Horse, please.

"Do you know, I had to pay for that woman a drink! I could have bought myself six glasses of beer with the money her one Scotch cost, whilst the men was passing up and down the bar, looking from her head to her haunches and back, whistling at her with their eyes. If I hadn't been there, I expect Minnie would have been asked some very direct questions, setting there with that Halloween streak down the middle of her head! I wish she was no relation to me."

"Don't take it so hard," I said. "When the fad blows over, Minnie's hair will go back to nature. Like two-tone cars, two-tone hair is just a fad, and a rather amusing one, I think. At least it makes a man stop and stare."

"Will you be so kind as to buy me a beer? Fact is, make it a whiskey. A double, if you can stand it, daddy-o. I need something strong to take my mind off of Cousin Minnie."

Cousin Minnie Wins

"IT is better to be wore out from living than to be worn out from worry," said Simple. "Them that lives to the hilt and wears their worries like a loose garment lives the longest. I do believe my Cousin Minnie is going to live to be one hundred and ten. She worries about nothing, except sometimes wondering can she borrow Five Dollars from me. When I say no, she frowns up."

"I thought I heard you say lately you had put your Cousin Minnie down," I said.

"I did," said Simple. "I put her down, but she took me up again. I stopped going to the bars where I thought she went, but I find out that she goes to all bars. Every bar I go in in Harlem, in steps Minnie. That woman really makes the rounds, which is why our cousinship is going on the rocks these days. I do not like a woman that gets around to more places than I do. And since I been married to Joyce, I do not get around much any more. But my cousin, she is here, there, everywhere each and every night. I says to Minnie once, 'Don't you even take off Monday from gallivanting?'

"Do you know what Minnie says to me? She says, 'Monday? Why, Monday ain't even on my calendar. I call it *Hon*-day, meaning HONEY day—the day to catch up with all the sweet things you might have missed on Sunday. Monday is Honey-day, Jesse Semple. If I has nothing better to do, I come to call on you, my favorite cousin.'

" 'You are not *my* favorite cousin, Minnie,' I says, 'especially since you can out-drink me. Our cousinship has gone adrift on a sea of licker.'

" 'You talk as if you bought me all them drinks, old Simple Negro, whereas you has not spent hardly a dime on me at this bar all summer. You know I has friends who will treat me every time they greet me, wine me before they dine me, and dance whenever I want to prance.'

" 'Minnie,' says I, 'if you would work as much as you dance, you might have some money of your own in your pocketbook sometimes, and not have to depend on others for a treat.'

" 'Honey,' says Minnie, 'other folks' treats is most sweet. Besides, you know I told you, that last white lady for who I worked lived in a duplex apartment, and she had too many steps for me to be running up. Steps get me down.'

" 'How come dancing don't get you down, too? I have seen you dance all night and not pant a pant.'

" 'Dancing do not seem to tell on a body like climbing steps do,' said Minnie. 'I could dance all night, like the song says, without feeling it. But just let me climb up and down steps half a day, and my wind is gone. I were not that way in my youthhood. Do you think I am getting old?'

" 'You do look kinder ageable,' I said. 'But I am sure it is not from work, neither from worriation.'

" 'Work and worry will get a woman down,' said Minnie. 'I do not wish to go under. If I do, I had rather it be from a good time than from a good job. I have never yet had no job in the world I was willing to give my life to, no matter how good. Why, I worked for a rich old white lady once who paid me just to *be* there, since she were kind of invalidded like, and could not answer her own doorbell. But just being there bugged me. I got to thinking about all the other nice places I could be, and I quit. Facts is, Jess, I am not working nowhere now. Lend me Five.'

" 'I will not,' I says, 'because all you want money for is to live it up or drink it up. I can live up and drink up my own money.'

" 'Then let's drink up your Five together, Coz,' coos Minnie, 'and it won't be a worriation to either of us.' Facts is, that is just about what had already happened. Minnie had had three Scotches whilst we was talking, and I had had six beers.

" 'You wins, Min,' I said.

" 'I won, hon! I almost always wins with men,' she said. 'Lemme tell you how once I won. That were back in the days when I used to take care of men, instead of letting men take care of me. I were in love with that young stud—a dude named Luther McWilliams Warren—deep in love, money-spending, cooking-and-scrubbing, working-my-fingers-to-the-bone for his sake, crazy in love. He took me for a play toy. He went around telling folks I wasn't nothing but his rag doll till his china doll comes.

" 'When I heard that, I said to myself, "I better not catch you with no china doll, Luther McWilliams Warren! If I do, I will fix your wagon!"

" 'Misfortunately for him, I heard at the beauty shop about his other woman. I told him that night, "Baby, you better watch your step." Luther Warren did not believe me, so I just waited a few months till winter came—because I knowed Luther did not like the cold. I also knowed he did not like to be hungry, neither poorly dressed. Neither to be out of pocket change. In them days it was me who paid the gas bill, me who bought the food, and me who give him spending change, also new shirts, shoes, and suits. And him with a china doll at the other end of town all the time—a meriney hussy with a blond streak in her head what paid Five Dollars at the beauty shop to have that streak put in. Name of Dorinda. I found out who she was. But by that time I were tired of Luther Warren, anyhow. I thought to myself, let Dorinda *take care* of him awhile—which I knowed she wouldn't do, since she were the type who expected to reap, not *sow*, to take, not *put*—which, in later years, I have learned to do myself.

" 'Meantime, Luther sported with his china doll—endangering his life and laying himself liable, because she had a husband. I did not let him know how much I cared, or how jealous-hearted I were—beyond crying once in a while and twice pitching a boogie. But by fall, jealousy had died in me, and I had made my plans.

" 'On Thanksgiving, I fixed him a turkey—but I did not put no poison in the dressing. I wanted that man to *live* and suffer, not suffer and *die*. Time went by. Soon he come asking me what was

I going to give him for Christmas. Would I buy him that new pinstripe suit he wanted? I said, *Um-hunnn-nn-n*! He thought when I purred like that, I meant yes, but I fooled that joker.

" 'The night before the day I pulled my trick, I were as sweet to him as sweet could be. I even give him Ten Dollars to go out with. I knowed where he went—Dorinda's. But I did not let on like I knowed. I had waited for the thermometer to drop. Radio said it would be zero come morning. I had already purchased my train ticket North. All I wanted were this real cold day to depart, and I was hoping he would not come home before afternoon. He didn't. He slept late—but elsewhere—not with me. I were glad. A well-prepared revenge is sweet.

" 'I called the gas man early that morning and had the gas turned off and the meter taken out. Electricity I had cut off, too. I told the grocery man I were canceling my bill. I called the phone man and had the phone, *not only cut off*, but removed. All of Luther's clothes in the closet I sold to the junk man. His hair oil I throwed in the garbage. His address books I tore up so he could not write nobody for help. I notified the rent man I were moving. I told that city goodbye and headed North to Freedomland. I always did want to come North, anyhow. So I came. I not only got rid of Luther, but rid of the South—all with one stone and a single ticket. I were not there when Luther McWilliams Warren tore his self away from his china doll that day and come home. I were gone.

" 'Home was not what it used to be to that joker, not no more. He liked to eat—but he found no meal. He liked heat—but he could strike a match to the gas burners all he wanted to—no blaze. He liked a hot bath. The tank was cold. I even pulled out the ball in the flush box so the toilet wouldn't flush. I also took out the light bulbs. Let him set there now and read the *Racing Form*! Luther Warren liked nice clothes. His clothes were sold, his drawers empty, his closet bare. He liked a bed to sleep on. I sold our bed to the second-hand store. He liked a roof over his head. Where we lived, rent was paid by the week, and the week was up. He liked company. Now not even me was around. Me, what he called his rag doll, had cut out, flew the coop, gone. And I did not even leave that man cigarette money—nothing but an empty house. Luther Warren was a picked chicken when I got through, with no hen house in which to find a roost, no yard in which to crow, and nothing to crow on. He must have been cold that day, too, in a cold house, in a cold world. I left him a note which said:

" '*Your rag doll leaves you, daddy,*
Your rag doll is gone.
Let your china doll feed you, daddy,
From now on.
Signed: *Minnie—on my moving day.*'

" 'The last time I heard tell of Luther McWilliams Warren, he were poor as a church mouse. His sins had caught up with him. *I won!*' "

Self-protection

"SHE crowned him king of kings," said Simple, "not to mention lord of lords. When my Cousin Minnie hit that man with a beer bottle, he were conked and crowned both all at once. Minnie raised a knot on his head bigger than the Koorinoor Diamond, which, I hear, were the biggest diamond ever to be set in a crown."

"Why did your cousin attack the poor fellow in so positive a manner?" I asked.

"That man evidently did not know my Cousin Minnie very well, in spite of the fact he were her steady boy friend since last Thanksgivings," said Simple. "I could see trouble coming before the holidays. In the first place, that man did not buy Cousin Minnie what she wanted for Christmas, which were a fur stole. 'I did not ask him for a fur coat,' said Minnie, 'just a stole—and he did not even get that. Come explaining that his funds was short.'

"Well, I knew Minnie were not happy. Still and yet, it being the season of Peace on Earth, she put up with the joker. She even took him out sporting New Year's Eve on her own money. But, Minnie told me, he got so high before the bells tolled that he wanted to send *her* home. He wanted to stay out and run the streets all the night without being bothered with his old lady. Minnie allowed as how that would never do, not with her money that she had lent him to celebrate in his pocket. Whereupon, one word led to another, so he upped his hand at Minnie. Howsoever, Minnie acted like a lady and backed away. She said, 'Daddy, do not show your color in the Mill Ritz Bar. Let's not end the Old Year on a low note.'

"But Rombow were drunk. He must not have read that sign up over the bar which says WE GROW OLD SO QUICK, BUT GROW WISE SO SLOW. When Rombow upped his hand at Cousin Minnie, he did not use common sense. Minnie is a woman not afraid of man, beast, or devil. She is also no respecter of persons. Minnie were just respecting Rombow because they were out in public, it were New Year's Eve, and the bells had not yet tolled. She also at times tried to be a lady, and she did not wish to end the Old Year on a low note. Minnie said again, 'Rombow, I done spoke nice now, but listen, I can raise my voice, too.'

" 'You better not raise it at me,' says Rombow.

"Whereupon, Minnie said, 'What?' so loud everybody in the bar heard her, in spite of all the noise going on plus Ray Charles on the juke box. 'What did you say?' says Minnie.

" 'If you can't hear my voice,' says Rombow, 'you can sure feel my hand.' Whiz! He thought he were fast, but Minnie was faster. When Rombow went to slap her, Minnie squatted. The blow went over her head. When Minnie come up, the nearest beer bottle were in her hand. With this Minnie christened, crowned, and conked Rombow all at once.

"Minnie said, 'If you want to be a king, Rom, I will crown you.' She did. A knot sprung out on Rombow's head the size of a hen's egg. But neither the bottle nor his head broke. However, what little sense he had must have been knocked from his head to his feet, because his feet had sense enough to carry him backwards fast, out of Minnie's way, and when he fell, he fell against the juke box. Rombow were stunned, shook up, shocked, and unconscious.

" 'You must be out of your mind,' said Minnie.

"He were, because when he came to, the bells had tolled. Minnie were surrounded by friends drinking to her health, and everybody had yelled *Happy New Year* so much that they were hoarse.

"It was about that time that I come into the bar, having taken Joyce home from Watch Meeting. I spied my Cousin Minnie and she told me her tale. I said, 'Coz, I should have been here to protect you.'

" 'There is as much difference between *should* and *is* as between last year and this,' says Minnie. '*Should* has gone down the drain, but *is* is here. I am able to protect myself. Happy New Year to you!' "

Ladyhood

"WHEN the man on the next stool last night asked my Cousin Minnie how old she were," said Simple, "she told him, 'Oh, about eleventeen! A man should not ask a lady's age,' she said, 'no more than he should ask if she has a wig on—which I do not tonight. Every strand is my own hair.'

" 'Can you do the Monkey?' asked the man.

" 'Backforwards and forwards,' said Minnie, 'including the Jerk.'

"Whereupon, the man put a quarter in the juke box and him and Minnie performed, until the bartender pointed at the sign NO DANCING and made them stop because it had been five minutes since they had last bought a drink, and the barman's point and purpose is to keep his licker moving."

"I don't see how the bar makes much off of you, then," I said to Simple. "But where is your Cousin Minnie tonight?"

"Home resting up until Friday—when the studs get paid," said Simple. "Minnie do not come out on quiet nights. She knows I do not treat relatives—except on Christmas—so she need not look to me to quench her thirst. To be a girl-cousin, Minnie can drink awhile, Jack, yet I have never seen her stagger, let alone reel. Minnie goes out of any bar under her own steam, no matter how many Scotches and sodas she has put away. You have to give it to Minnie—that chick carries her licker well and protects her ladyhood, too. Minnie knows she is a lone woman in this big city—except for me, her Cousin Jess."

"Your Cousin Minnie seems quite self-reliant."

"She is used to making her way in the world, if that is what you mean," said Simple. "If necessary, Minnie will even work to keep her head above water. But not if any other kind of lifeboat or lifeguard is in sight. To be a big woman, Minnie can look so little and lost and lone and helpless sometimes, setting on a bar stool with nothing but a little glass of Scotch when what she really craves is a double, that almost any strange man will take pity on her and say, 'Baby, I beg your pardon, perhaps you would accept some refreshments on me.'

"If he makes a polite approach, Minnie will turn her head to one side, somewhat down, and reply, 'With utmost pleasure—if you introduced yourself. But I do not drink with no man I do not know.'

" 'My name is So-and-so-and-so,' says the stud.

"Whereupon, Minnie says her name is Minnette, and that she were a Johnson before her mother married her third stepfather. Then, says Minnie, she took the name of Ashmore. But sometimes Minnie forgets which stepfather's name she took—*Butler* or *Ashmore*—which makes no difference because by then she has ordered a double Scotch on the man and their friendship is cemented. Minnie do not spend another dime of her own money that evening.

My Cousin Minnie has a way with men, Boyd. She makes chumps out of them so sweet-like. It might take a man several months to find out Minnie can be big, bad, bold, and boisterous if she wants to. If a man goes too far with Minnie, she can raise her voice and embarrass him proper. Ray Charles can be screaming on the TV and Bill Doggett yelling on the juke box both at once, but you can still hear Minnie in the bar above all that noise telling some old joker, 'Don't let your licker go to your head, daddy, because if you do, I'll blow you off your feet. You done barked up the wrong tree, insulting me. Bartender, tell this man to vacate my person.'

"But by that time it is nearly closing, and the man has spent all his money anyhow. If he makes no argument, Minnie will calm down and say real ladylike, as she rises to leave—alone—'Good night.'

"But if the man raises his voice and asserts his manhood, it is not good night that Minnie says to that cat as she goes out the door. Oh, no, it is not good night. It is a word that begins with a letter I do not like to mention. Minnie knows more bad words than I do. To tell the truth, sometimes I think my Cousin Minnie is a disgrace to the race."

"Why?" I asked.

"Because, in protecting her ladyhood, Minnie does not always act like a lady. I told you about the time she hit that man in the bar with a beer bottle New Year's Eve, did I not?"

"You did. So?"

"It would have been more politer—and cheaper, too—had Minnie hit him with something that did not contain good alcohol," said Simple. "Or if she had screamed and throwed a glass. But Minnie did not scream. She just up and knocked the man out with a bottle. Should not a lady settle things in a more gentler manner? Maybe even faint first?"

"Your concept of the word 'lady' evidently comes from remote romantic sources," I said. "Gentle ladies in the days of antiquity never had to face the problems Minnie has to face. In fact, the whole conventional concept of the word 'lady' is tied up with wealth, high standing, and a sheltered life for women. Minnie has to face the world every day, in fact do battle with it."

"True," said Simple, "to remain a lady, Minnie often has to fight. It is not always easy for a colored lady to keep her ladyhood."

"You are bringing up race again," I said. "But this time I think you put your finger on the crux of the argument."

"The crust of the argument is that Minnie believes in peace so much she will fight for it," said Simple. "When Minnie wants the right to be let alone, she means to *be let alone*. Yet she will lead a man on, let him spend his whole wages on Scotch, beer, or wine —it depending on how much wages he has got as to which class she puts him in. Then when the man wants to bother Minnie, she does not wish to be bothered. That is what leads to trouble. I have told my cousin that mens were not made to be taken advantage of. But ever since Eve, that is what womens have done. I reckon I cannot change Minnie."

"Men do not have to let women run away with their senses," I said.

"No," said Simple, "but they do. There was a time when a woman could twist me, as much sense as I got, around her little finger. In fact, at one time Zarita had me all balled up in her little tiny fist. But that were before I met Joyce, my wife, who now has got me tied to her apron strings."

"Not very tightly," I said, "as often as I see you here in Paddy's Bar."

"Before I got married, I used to be in here every night the Lord sent," said Simple. "Now I am only in here every other night—or so."

"Or so, is right," I said.

"But I do not drink like I once did," claimed Simple. "Neither do I stray. My eyes might roam, but I stay home. I have got a good home, pal, which I mean to keep. What I wish is that my Cousin Minnie would settle down and make herself a good marriage, too. Minnie has been in Harlem long enough to get the country out of her hair now, and Virginia out of her system. Yet Minnie is in this bar more often than me. She is getting to be a settled woman now, so she ought to settle down—and not on a bar stool neither. A lady should not hang out in places which are shady. I have told Minnie she is liable to get hurt sometimes, the way she does her boy friends. A man can put up with so much, but Minnie sometimes piles it on."

"From all you have told me about Minnie, she can protect herself," I said.

"At the expense of her ladyhood," said Simple. "A woman should not put herself in a position where she has to fight her way out."

"You never forced a woman into such a position yourself?" I asked.

"Being a man, naturally, I have sometimes tried to make my point—and over-made it," admitted Simple. "My first wife, Isabel, once attacked me so ferocious, the neighbors had to help me get out of the house. That were in Baltimore. Since I come to New York, I have got more sense. Yet there is some chumps in Harlem who take one look at any woman, including Minnie, and their senses desert them. What is it about womens that makes a man lose his mind?"

"You answer that, if you can."

"I reckon it must be their ladyhood," declared Simple.

Lynn Clarisse

"How nice to be respectably dirty," said Simple's cousin Lynn Clarisse, who had one of those double names like many girls, colored and noncolored, have down South. "How nice," she said, "to be able to read *Another Country* and *The Carpetbaggers* and William Burroughs and Henry Miller and *The Messenger*, even *City of Night* and *Last Exit to Brooklyn* without blushing—because everybody else is reading them. There are lots of things in those books I know, of course, since I am full-grown and adult. But there are more things I don't know, at least not from experience."

"Let's experience a few," I said—testing her out, of course.

"We can't even get started on the spur of the moment, Mr. Boyd," she said, coming right back with an answer without blushing. No stammering. She wasn't a bit "country."

"You must have gone to a sophisticated college," I said. "Was it white, black, or integrated?"

"Fisk, as I know *you know* I told you," she said.

"Yes, you did," I remembered, "last night when Simple took me by his house to meet you. How come you have a cousin like Simple?"

"He's in the family," said Lynn Clarisse, "and is one relative who happens to be down with it. I love that cat, and I love his Harlem."

"I do, too," I said. "He told me you were colleged. But I sort of expected a girl whose mind did not go beyond the classroom, you know, conventional."

"There are no limits to where the mind or body goes," said Lynn Clarisse. "My body has been on Freedom Rides. See that scar where an Alabama cop tried to break my neck with his billy club. He just broke my shoulder, but it left a scar on my neck where his club burst the skin open. It might sound pretentious to say it, but while my body was in Alabama that night, my mind was on Sartre and Genet."

"Are you really colored?" I asked, just playing, of course.

"Are you blind?" she replied. She laughed. I laughed. "I am darker than dark brownskin." But the mystery was not solved. She had never been North before, Lynn Clarisse. So, how come so suave, so bright, so—well?

"Maybe you don't know it," she said, "but we do have libraries in Nashville, too. Integrated just like New York. And Fisk, a colored college, you know, only slightly integrated, has one of the best libraries in the country, and a librarian who helps students choose good books. We have a browsing room where some can browse, and others can sleep, whisper sweet nothings, or just clean their fingernails—sort of nice place. As for reading books, even far-out books, even beatnik books, fine. Only there are not enough books for me down South, which is one reason I came to New York. Or maybe I came to see books in action. Slow motion, though, so don't rush me, Mr. Boyd."

"I'm too flabbergasted," I said. "I can't believe you are Jesse B. Semple's cousin."

"Flesh and blood," she replied. "And he brought me in this café, which is the nicest one, so he says, on 125th Street. You know he's up there at the bar, so if you still don't believe I'm his cousin, call him and ask him."

"Let's not bother Simple this moment," I said. "We're cozy back here in this booth. Say, Lynn Clarisse, have you seen any plays in New York?"

"Not yet."

"Could I take you to see some? What do you want to see?"

"Anything with my people in it," said Lynn Clarisse, "the Sammy Davis musical, Ruby Dee in Shakespeare, Gilbert Price, Diana Sands, a LeRoi Jones play if any are running, *Othello*."

"You are a race woman for true," I said.

"I've got to keep up with my own culture," said Lynn Clarisse. "Those plays will hardly be touring down South."

"I thought you were going to stay up North awhile?"

"A few weeks. Then I'm going back South. We've got things to do."

"More Freedom Rides?"

"Voter Registration."

"I'll miss you when you leave."

"Come down South," said Lynn Clarisse.

"We've got things to do in Harlem, too," I said.

"And me, I have got something to do right now," interrupted Simple at the edge of our booth. "I have got to go home."

"All married men should be home by midnight," I said, motioning him away.

"Also all young ladies who come out in the evening with their cousins in Harlem," added Lynn Clarisse. "So good night, Mr. Boyd."

"You are both going and leave me all alone in this bar?" I asked.

"With fifty-odd Negroes and the white proprietor, you'll have company," said Simple. "I will even order you a beer on me and drop a quarter in the juke box before I depart, so you can listen to Nina Simone. Good night, old boy."

"Good night, my erstwhile friend."

"Good night, Mr. Boyd," said Lynn Clarisse.

"Good night!"

Riddles

"UNTIL I met Joyce," said Simple, "I did not eat regular on a tablecloth. Now that we are married, each and every day we eat on a tablecloth, even if it does keep me running to the laundrymat—which I would only do for Joyce. Joyce says she will not eat her dinner on plastics. Breakfast, yes. Dinner, no! Joyce says she et on newspapers, linoleum, and so on, in rooming houses long enough. She says she did not marry me to go backwards.

"I said, when we first got married, 'Baby, you look good presiding over a nice table.'

"Joyce said, 'You look good, too, Jess, sitting over a plate. You are the apple of my eye, the cog in my wheel, the sugar in my tea. In fact, you are all in all to me.' "

"I believe you are a prevaricator," I said to Simple.

"Which means what?" he asked.

"A liar," I said.

"Don't talk so much truth, Boyd, you might offend me." Simple grinned. "Anyhow, I was reading in an old paper I picked up to line the garbage pail where Einstein tackled the riddle of the universe and ended up with the atom bomb, which, says the paper, he did not aim to do. Einstein were trying to solve the riddle of the universe. Only thing is, them equations of Mr. Einstein's which they printed on the front page of the paper—everything down there equals zero, nothing, naught, I mean 0. Now, why is that?"

"Zero with Einstein was probably only a symbol for something else," I explained.

"For what?"

"Relativity," I said.

"Well, he put it all down to equal nothing, naught, 0, zero—which may be true for relativity, but it dead sure ain't true for me."

"In the overall picture, his equations may all add up to nothing," I said, "since everything is relative."

"My relatives didn't have nothing," said Simple. "But in spite of that, I, me—my mother's boy, Jesse B.—I do not add up to nothing. Neither does my life, which is at least biscuits and gravy, corn bread and ham, whiskey and womens, daytime working, nighttime loving. That is my life—not no zero."

"Einstein's theory had no direct relation to you, my dear fellow. He was dealing in pure science, which relates to the basic sources of matter and material, the great principles of the universe, the paths of the stars, the vast whirl of the zodiac, and the mysteries of infinity. When Einstein wrote that *phi* over *psi* divided by *gamma* multiplied by the square root of *p* equals *naught*, he did not have you in mind. You are an infinitesimal unit in the great complexity of the cosmos."

"Um-huh!" said Simple. "Well, at the corner of 125th Street and Seventh Avenue in Harlem, U.S.A., also at 135th and Lenox, not to speak of in front of Paddy's Bar and Grill, I am my baby's favorite guy, and my, my, my! No lie! So I do not add up to zero. I think Einstein must have done got old when he put down that all that figuring equals nothing. Besides, them formulas he put on that paper ain't the riddles of the universe."

"Well, just what do you figure, then, is the riddle of the universe?" I asked.

"Womens," said Simple.

"Don't be absurd," I said. "Women have nothing to do with the vast complexities of the cosmos. They are not the riddle of the universe."

"Then it must be white folks," said Simple.

"Racist!" I said.

"My wife is colored," said Simple. "And to tell the truth, Boyd, I don't think womens is too much riddles, after all, especially if you be around them long. You know, when I was young I used to be always reaching for the moon," said Simple; "then I found Joyce—who is just a good wife and a good cook."

"Less than the moon, I presume."

"More," said Simple. "The moon is beyond a man's reach—but I got Joyce. She is a wonderful woman. Eve in the garden could not be no better, because Eve had no stove on which to cook. She lived under a tree. How do you reckon Adam got his meals?"

"An apple," I said.

"And that came from Satan raw. But my wife can cook fried apples real good. Do you know, I love that woman."

"You ought to," I said, "but I seem to remember you were married once before—with less fortunate results."

"Isabel—that chick in Baltimore!" cried Simple. "In them days I were reaching for the moon. I saw them pictures of them pretty stage girls and colored models in the *Afro* and I thought I ought to marry one myself. So I hooked a waitress—the prettiest one on Pennsylvania Avenue—which were the Lenox Avenue or South Parkway of Baltimore. I thought I hooked her—but she hooked me. That Isabel were a lulu! A bodiddling! A rib out of Adam's wrong side. My first wife led me a dog's life—which is why I say, don't reach for no moon. Take what you can handle. If you be a normal man, try to find a normal woman. Not no picture-book-stage-footlights-radio-TV famous chick. Such a broad will drive you crazy.

In the first place, how you gonna know how many millions of other mens is in love with her? How you gonna know who else saw her picture in the papers? With so many mens to pick and choose from, how do you know she is gonna like you, just you, for yourself alone? Huh? I am asking?"

"Don't ask me," I said. "I have never been married."

"But you's colleged," said Simple. "You have studied on these things, them things, and all kinds of things. Not only college, but you's psycolleged, so you told me."

"I have studied psychology," I said, "but I don't know everything. And I did not specialize in sex and marriage."

"I am knowledged on both," said Simple, "including somewhatly the riddle of the universe. Womens has been my pleasure in life. I works for a living, but I loves for fun. When it comes to a woman, this is what I would advise: Don't reach for the moon. Golden blondes is out. Charcoal blondes is better. Color makes no difference, and hair any beauty parlor can take care of. Rose Meta will see to the hair. Age also is not so much of a difference. If a woman is too young, she will be flighty. If she is too old, you will not marry her anyhow. Disposition, that is important. If you cannot get along with her, love her and leave her, but do not marry her. Cookery, a main item. Do she cook good? Will she cook regular? Do she like to eat her own self, and is therefore familiar with the kitchen? And do she, or don't she, lose all interest when the meal is over? Will she also wash dishes, or will she say, 'Baby, now it is your turn,' just when you are ready to take off your shoes and look at TV? In other words, will she understand that a man is a man?

"If she understands, then that is the woman for me. I do not know nothing about no woman in the moon, nor man in the moon neither. And being no astronaught, I know I cannot reach no moon. If there was a woman in the moon, anyhow, I would not want her. My choice is Joyce. She is right here on earth, right here in Harlem—my complexion, my size, all right, my delight! And I done got wise. Listen to me—I tells all mens to stop reaching for the moon. Take what you can get, and in that way one and one will make a better two. You know what Pearl Bailey sings? 'Takes Two to Tango.' Then get your partner not off no moon, man. Leave the moon alone. Reach where your arms can reach—then you can keep what your arms can hold. So says me, Jesse B.—Amen!"

Part Two

RACE, RIOTS, POLICE, PRICES, AND POLITICS

Ways and Means

"YOU see this, don't you?" said Simple, showing me his N.A.A.C.P. card. "I have just joined the National Organization for the Association of Colored Folks and it is fine."

"You mean the National Association for the Advancement of Colored People," I said.

"Um-hum!" said Simple, "but they tell me it has white people in it, too."

"That's right, it does."

"I did not see none at the meeting where me and Joyce went this evening," said Simple.

"No?"

"No! There should have been some present because that *fine* colored speaker was getting white folks told—except that there was no white folks there to be told."

"They just do not come to Negro neighborhoods to meetings," I said, "although they may belong."

"Then we ought to hold some meetings downtown so that they can learn what this Negro problem is all about," said Simple. "It does not make sense to be always talking to ourselves. We know we got troubles. But every last Italian, Jew, and Greek what owns a business all up and down Seventh Avenue and Eighth Avenue and Lenox in Harlem ought to have been there. Do you reckon they belong to anything colored?"

"I don't expect they do," I said.

"Well, next time I go to a A.A.C.P. meeting . . ."

"N–A–A–C–P meeting," I said.

". . . N.A.A.C.P. meeting, I am going to move that everybody get a coin can," said Simple, "and go from store to store and bar to bar and hash-house to hash-house and take up collection for the N.A.A.C.P., from all these white folks making money in colored neighborhoods. If they don't give, I will figure they do not care nothing about my race. White folks are always taking up collections from *me* for the Red Cross or the Community Chest or the Cancer Drive or the March of Dimes or something or other. They are always shaking their cans in *my* face. Why shouldn't I shake my can in *their* face?"

"It would be better," I said, "if you got them all to be *members* of the N.A.A.C.P., not just to give a contribution."

"Every last white businessman in Harlem ought to belong to the N.A.A.C.P., but do you reckon they would ever come to meetings? They practically all live in the suburbans."

"They come to Harlem on business," I said, "so why shouldn't they come to the meetings?"

"That is why they go to the suburbans, to get away from the Negroes they have been selling clothes and groceries and victuals and beer all day. They do not want to be bothered with me when they close up their shops."

"Do you blame them?" I said.

"I do," said Simple. "Long as the cash register is ringing, they can be bothered with me, so why can't they come to an N.A.A.C.P. meeting?"

"Have I ever heard of you going out to the Italian or Jewish or Irish neighborhoods to any of their meetings to help them with their problems?" I asked.

"I do not have any stores in the Italian or Jewish neighborhoods," said Simple. "Neither do I own nary pool hall in an Irish neighborhood, nor nary Greek restaurant, nor nary white apartment house from which I get rent. I do not own no beer halls where Jews and Italians come to spend their money. If I did, I would join the Jewish N.A.A.C.P., and the Italian one, too! I would also join the Greek N.A.A.C.P. if I owned a hash-house where nothing but Greeks spent money all day long like I spend money in their Greasy Spoons."

"You put social co-operation on such a mercenary basis," I said.

"They would want me to have mercy on them if they was in my fix," said Simple.

"I did not say anything about mercy. I said *mercenary*—I mean a buying-and-selling basis."

"They could buy and sell me," said Simple.

"What I mean is, you should not have to have a business in a Jewish neighborhood to be interested in Jewish problems, or own a spaghetti stand to be interested in Italians, or a bar to care about the Irish. In a democracy, everybody's problems are related, and it's up to all of us to help solve them."

"If I did not have a business reason to be interested in *their* business," said Simple, "then what business would I have being interested in *their* business?"

"Just a human reason," I said. "It's all human business."

"Maybe that is why they don't join the N.A.A.C.P.," said Simple. "Because they do not think a Negro is human."

"If I were you, I would not speak so drastically unless I had some facts to go on. Have you ever asked any of the white businessmen where you trade to join the N.A.A.C.P.—the man who runs your laundry, or manages the movies where you go, or the Greek who owns the restaurant? Have you asked any of them to join?"

"No, I have not. Neither have I asked my colored landlady's white landlord."

"Well, ask them and see what they say."

"I sure will," said Simple; "then if they do not join, I will know they don't care nothing about me."

"You make it very simple," I said.

"It is simple, because everybody knew what stores to pick out the night of the riot."

"I was in Chicago that summer of '43, so I missed the riot."

"I was in it," said Simple.

"You don't say! Tell me about it. Where were you that night?"

"All up and down," said Simple.

"Grabbing hams out of broken windows?"

"No," said Simple, "I did not want no ham. I wanted Justice."

"What do you mean, Justice?"

"You know what I mean," Simple answered. "That cop had no business shooting a colored soldier!"

"You had no business breaking up stores, either," I said. "That is no way to get Justice."

"That is the way the Allies got it—breaking up Germany, breaking up Hiroshima, and everything in sight. But these white folks are more scared of Negroes in the U.S.A. than they ever was of Hitler, otherwise why would they make Jackie Robinson stop playing baseball to come to Washington and testify how loyal we is? I remember that night after the riots they turned on all the street lights in Harlem, although it was during the war and New York had a dim-out. Wasn't no dim-out in Harlem—lights just blazing in the middle of the war. The air-raid drill was called off, likewise the blackout. Suppose them German planes had come with *all* our lights on full."

"You're so dark the cops couldn't see *you* in a dim-out, so they had to turn on the lights."

"Make no remarks about my color, pal! You are the same complexion. And I'll bet if you'd been in New York when the riot started, you would have been out there in the streets with me."

"I would have emerged to see the excitement, yes, but not to break windows looking for Justice."

"Well, *I* was looking for Justice," said Simple. "I was tired."

"Tired of what?"

"Of hearing the radio talking about the Four Freedoms all day long during the war and me living in Harlem where nary one of them Freedoms worked—nor the ceiling prices neither."

"So?"

"So I threw a couple of bricks through a couple of windows when the riots started, and I felt better."

"Did you pick your windows or did you just throw?"

"Man, there wasn't no time to pick windows because the si-reens was blowing and the P.D.'s coming. But I aimed my foot at one grocery and my bricks at two big windows in a shoe store that cost them white folks plenty money to put back in."

"And that made you feel better?"

"Yes."

"Why?"

"Well, I figured, let them white men spend some of the profits they make out of Harlem putting those windows back. Let 'em spend some of that money they made out of these high rents in Harlem all these years to put them windows back. Also let 'em use some of that money to put them windows back that they owe my grandmother and my great-grandmother and her mother before that for working all them years in slavery for nothing. Let 'em take *that* back pay due my race and put them windows back!"

"You have things all mixed up, old man," I said, "which is one reason why I am glad you have joined the N.A.A.C.P., so that the next time a crisis comes up, you will have a more legitimate outlet for your energies. There are more effective ways and means of achieving justice than through violence. The N.A.A.C.P. believes in propaganda, education, political action, and legal redress. Besides, the men who owned that shoe store you threw those bricks in probably were way over in Europe when you were born. Certainly they had nothing to do with slavery, let alone your grandma's back pay."

"But they don't have nothing to do now with *Grandma's grandson* either—except to take my money over the counter, then go on downtown to Stuyvesant Town where I can't live, or out to them pretty suburbans, and leave me in Harlem holding the bag. I ain't no fool. When the riot broke out, I went looking for Justice."

"With a brick."

"No! Two bricks," said Simple.

The Law

"I DEFINITELY do not like the Law," said Simple, using the word with a capital letter to mean *police* and *courts* combined.

"Why?" I asked.

"Because the Law beats my head. Also because the Law will give a white man One Year and give me Ten."

"But if it wasn't for the Law," I said, "you would not have any protection."

"Protection?" yelled Simple. "The Law always protects a white man. But if *I* holler for the Law, the Law says, 'What do you want, Negro?' Only most white polices do not say 'Negro.' "

"Oh, I see. You are talking about the police, not the Law in general."

"Yes, I am talking about the polices."

"You have a bad opinion of the Law," I said.

"The Law has a bad opinion of me," said Simple. "The Law thinks *all* Negroes are in the criminal class. The Law'll stop me on the streets and shake me down—me, a workingman—as quick as they will any old weed-headed hustler or two-bit rounder. I do not like polices."

"You must be talking about the way-down-home-in-Dixie Law," I said, "not up North."

"I am talking about the Law *all over* America," said Simple, "North or South. Insofar as I am concerned, a police is no good. It was the Law that started the Harlem riots by shooting that soldier-boy. Take a cracker down South or an ofay up North—as soon as he puts on a badge he wants to try out his billy club on some Negro's head. I tell you police are no good! If they was, they wouldn't be polices."

"Listen," I said, "you are generalizing too much. Not all cops are bad. There are some decent policemen—particularly in New York. You yourself told me about that good Irish cop downtown who made an insistent Southerner get out of a Negro's cab."

"I admit since the riots the cops ain't so bad in Harlem, and downtown there are some right nice ones. But outside of New York, you can count the good polices on the fingers of one glove," said Simple. "They are in the minorality."

"You mean *minority*. But what about the colored cops?" I asked. "Not all cops are white."

"Man!" said Simple. "Colored cops are *colored*, so they can't bully *nobody* but me—which makes it worse. You know colored cops ain't gonna hit no white man. So when the black Law does get a chance to hit somebody once, they have to hit me *twice*. Colored cops is worse than white. A black Law is terrible!"

"I do not agree with you," I said. "I think there ought to be more colored cops."

"You can add, can't you?" asked Simple.

"Yes."

"Then use your rithematics. A black Law cannot lock up a white man in most cities, and he better not try. So when a colored cop does some arresting he has to lock up *two* or *three* of *me* to fill his quota—otherwise he never would get promoted."

"Well, anyhow, if it wasn't for the police, who would keep you from being robbed and mugged?"

"I have been robbed and mugged both," said Simple, "and there was not a cop nowhere to be found. I could not even find a P.D. car."

"Did you report being robbed?"

"I did the first time, but not no more. Them polices down at the precinct station looked at me like *I* were the robber. They asked me for all kinds of identifications from my driving license to my draft card. That was during the war. I told them, 'How can I show you my draft card when it was in my pocketbook and my pocketbook is just stole?' They wanted to lock me up for having no draft card."

"That does not sound plausible," I said.

"It may not sound possible—but it was," said Simple. "I told the Desk Sergeant that them mugs taken Eighty Dollars off of me at the point of a gun. The Desk Sergeant asked me *where did I get Eighty Dollars*! I showed him my hands. I said, 'See these here calluses? I work for my money,' I said. 'I do not graft, neither do I steal.'

"The Desk Sergeant hollered, 'Don't get smart, boy, or I'll throw *you* in the jug!' That is why I would not go back to no police station to report *nothing* no more."

"Maybe you'll be better treated next time."

"Not as long as I am black," said Simple.

"You look at everything, I regret to say, in terms of black and white."

"So does the Law," said Simple.

American Dilemma

"When I come around the corner last night here in Harlem," said Simple, "and nearly run into a white cop strolling around the corner from the other way, I almost said, 'Birmingham.' "

"Almost? What did you say instead?" I asked.

"Nothing," said Simple.

"What did the cop say?"

"Nothing, neither," said Simple. "If he had been a colored cop and I had bumped into him, I would have said, 'Excuse me.' But he being white, I did not say nothing. And what I thought was Birmingham."

"Seemingly, then, you equate all white people with the brutalities of Birmingham, even whites in New York."

"I do," said Simple. "After dark, Harlem is black, except for cops.

Here of lately, it looks like there is more white cops than ever strolling around our corners at night. They must be expecting more trouble."

"What 'they'?" I asked.

"The white folks downtown. If there was as many black cops downtown in New York as there is white cops uptown in Harlem, you would know something was wrong. I reckon it is Alabama and Mississippi making the white folks downtown afraid Harlem might get mad again and start breaking up things, like they did in the riots."

"I admit there is often tension in the air," I said. "But do you think it will reach riot proportions again?"

"All I know is, when I come around that corner last night off Lenox Avenue and run into that white cop, when he saw me he looked like he was scared. You know I am no dangerous man. I am what folks calls an ordinary citizen. Me, I work, pay my rent, and taxes, and try to get along. But that young white cop looked at me like he were afraid of me. I do not much blame him, up here in Harlem all by hisself at midnight A.M. in the middle of Negroes. Lenox Avenue can get real lonesome-looking late at night. When I saw that cop and thought about Birmingham, I bet he saw me and thought about riots.

"He were a young cop. Maybe he just recently got on the force. Maybe he needs to earn some steady money to take care of his wife and kids and buy hisself a house in some neighborhood where there is no Negroes. None of these white cops here in Harlem ever live in Harlem. They say Harlem is the place where the Police Department puts rookies and green young cops to break them in. Or else they put old cops who has done wrong in some other part of New York, maybe taken graft that should have gone to the precinct captain, or something like that. So they put them up in Harlem for a punishment. Anyhow, the other night, here is this young white cop coming around the corner, and here is me coming around the corner. We almost bump. I pass, he passes, and nobody says nothing.

"In a way, I felt sorry for that young white cop. Was I not colored and he not white, I would have said, 'Good evening! It's kind of quiet tonight, ain't it?' And maybe he would have said, 'Good evening,' back. But neither one of us said nothing. I almost bumped into him. He almost bumped into me, curving that corner, and nobody even said, 'Good evening,' let alone, 'Excuse me.' All I thought about was Birmingham. What he thought I do not know."

"I gather, then, that there was no friendly word exchanged between you—you, citizen, and he, policeman, guardian of the law."

"No friendly word," said Simple.

Color of the Law

"LAST Sunday I walked some thirty blocks down Seventh Avenue straight through Harlem, and in all them thirty blocks I did not see a single *white* person, other than cops—nothing but Negroes. Harlem is really a colored community. Of course, this were Sunday. Weekdays you see plenty of white folks in Harlem, since they own most of the stores, bars, banks, and number banks. But they do not live with us. On Saturday nights, these white folks take their money they have got from Negroes and go home to big apartments downtown, or nice houses with lawns out on Long Island—and leave me here in Harlem. They do not ever invite me to their homes for Sunday dinner—yet it's me what pays for their dinners. They make their money out of me. Then they want to tell me *not* to vote for Adam Powell or listen to Malcolm X because they raises too much hell! Do I tell them how to vote or who to listen to?

"The only white folks you see in Harlem on Sundays is cops, and of them you see plenty, two and three on every corner, and most of them white. They have some fine colored cops in New York, but where are they at? Off on Sundays? It looks like to me every day in Harlem they got white cops to spare. On Marcus Garvey Day they even had white cops on the roofs looking down on the Negroes—to keep us from running riot, I reckon. I guess they have not forgot the Harlem riots yet downtown. And now Negroes do get kind of evil.

"I feels evil myself when I sees a white cop talking smart to a colored woman, like I did the other day. A middle-aged brownskin lady had run through a red light on Lenox Avenue by accident, and this cop were glaring at her as if she had committed some kind of major crime. He was asking her what did she think the streets was for, to use for a speedway—as if twenty miles an hour were speeding. So I says to the cop, 'Would you talk that way to your mama?'

"He ignored me. And as good luck would have it, he did not know I had put him in the dozens. By that time quite a crowd had gathered around. When he saw all them black faces, he lowered his voice, in fact shut up altogether, and just wrote that old lady a ticket, since he did not see any colored cops nearby to call to protect him. In Harlem nowadays, when colored cops are around, they do all the loud talking, whilst the white cops just stand by—in case. Since the Harlem riots way back in the forties, white cops uptown ain't as rambunctious as they used to be—not unless they got six squad cars with them. Still and yet, they know the law is white, and *white* makes right insofar as the law goes—which is why I votes black. I will vote for Adam Powell as long as he claims to be colored.

"There were four white cops in the polling place where I went to vote. Right in the middle of Harlem, four white cops. Everybody else there were colored, voters all colored, officials all colored registering the books, only the cops white—to remind me of which color is the law. I went inside that voting booth and shut the door and stood there all by myself and put the biggest black mark I could make in front of every black name on the ballot. At least up North I can vote black. If enough of us votes black in Harlem, maybe someday we can change the color of the law. At any rate, I, Jesse B. Semple, have put down my vote."

After Hours

"BARTENDER!" Simple cried in a loud voice as though he were going to treat everyone in the place. "Once around the bar." Then, pointing to ourselves, "This far—from my buddy to me."

By the time the beers were drawn, Simple had begun to recount a story.

"You know," he began, "I was way down under in Harlem the other night, way, way down on Lenox Avenue." I could see it was a serious story because he forgot his beer, allowing his glass to remain on the bar.

"It was so cold I went into a barbecue place thinking I might take a order of spareribs and coleslaw to Joyce if I had enough change —and at the same time get warm. Man, the juke box was playing up a breeze, flashing colored lights, and the joint was full of young kids and girls not buying nothing much but drinking Pepsis and jiving around the juke box. I looked at them kids and I felt sorry. I can see now why these girls wear open-worked shoes in zero weather because them cheap soles are so thin they couldn't keep their feet warm anyhow, so they'd just as well be open-worked.

"And the boys," continued Simple, "with them army-store raincoats on and last spring's imitation camel's hairs—which would not keep nobody warm—because they ain't had the money this winter to buy an overcoat. They was just jiving and jitterbugging quietly-like, till the woman hollered, 'Stop!' because there was a big sign up:

NO DANCING POSITIVELY

"They also had a sign up:

DON'T ASK FOR CREDIT—HE'S DEAD

"I reckon that is why those kids could not eat much, on account of credit being dead. But they had to move to keep warm because it was kinder cold in that place, the only heat being from that thing where the barbecue turns and that was not much. It were a Greek place or some kind of foreigner's, but at least they had colored help. The foreigner just set behind the cash register and took the money.

"While I was setting there waiting for the woman to wrap up my sandwich and coleslaw for Joyce, a half-dozen little old teen-age boys come in and stood around listening to the juke box, singing with the records and rubbing their ears to get warm. By and by a quarrel started amongst them and before you could say 'Hush,' one of them let a blackjack a foot long slide out of his sleeve and another one drew a knife. They all started cussing and damning.

"The woman behind the counter said, 'Somebody ought to call the Law,' which kinder riled me the wrong way because, after all, they was nothing but kids.

"So I said, 'Madam, the cops could only lock them kids up. The cops could not make their papa's kitchenette big enough for them to invite their young friends to come home and have fun in and not have to look for it in the streets. I bet where these boys live there are forty-eleven names in the doorbell, the house is so crowded. Also some roomer has the spare bed.'

"The woman said, 'I reckon you right. There are about that many names in the bell where I live, too. But I just don't want these boys to fight in here, that's all. They make me nervous.'

"The boys didn't fight. They finally put up their weapons, and I took my sandwich and coleslaw and went on up the street. Zero outside, man! And cold enough to freeze a brass monkey! But all the way to Joyce's I kept thinking about them kids that didn't have no place to go in the evening but to that juke-box joint with a sign up:

NO DANCING POSITIVELY

"I said to myself, 'If I ever have a kid, I will have a juke box *at home* and his friends can come in and dance as much as they want.' "

"A Victrola would be more appropriate for the home," I said.

"A juke box is more sociable," declared Simple; "then they wouldn't get into the habit of wanting to be out in the streets so much and later when they got grown start to running around to bars and after-hour joints."

"Like you," I said.

"Yes, like me," said Simple. "I almost got caught in a raid the other night. But the cops phoned first that they was coming. The raid were just a polite hint to the houseman to keep their graft up to date and let the Law have theirs on time. I guess the reason cops are so hard on after-hour spots, and them folks who run them have to pay off so steep to stay open, is because they serve such bad bodacious licker."

"There must be some after-hour spots that serve good liquor."

"They are few and far between," said Simple. "Just because it was cold outside, I went into one of them gyp joints night before last and I have not got over my hangover yet. In fact, it is just like one of them prohibition hangovers—the kind of licker that hits you in the head like a baseball bat, cracks your skull inside, and mighty near blinds you besides. If the licker ain't bad, then it's like up at Mamie Lou's last Saturday—cut so much it wouldn't even make you high, let alone leave you with a hangover. In these after-hour joints, either they gyp you or try to kill you, one.

"At that place I went the other night, Mojo Mike's King Kong Palace, basement floor, last apartment, down the hall off Lenox, the guy sold me a half pint of pure white mule mixed with blue lightning. I thought my tonsils would explode.

"I said, 'What *is* this? It looks like water and tastes like fire.'

"He said, 'That is some of this new atomic licker. It will make you Nagasaki, then go up in smoke. For Thirty-five Cents you can solid blow your top, I mean anatomize your wig.'

"I said, 'It's too big a bargain for me.' But since I'd paid for it, naturally, I drunk it. And, boy, what a hangover!"

"I don't sympathize with you," I said.

"I do not expect you to," said Simple. "I guess you have never oversported *yourself*—therefore you cannot understand. If you don't understand, you cannot sympathize. It is just like somebody who never had the toothache and don't know what it is."

"I've had a toothache," I said.

"Then you can sympathize with me when I have the toothache. But you cannot sympathize with me if I have a hangover."

"The wise thing to do," I said, "would be to avoid bootleg liquor and stay out of after-hour joints."

"Then where would a human go after the bars close?"

"Home," I said.

"That would be too simple," said Simple. "A man can *always* go home."

"It would be better for your health, your reputation, and your pocketbook if you would go home at a reasonable hour," I said. "You're getting too old to be running around all night. You ought to know better."

"Age has nothing to do with wisdom," said Simple. "I know a man fifty-two years old who never does go home except to take a bath and change his underwear. And sometimes, before he can do that, his wife runs him out of the house. A woman can really be a thorn in a man's side when she does not understand him. My wife did not understand me: that is why I am out here in the streets tonight."

"Joyce understands you quite well," I said, "yet I see you are not keeping her company this evening."

"I was with her last night," said Simple. "And I am somewhatly doubtful of her understanding. You know the first thing she asked me? She said, 'Where was you the night before?'

"I said, 'I was out, baby, in an after-hour place, and I did not get home till late.'

"She said, 'That is no excuse for you to come around to my house and set up and snooze. I do not pay rent here to receive sleepers. Suppose my landlady was to walk in and catch you sleeping in her parlor.'

"I said, 'So what? When a man is tired, he has to sleep. Besides, I got a headache.'

"She said, 'A licker-ache, that's what! I can smell wood alcohol from your end of the couch to mine. Get out of here and go on home. You ain't no company to me in your condition.'

"Joyce were mad! That is why I am not keeping her company this evening. And that is what I am telling you about a woman not understanding a man. The very time you need to be understood most is the time they let you down. Hangovered as I was, Joyce should have said, 'Baby, lemme put a cold towel on your head.' Instead of that, she said, 'Get out of here and go home! You ain't no company for me.' Now, if Joyce had come to see me feeling bad, I would have tried to comfort her."

"You would not be going with Joyce if she were the kind of girl who gets drunk and has hangovers," I said.

"True," answered Simple.

"Then why do you expect her to understand you when you come up in that condition?"

"*Because I am a man,*" said Simple, "and a woman is suppose to understand. There is nothing worse than a hangover. So if *ever* there is a time to understand, that time is it. I am disappointed in Joyce."

"Joyce is probably disappointed in you," I said, "spending your money collecting hangovers in joints like Mojo Mike's after hours."

"After hours is when I needs most to be understood," said Simple, "especially *after* after hours."

When a Man Sees Red

"I MAY not be a red," he said as he banged on the bar, "but sometimes I see red."

"What do you mean?"

"The way some of these people a man has to work for talks to a man, I see red. The other day my boss come saying to me that I was laying down on the job—when all I was doing was just thinking about Joyce. I said, 'What do you mean, laying down on the job? Can't you see me standing up?'

"The boss said, 'You ain't doing as much work as you used to do.'

"I said, 'A Dollar don't do as much buying for me as *it* used to do, so I don't do as much for a Dollar. Pay me some more money, and I will do more work.' "

"What did he say then?"

"He said, 'You talk like a red.'

"I said, 'What do you mean, red?'

"He said, 'You know what I mean—*red, Communist*. After *all* this country has done for you Negroes, I didn't think you'd turn out to be a red.'

"I said, 'In my opinion, a man can be any color except yellow. I'd be yellow if I did not stand up for my rights.'

"The boss said, 'You have no right to draw wages and not work.'

"I said, 'I have *done* work, I *do* work, and I *will* work—but also a man is due to eat for his work, to have some clothes, and a roof over his head. For what little you are paying me, I can't hardly keep body and soul together. Don't you reckon I have a soul?' I said.

"Boss said, 'I have nothing to do with your soul. All I am concerned about is your work. You are talking like a Communist, and I will not have no reds in my plant.'

"I said, 'It wasn't so long ago you would not have no Negroes in your plant. Now you won't have no reds. You must be color-struck!'

"That got him. That made him mad. He said, 'I have six Negroes working for me now.'

"I said, 'Yes, out of six hundred men. You wouldn't have them if you could've got anybody else during the war. And what kind of work do you give us? The dirty work! The cheapest wages! Maintenance department—which is just another way for saying *clean up*. You know you don't care nothing about us Negroes. You getting ready to fire me right now. Well, if you fire me, I will be a red for sure, because I see red this morning. *I will see the union, if you fire me,*' I said.

" 'Just go on and do your work,' he said, and walked off. But I was hot, pal! I'm telling you! But he did not look back. He didn't want to have no trouble out of that union."

"Now I know he will think you are a red," I said.

"Is it red to want to earn decent wages? Is it red to want to keep your job? And not to want to take no stuff off a boss?"

"Don't yell at me," I said. "I'm not your boss. I didn't say a thing."

"No, but you implied," said Simple. "Just because you are not working for white folks, you implied."

"There you go bringing up the race issue again," I said. "I think you are too race-conscious."

"I am black," said Simple, "also I will be red if things get worse. But one thing sure, I will not be yellow. I will stand up for my rights till kingdom come."

"You'd better be careful or they will have you up before the Un-American Committee."

"I wish that old Southern chairman would send for me," said Simple. "I'd tell him more than he wants to know."

"For instance?" I said.

"For instant," said Simple, "I would say, 'Your Honery, I wish to inform you that I was born in America, I live in America, and long as I have been black, I been an American. Also I was a Democrat—but I didn't know Roosevelt was going to die.' Then I would ask them, 'How come you don't have any Negroes on your Un-American Committee?'

"And old Chairman Georgia would say, 'Because that is un-American.'

"Then I would say, 'It must also be un-American to run a train, because I do not see any colored engineers running trains. All I see Negroes doing on the railroads is sweeping out coaches and making beds. Is that American?'

"Old Chairman Georgia would say, 'Yes! Sweeping is American.'

"Then I would say, 'Well, I want to be un-American so I can run a train.'

"Old Chairman would say, 'You must be one of them Red Russians.'

" 'No, I ain't neither,' I would say. 'I was born down South, too, like you. But I do not like riding a Jim Crow car when I go home to Dixie. Also, I do not like being a Pullman porter *all the time.* Sometimes I want to *run* a train.'

" 'I know you are a Red Russian!' yells that old Chairman. 'You want to tear this country down!'

" 'Your Honery,' I says, 'I admit I would like to tear *half* of it down—the Southern half from Virginia to Mobile—just to build it over new. And when I built it over, I would put *you* in the Jim Crow car instead of me.'

" 'Hold that Negra in contempt of court!' yells Chairman Georgia.

" 'I thought you just said I was a Red Russian. Now here you go calling me a Negro. Which is I?'

" 'You're both,' says the Chairman.

" 'Why? Because I want to drive a train?'

" 'Yes,' yells the Chairman, 'because you want to drive a train! This is a white man's country. These is white men's trains! You cannot drive one. And down where I come from, neither can you ride in a WHITE coach.'

" 'You don't have any coaches for Red Russians,' I said.

" 'No,' yells the Chairman, 'but we will have them as soon as I can pass a law.'

" 'Then where would I ride?' I asked. 'In the COLORED coach or in the RED coach?'

" 'You will not ride nowhere,' yells the Chairman, 'because you will be in jail.'

" 'Then I will break your jail up,' I said, 'because I am entitled to liberty whilst pursuing happiness.'

" 'Contempt of court!' bangs the Chairman."

Just then the bartender flashed the lights off and on three times, indicating that it was time to close the bar, so I interrupted my friend's imaginary session of the Un-American Committee.

"Listen," I said, "you're intoxicated, and when you are intoxicated, you talk right simple. Things are not that simple."

"Neither am I," said Simple.

Simple and the High Prices

"LISTEN," said Simple, "how am I going to live with prices getting higher and higher and my weekly wages staying just the same?"

"I do not know," I said. "What I am worried about is how am I going to live myself."

"Now, buddy-o," said Simple, "you know if I live, you live."

"I do not know any such thing," I said, "because if you can't live yourself, how could you help me?"

"I can always borrow a couple of bucks from Joyce," said Simple.

"Joyce's wages are not getting any higher, either, are they?" I asked.

"Womens always seems to manage to make out somehow," said Simple.

"If you can so easily borrow a few dollars from Joyce," I said, "why do you so regularly borrow from me when your own funds have run short—nearly every Thursday or Friday? Why don't you borrow from Joyce if it is so easy?"

"I did not say it was easy," said Simple. "What I said is, I *can* borrow from Joyce, but it is not easy. And she does not approve of my drinking. But if I was hungry, she would lend me. And if you was hungry, I would lend you. And if I was hungry, you would lend me."

"I have never known you to be hungry," I said. "I have only known you to be thirsty."

"Prices have never been so high before," said Simple. "I am liable to get hungry and thirsty, too, now. And I am a man who must always eat before I drink. Beer is bad on an empty stomach."

"Suppose you got to the point where you could not eat—what would you do then?" I asked.

"Just drink," said Simple.

"You mean you would let poverty drive you to drink?"

"I would not have to be driven," said Simple.

"What you ought to do is think," I said. "How do you expect the human race to get out of the hole we are in if folks do not think?"

"That is what I pay my congressman for," said Simple. "Also the President. They are the government. Let them think."

"In the final analysis," I said, "you are the government—and if each citizen does not think for himself . . ."

"I am not talking about no *final analysis*," said Simple. "I am talking about *high prices*. If I was to think all night, meat would not be one cent cheaper."

"That is where you are wrong," I said. "If you were to think constructively, and make plans, perhaps you could reduce the price of meat."

"I had rather think how to raise my wages," said Simple.

"That is one-sided," I said. "If you raise your wages, the producer will raise his prices. Then we have a vicious circle all around."

"With me in the middle," said Simple, "so I go down!"

"Naturally you go down," I said, "because you are caught in a dilemma."

"I don't know about the 'lemma," said Simple, "but I sure am caught. Last week I went to buy a sport shirt for this warm weather coming up here, and the man said, 'Seven Fifty.' I said, 'Seven Fifty for what? I bought this shirt four years ago for Two Twenty-five.' The man said, 'Try and find it now.' I tried. At the next store, that self-same shirt was Eight. I said, 'Wait! Four years ago I bought . . . !' Before I could get it out good, the man said, 'You are four years too late.' "

"What did you do then?"

"I cut out, friend. And I did not buy the shirt."

"That is what makes depressions," I said. "You don't buy the shirt. The manufacturer can't pay his help. His help can't buy any shirts. No factories can pay anybody—and you end up out of work. That is the vicious circle."

"I am caught," said Simple.

"All of us are caught," I said.

"It sounds like W.P.A. to me," said Simple. "And if it is, I put my application in now."

"For relief?" I asked.

"For whatever they have to offer," said Simple.

Nickel for the Phone

"When I were knee-high to a duck I went to the circus and I saw there Jo-Jo the Dog-Faced Boy, or else it were Zip the Pinheaded Man. I never did know the difference because I were too little. I went with my grandpa and grandma before they died and I were sent back to my mama. Neither one of them old folks could read. They also disremembered what the side-show barker said afterwards, so when I got big I never did know if it were Jo-Jo the Dog-Faced Boy I saw or Zip the Pinheaded Man. Anyway, whichever one it were, *he were awful.*"

"What makes you think of that now?" I asked.

"Last night Joyce told me I looked like Zip. I am trying to figure out if it *was* Zip that I saw, because if I look like what I saw in that circus, I sure look *bad.*"

"You do not have a pinhead," I told him. "But, come to think of it, you could be said to have a dog-face."

"I know I am not good-looking," said Simple, "but I did not think I looked like a dog."

"The last time I saw her, Joyce told me she thought you were a fine-looking man," I said. "Why has she changed her mind?"

"Because I promised to pass by her house night before last night and I did not go."

"Why didn't you?"

"That's my business, but Joyce wants to make it hers. Womens is curious."

"Naturally."

"So when I did not tell her where I went Thursday night, she jumped salty. She said she did not care where I was nohow. So I says, 'Why do you keep on asking me, if you don't care?'

"She says, 'I *did* care, but you have drove all the care out of me, the way you do.' Then she started to cry. Now, when a woman starts to cry, I do not know what to do.

"So I says, 'Let's go down to the corner and have a rum-cola.'

"She says, 'I do not want to go nowhere with you and you looking like Zip!' That is when I started to wondering who Zip were."

"I have always wondered, too," I said, "never having seen that famous freak."

"Another thing I have wondered is, who is Cootie Brown? Last Saturday night somebody said to me, 'Man, you're drunk as Cootie Brown.' "

"Which meant high as a Georgia pine."

"I know what it meant, but I do not know who Cootie Brown was. Do you?"

"I guess he was just somebody who got pretty drunk all the time."

"And Zip were somebody who looked pretty bad all the time."

"That's about it. But did you effect a reconciliation with Joyce?"

"Only partly," said Simple. "A woman does not like to make up right away. They like to frown and pout so you will pet and beg 'em. But I do not beg nobody."

"What's your method, friend?"

"I leave—till they calm down, daddy-o. Just leave the house and let 'em cool off, put a little distance between troubles and me. Facts, I intend to put several days between myself and Joyce."

"You are not going by there and eat on Sunday as usual?"

"I can eat in Father's for Fifteen Cents—so why should I worry with Joyce?"

"Father Divine's is all very well. But his biscuits are nothing like Joyce's, that time she invited us to dinner last Easter."

"I do not care for biscuits when they are all mixed up with Who-Struck-John. Joyce must think a man don't have no place else to go except to her house. There's plenty womens in this world. And tonight I am dressed up, so I know I don't look like Zip. Lend me a nickel, boy."

"For what?"

"To phone, what you think? I want to see how Joyce talks this evening. If she answers with one of them sweet *Hello's*, then changes her voice to a gravel bass when she finds out it's me, I will know she's still got her habits on."

"I thought you said just now you weren't going around there tonight."

"I'm *not* going, no matter how sweet she talks. But what is a nickel? I would just juke-box it away on a record by Duke, so I might as well waste it on Joyce."

"You will want that nickel when times get hard."

"That's right," said Simple. "If this depression-recession gets any worse, *both* of us might want some of her biscuits, huh?"

"You have more foresight than I thought," I said. "Here's a nickel. Go call her up."

Possum, Race, and Face

"SINCE you just came in, how come you've got to go so soon? If you was a good buddy, you'd wait until I have one more beer," said Simple about 2 a.m. Saturday night in the crowded bar. "I have to get up kinder early in the morning myself, at least by noon. I am going to have Sunday dinner with Joyce! We have made up, man! And she is cooking especially for me. I wish I could invite you, but I can't, 'cause Joyce just invited me *alone*."

"I'm happy to hear you're reunited," I said. "In truth, I am delighted. How did you two effect your reconciliation?"

"We just couldn't stand not to see each other no longer."

"Who gave in first?" I asked. "You or Joyce?"

"We both gave in at once, man. You know how those things is. I forgived her—and she forgived me. Now she is cooking again—and I have got my appetite back."

"What are you going to eat tomorrow?"

"Chicken, since it is Sunday," said Simple, "but I wish it were possum."

"Possum! Now I know you are intoxicated. Where on earth can you get a possum in New York?"

"As many Negroes as there are in Harlem, there ought to be at least one possum around in the fall of the year. Listen, man, tonight if I had a lantern and a hound dog and a gun, and if there was a persimmon tree on Sugar Hill and that possum was up that tree,

I'll bet you I would get myself a possum this very night. I bet on that!"

"So you used to hunt possum down home?"

"He could be up a nut tree, too, or whatever kind of tree he was up, me and my hound would find him out and bring him down," declared Simple.

"Do you suppose Joyce knows how to cook a possum?" I asked.

"She might not admit it," said Simple, "but I'll bet you if I brought her one, she would not give it up for silver nor gold. Between her and an oven, that possum would come out good. But I don't reckon nobody in America could cook a possum like my Uncle Tige. The way Uncle Tige cooked a possum, man, you would not want nothing better on this earth, *never*!"

"I never heard tell of your Uncle Tige before. Who was he?"

"I lived with him and Aunt Mandy for a time when I were ten, eleven, twelve."

"You sure lived with a lot of different relatives."

"I was passed around," explained Simple. "When I were a child, I was passed around. But not even with Grandma Arcie did I eat so good. Not *no* place did I eat so good as with Uncle Tige. Him and Aunt Mandy both liked to eat. They both could cook. And sometimes they would see who could outcook the other. Chitterlings—man, don't talk! Hog jowl, hog maw, pig tails, pig feets! They tasted like the Waldorf-Astoria *ought* to taste—but I know it don't. Corn dumplings, turnip greens, young onions! Catfish, buffalo fish, also perch! Cabbage with cayenne pepper! Tripe! Chine bones and kraut! On Sunday two hens stuffed with sage dressing! Also apple dumpling! Umm-m-huh!

"When they sent me back to my Aunt Lucy, I was so big and fat the schoolteacher looked at me and said, 'Boy, how come you're only in the fourth grade? Big as you is, you ought to be in the low ninth.'

"I had done et so much cracklin' bread I was oozing out grease and so many hominy grits with gravy till my hair was oily and laid down just like a Indian's. I did not have to use no Murray's Pomade then. But that was long ago. And I have not et like that since I come to New York. I would give all the ducks, chickens, and turkeys in the world for a possum.

"A possum for Sunday dinner, man, would be perfect, cooked like my Uncle Tige used to cook him. First singe him in hot ashes, then clean him, then bake him—and that possum all stuffed with apples and fruits and pineapples with great big old red yams laid around his sides, plenty of piccalilli and chowchow and watermelon-rind pickles setting in little cut-glass dishes all around the table. And a great big old jug of hard cider to drink along with that possum. Aw, man, Sunday would be perfect then! But since we will not have a possum, I will have a good dinner tomorrow right on. Joyce is making hot biscuits. And if there is anything I like in this world, it is biscuits."

"Me, too," I said.

"I also like beer," said Simple.

"Then why don't you set us up?"

"Because I haven't got a dime left. I stashed my money home this week since I intend to take Joyce out to a show or something every night now that we made up. But if I ever get hold of a possum in Harlem, you will get some of it. You are my friend."

"Give us a beer, Tony," I said. But the bartender didn't hear me with the juke box going.

"Sometimes I set and remember when I were nothing but a child," Simple continued. "In this noisy old bar I set sometimes and remember when I were a child, and I would not want to be a child again. But some things about it was good—like possum. There was other things I don't like to remember. Some of them things keep coming back to me sometimes when I set in this bar and look in the bottom of my beer glass and there ain't no more beer."

"Another round, Tony!"

"When I were a growing boy and lived with my Aunt Lucy, I used to hear the old folks saying, 'Take all this world and gimme Jesus!' Aunt Lucy were a great Christian, so she used to go to church all the time, facts, she were a pillar of the church. It was her determination to go to Beulah Land, and I do believe she went. In this life she had very little to look forward to—except some more hard work. So no wonder she said, 'Take all this world—but gimme Jesus!' Well, the white folks have taken this world."

"What makes you think that?"

"The earth don't belong to me," said Simple. "Not even no parts of it. This bar does not belong to me. It belongs to Italians. The house I live in does not belong to me. It belongs to Jews. The place I work at belongs to an Irishman. He can fire me any time he gets ready. The insurance I'm in belongs to white folks. And I reckon the cemetery I'll be buried in belongs to them, too. The only thing I own is the clothes on my back—and I bought them from a white store."

"You could at least belong to a colored insurance," I said.

"My mama put me in the Metropolitan when I were knee-high to a duck, and I never did get around to changing my policy," said Simple. "But you are getting me off my point—which is that this *world* belongs to white folks."

"Have you been all over the world?"

"No," said Simple, "but I reads. I listens to world news on the radio every day. I am no dumbbell. I hear all about the Dutch in Java, the Americans in Japan, and the English in Africa, where I hear they have Jim Crow cars. Don't tell me ofays don't own the world."

"That doesn't necessarily mean they are going to keep it forever," I said, competing with the music on the juke box and the noise at the bar. "The colonial system is bound to come to an end."

"When?" asked Simple.

"Before long. The British Empire is on its last legs. The Dutch haven't got much left."

"But the crackers still have Mississippi, Georgia, Alabama, and Washington, D.C.," said Simple.

"I admit that, but when we start voting in greater numbers down

South, and using the ballot as we ought to up North, they won't be as strong as they might have been."

"I hope I live to see that day," said Simple. "Anyhow, the next time I go to church, I am going to pray for the Lord to give back some of this world to colored folks."

"I am glad you intend to go to church. But what you ought to pray is *not* to have the world split up between colored and white nations, but instead, to have the spirit of co-operation enter into *everybody's* soul so that we all could build a decent world together."

"If I was to really pray what is in my mind," said Simple, "the Lord would shut up His ears and not listen to me at all. If I was to pray what is in my mind, I would pray for the Lord to wipe white folks off the face of the earth. Let 'em go! Let 'em go! *And let me rule awhile!*"

"I'll bet you would do a fine job of ruling," I said sarcastically.

"I would do better than they have done. First place, with white folks wiped out, I would stop charging such high rents—so my landlady could charge *me* less. Second place, I would stop hoarding up all the good jobs for white folks—so I could get ahead myself. Third place, I would make the South behave. Fourth place, I would let Asia and Africa go free, and I would build them all schools and air-cooled movies and barbecue pits—and give everybody enough to eat, including possum. Then I would say, 'If you-all colored folks in Africa and Asia and elsewhere, including Harlem, don't behave yourselves, I will drop an atom bomb on you and wipe you out, too—just like the Lord wiped out the white folks!' I would make everybody behave themselves."

"In other words, you would repeat the same old mistake of force and violence that the white nations have been guilty of," I said.

"Except that I would *force* people to be *good*, and get educated, and run themselves, and enjoy Lena Horne and Bing Crosby, and eat aplenty. I would make people do *right*. I would not let them do wrong."

"You would do more than God is doing," I said.

"Man, I would be *a hell*," cried Simple, "a natural hell!"

"I think you must be drunk," I said. "Stop yelling so loud, or that white bartender will think you're a disgrace to the race."

"Oh," sighed Simple, "there are certainly a lot of disadvantages in being colored. The way that juke box is blaring, a body has to yell. Yet you can't even holler out loud without somebody saying, 'Shsss-ss-s! Don't be so rowdy in front of white folks.' You can't even get drunk and walk staggle-legged down the street without somebody accusing you of disgracing the race. I think Negroes should have as much right to get drunk and misbehave in front of anybody as the next person has, without somebody always throwing it up in our faces about disgracing the race."

Simple paused for a long drink of beer, gulped, took a deep breath, and went on.

"If a colored man even gambles a little penny ante and the place gets raided, there is a big headline in the papers:

HARLEM VICE DEN RAIDED

"But at them downtown clubs they gambles hundreds of dollars every night, never do get raided, and nobody calls them a vice den. But just let a colored man roll one roll—and he is a disgrace to the race. Or take murder and manslaughter, for instant. A white man can kill his wife, cut her up, put her in a trunk, ship her to California, and never get her body out of the baggage room, yet nobody talks about he is a disgrace to the white race. But just let a Negro carve somebody once lightly with a small knife and the papers say:

BIG BLACK BUCK RUNS AMUCK

"Then everybody in Harlem says, 'What a shame for a Negro to act that way,' and 'How is the race ever gonna get anywhere?' Why, hundreds of white folks kills hundreds of other white folks every day, and nobody says, 'What a shame for a white man to act like that.' "

"Well, being a minority race," I said, "we have to save face. We have to act better than white people act, so they won't brand us as being worse."

"Being worse?" cried Simple, topping Louis Jordan's loudest riff on the juke box. "How could colored folks be worse? Hitler was white and he killed up more folks in *three years* than all the Negroes put together have kilt since B.C. Just look at all them colored mens Southerners have lynched and burnt! How could we be any worse? But me—if I even have one *small* penknife in my pocket that I never use, and I get caught and locked up, they fingerprint me, take my picture, and put it in the papers with a big headline:

HARLEMITE BRANDISHES WEAPON

and make out like I am a black disgrace to the U.S.A. I do not think that is right, and if I was ruling the world it would not be. I think I should have as much right as the next one to be a disgrace—if I want to be—without anybody talking about my race."

"*Nobody* has a right to be a disgrace," I said. "That is where you are wrong. I do not appreciate your argument."

"I don't mean people *ought* to kill and murder," said Simple. "But let's get back to what I started with, getting drunk. I see plenty of white men get on the buses drunk, and nobody says that a white man is a disgrace to his race. But just let a colored man get on the bus drunk! Everybody says, 'Tuc-tuc-tuc!' The white folks say, 'That's just like a Negro.' And the colored folks say, 'It's a shame. A disgrace to our group.' Yet the poor man hasn't done a thing but get drunk."

"Nobody, white or colored, has any business getting on a bus or streetcar drunk," I said. "If you are drunk, you should take a taxi home. Drunks are nuisances, staggering around and talking out of turn—like you when you are high. I do not agree with you this evening."

"If you agreed, there would be no point in having an argument," said Simple, pushing back his glass.

"There is not very much point to *your* argument," I said.

"Except," said Simple solemnly, "that I think colored folks should have the same right to get drunk as white folks."

"That is a very ordinary desire," I said. "You ought to want to have the right to be President, or something like that."

"Very few men can become President," said Simple. "And only one at a time. But almost anybody can get drunk. Even I can get drunk."

"Then you ought to take a taxi home, and not get on the bus smelling like a distillery," I said, "staggering and disgracing the race."

"I keep trying to tell you, if I was white, wouldn't nobody say I was disgracing no race!"

"You definitely are not white," I said.

"You got something there," said Simple. "Lend me taxi fare and I will ride home."

Everybody's Difference

"I AM a good-looking man, if I do say so myself," said Simple. "Sometimes I say to my wife, 'Joyce, baby, you have married a nice-looking joker.' And do you know what Joyce answers?"

"No," I said.

"Joyce says, 'You would be O.K. if you didn't act so simple.' "

"And why does she cast such an aspersion upon you?" I asked.

"Because sometimes I am simple," said Simple. "But it is not by intention. It is just the way God made me. But I am glad He did not make me bowlegged. I once knew a man who was so bowlegged he looked like a Japanese bridge. I also once knew a girl who was bench-legged. She looked like she was standing in two places at once. But if I was a girl I had rather be bench-legged than bow-legged—which for a woman, being bowlegged looks like such an open invitation.

"Now, take my Uncle Tige, he were so knock-kneed, and slue-footed, he looked like one foot was going left, and one foot was going right. Also he could of played golf with either foot and knock a ball *wham* and gone! Uncle Tige rolled like a sailor, too, when he walked."

"Uh! Uh! Uh!" I said.

"That's the way he navigated," continued Simple. "But talking about walking, you know my Cousin Minnie?"

"Of course," I said.

"Well, she has got what I call a bebop walk," said Simple. "When my Cousin Minnie walks down the street, one hip says BEE and the other hip says BOP—just like a seesaw, up, down—up, down! rock, roll—rock, roll. No wonder the mens turn around to look at Minnie. The Lord, I reckon, gave her them ball-bearing hips, but the Devil must of taught her how to use them. When Minnie turns into a bar, seven jokers follow her. And out of that seven, at least six will buy her a drink. Minnie has a way of leading men down the primrose path to poverty each and every payday. I have seen Minnie drink as many as seventeen drinks on a weekend night and not fall off the stool. As long as a man will buy, Minnie will try. Then get up and bebop on home *by herself*. Jokers turn their pockets inside out and say, 'I thought I had a dollar left.' But they do not even have bus fare home. By that time, Minnie has also done borrowed from each and every one of them, so she can take herself a taxi to her door. If nature is going to make a woman offbeat in the hips, it is not bad to be made like Minnie, who walks like jelly on a plate. If Minnie were as pretty as my old used-to-be, Zarita, she would be irresistible.

"I am married to the best woman in the world, but you know, the other day I saw Zarita, and I could not help but cast a manly eye on her. I know I would be simple to take up with that woman again, and I won't. But sometimes your mind do not pay any attention to your judgment. Oh, well, the Lord made everybody different—some bowlegged, some knock-kneed, some pigeon-toed, some slue-footed, others bebop-hipped, and some on the simple side. But I reckon God knows what He was doing. He gives everybody their difference.

"God also made good and evil. And He made some people too

evil for their own good. Take Cojo and Whitney, who are fighting souls. I hates to see two mens get hurted. But when they are as bad as Cojo and Whitney, I would not stop them from fighting each other. Let them go ahead and hurt themselves and hurt each other. That, I figure, is better than them hurting me if I come in between. Cojo and Whitney is fighting characters, both. Them boys has got so many scars on them that one more scar do not make no difference. They done lost so much blood in their time that either one of them could start a blood bank.

"Cojo and Whitney is the kind of Negroes who will back up integration and anything else to the last drop of blood. They do not care. They is the fighting forces of the race, the core of the last resort. They do not respect God, man, each other, nor white folks. Also they has no fear of razors, knives, guns, clubs, nor brass knucks. Now, take me. I had rather get shot than cut by a knife. To Cojo a knife is a play toy. To Whitney a razor amounts to no more than a rubber band in a child's slingshot. A bullet either one of them can duck. A baseball bat would just bounce off their heads. If Whitney and Cojo was due to be dead, they would have been died long ago. They is hard Negroes."

"I always thought they were friends," I said, "so why do they fight each other?"

"Is it not Saturday?" asked Simple. "Have they not 'over-indulged,' as says my wife, Joyce? And do they not feel playful? Therefore they fights."

"Those are slight provocations," I said; "in fact, no provocations at all."

"Sometimes just the sight of Whitney provokes Cojo," said Simple, "and the sight of Cojo provokes Whitney. Both is too evil for the other's good, even if they is friends. But you seen how tonight they done fit, fought, and re-fit. Is either one of them dead, kilt, grave wounded, or even sent to the hospital? No! Cojo is just gone around the corner to change his shirt, and Whitney is setting across the street in the fish joint ordering a catfish sandwich with his bleeding arm wrapped in the cook's dish towel. Was I to bleed so much, I would be in Harlem Hospital right now with Joyce sending for a minister to pray over my carcass, thinking I am about to die. They do not die of no little old things like a stab wound, a slit, or a cut. They bleeds, but they stops their own blood. They are hurt, but they do not groan, moan, or ask for sympathy.

"Looks like to me, with a blade flashing in his face, a man would be scared. Whitney do not even turn pale. Cojo do not tremble. Them kind of men have got the kind of steel in their souls, I reckon, which weapons do not touch, which no kind of afraidness can scratch, which an uppercut to the jaw do not faze, which can take a whole lot of punishment because their souls is unshootable, uncuttable, and unbeatable. Them is the kind of Negroes in slavery time who gave Old Master a Little Rock hangover—from which he has not recovered yet. Them is the kind of jokers who take no tea for the fever, who do not think now and *act* afterwards, but acts then and there, when and where, sooner than soon and quicker than a rocket taking off for the moon. What the other man has got in the way of weapons makes no difference, and what you *say* you will do does not matter, because what Whitney and Cojo have *done* by the time you have *said* what you *will* do is IT. By the time you finish talking about what you *will* do, your mouth may have to place a long-distance call to your ear! But Whitney and Cojo are still here, all in one piece—even if one or two parts is bleeding. Which is why, if they go to fighting in my front parlor, I would not come between them."

"I see the wisdom of your position," I said. "But you said God made good and evil. All you have described with Cojo and Whitney is evil. What about the good?"

"The good is friends like you who might treat me to another cold beer," said Simple.

"In that case," I said, "the good will have to say, 'Good night.' "

Coffee Break

"MY boss is white," said Simple.

"Most bosses are," I said.

"And being white and curious, my boss keeps asking me just what does THE Negro want. Yesterday he tackled me during the coffee break, talking about THE Negro. He always says 'THE Negro,' as if there was not fifty-eleven different kinds of Negroes in the U.S.A.," complained Simple. "My boss says, 'Now that you-all have got the Civil Rights Bill and the Supreme Court, Adam Powell in Congress, Ralph Bunche in the United Nations, and Leontyne Price singing in the Metropolitan Opera, plus Dr. Martin Luther King getting the Nobel Prize, what more do you want? I am asking you, just what does THE Negro want?'

" 'I am not THE Negro,' I says. 'I am *me*.'

" 'Well,' says my boss, 'you represent THE Negro.'

" 'I do not,' I says. 'I represent my own self.'

" 'Ralph Bunche represents you, then,' says my boss, 'and Thurgood Marshall and Martin Luther King. Do they not?'

" 'I am proud to be represented by such men, if you say they represent me,' I said. 'But all them men you name are *way* up there, and they do not drink beer in my bar. I have never seen a single one of them mens on Lenox Avenue in my natural life. So far as I know, they do not even live in Harlem. I cannot find them in the telephone book. They all got private numbers. But since you say they represent THE Negro, why do you not ask them what THE Negro wants?'

" 'I cannot get to them,' says my boss.

" 'Neither can I,' I says, 'so we both is in the same boat.'

" 'Well then, to come nearer home,' says my boss, 'Roy Wilkins fights your battles, also James Farmer.'

" 'They do not drink in my bar, neither,' I said.

" 'Don't Wilkins and Farmer live in Harlem?' he asked.

" 'Not to my knowledge,' I said. 'And I bet they have not been to the Apollo since Jackie Mabley cracked the first joke.'

" 'I do not know him,' said my boss, 'but I see Nipsey Russell and Bill Cosby on TV.'

" 'Jackie Mabley is no *him*,' I said. 'She is a *she*—better known as Moms.'

" 'Oh,' said my boss.

" 'And Moms Mabley has a story on one of her records about Little Cindy Ella and the magic slippers going to the Junior Prom at Ole Miss which tells all about what THE Negro wants.'

" 'What's its conclusion?' asked my boss.

" 'When the clock strikes midnight, Little Cindy Ella is dancing with the president of the Ku Klux Klan, says Moms, but at the stroke of twelve, Cindy Ella turns back to her natural self, black, and her blond wig turns to a stocking cap—and her trial comes up next week.'

" 'A symbolic tale,' says my boss, 'meaning, I take it, that THE Negro is in jail. But you are not in jail.'

" 'That's what you think,' I said.

" 'Anyhow, you claim you are not THE Negro,' said my boss.

" 'I am not,' I said. 'I am *this* Negro.'

" 'Then what do *you* want?' asked my boss.

" 'To get out of jail,' I said.

" 'What jail?'

" 'The jail you got me in.'

" 'Me?' yells my boss. 'I have not got you in jail. Why, boy, I like you. I am a liberal. I voted for Kennedy. And this time for Johnson. I believe in integration. Now that you got it, though, what more do you want?'

" 'Reintegration,' I said.

" 'Meaning by that, what?'

" 'That you be integrated with *me*, not me with you.'

" 'Do you mean that I come and live in Harlem?' asked my boss. 'Never!'

" 'I live in Harlem,' I said.

" 'You are adjusted to it,' said my boss. 'But there is so much crime in Harlem.'

" 'There are no two-hundred-thousand-dollar bank robberies, though,' I said, 'of which there was three lately *elsewhere*—all done by white folks, and nary one in Harlem. The biggest and best crime is outside of Harlem. We never has no half-million-dollar jewelry robberies, no missing star sapphires. You better come uptown with me and reintegrate.'

" 'Negroes are the ones who want to be integrated,' said my boss.

" 'And white folks are the ones who do *not* want to be,' I said.

" 'Up to a point, we do,' said my boss.

" 'That is what THE Negro wants,' I said, 'to remove that *point*.'

" 'The coffee break is over,' said my boss."

Intermarriage

"I BEEN reading in the papers about Sammy Davis turning himself into a Jew," said Simple, "but in his pictures, he still looks colored to me."

"Because a man changes his religion does not mean he changes his complexion, too," I said. "Sammy Davis *is* colored."

"But his race is now Jewish," said Simple.

"No," I said, "his *religion* is Jewish."

"I thought Jews were a race of people," said Simple.

"Judaism is a religion," I said, "and anybody can become a Jew in the religious sense by adopting the Hebrew faith—which is what Sammy Davis did."

"I think he made a mistake," said Simple.

"Why?" I asked.

"Because in a little while Jews are going to start trying to be colored," said Simple, "and Sammy Davis will just have to turn around and come back where he started from in order to be saved, because if the Jews are wise, they will not try to stick with the rest of the white folks from here on out. Instead they will come with us."

"What do you mean, 'come with us'?" I asked.

"I mean run WITH us—if they don't want to run FROM us like the white folks are doing in the Congo when they hear them Congo drums. There ain't but two ways to go tomorrow—ALONG WITH us or AWAY FROM us. Right now, most white folks is trying to run away from us, everywhere in the world—even when we are not chasing them. But we here in the U.S.A. is not chasing nobody when we buy a house next door to some white family. Yet and still, them white folks run like mad, be they Jewish or otherwise. Do you reckon if me and Joyce was to buy a house next door to Sammy Davis, he would run, too?"

"Sammy is probably a liberal Jew," I said.

"I am not talking about stingy," said Simple.

"I am not talking about being liberal with money, either," I explained. "I mean liberal in a racial and religious sense, accepting everyone equally."

"My wife is upset about Sammy marrying white," said Simple. "In fact, Joyce is mad."

"Your wife is like a great many other colored women. Their tolerance doesn't encompass interracial marriage," I said. "On that they take a rather narrow-minded view, especially when the male involved is a celebrity."

"And more so when that Negro is up in the money," said Simple. "Joyce says, 'Just let a Negro get a little money, he ups and marries a white woman—and his new wife is the one that wears furs and diamonds. Usually his first wife, colored, is left out in the cold when the money starts coming in,' says Joyce.

"The more Joyce talks, the madder she gets on that subject. Then she switches to colored women and white men. 'Lena Horne, Pearl Bailey, Katherine Dunham, Diahann Carroll, Dorothy Dandridge, Josephine Baker, Eartha Kitt—every last famous woman we got in show business almost—except Ethel Waters, who is rather old for wedding veils—has up and married white. So who shares all these rich colored women's money?'

"I said, 'Joyce, you are making me mad because I am not white—then I could marry me a well-off star.'

"That were a mistake which I should not have said, because then my wife got mad at me. Joyce yelled, 'I wouldn't put anything past you, Jess Simple. You just try to quit me for some blonde—and I will fix your little red wagon!' After that, she said some other things that were not nice at all. How come colored womens can't even talk calm about marrying white?"

Joyce Objects

"THAT Joyce is still talking about the nerve of Jimboy introducing his white wife to her friends at the formal," said Simple, calling for another beer. "When I went by the house tonight, Joyce and her old landlady was still low-rating Jimboy. Besides, they had just read in the *Afro-American* where another famous Negro had married a white woman. These colored papers can really upset you, if you are colored. One week it's lynchings. Next week it's race riots. Another time you can't vote in South Carolina. Or you can't eat some place else. Or you can't rent a house here.

"But now it ain't what you *can't* do that's got Joyce upset. It's what you *can* do—leastwise up North—and that is marry white. Joyce is almost as upset as Talmadge or Rankin would be about intermarriage. In fact, she is mad. Joyce says she don't see why a colored woman is not good enough for any of our colored big shots. Why should so many band leaders, race leaders, prize fighters, and musicianers marry white, Joyce wants to know. She declares it ain't right. According to her, white women are out to wreck and ruin the Negro race."

"I have always considered marriage a private matter," I said, "so I cannot agree with Joyce."

"That is what I would say, too," said Simple, "if I dared to say anything. But I eat Joyce's food almost every night, so I daresn't open my mouth. Intermarriage is a sore subject with Joyce. And her big old landlady backs her up on it. Both of them says when a colored man is in public life, he *belongs* to the public. He has got no business letting the race down by marrying a white woman. Besides, Joyce says, too many big Negroes with good incomes are up and marrying white—and she never reads about no white woman marrying a *poor* Negro. Since Jimboy makes a good salary playing the piano, according to Joyce, women like his wife are just taking money away from the race."

"Joyce has love and economics slightly mixed up."

"Um-m-m!" said Simple. "But I dare not dispute her, riled as she is about my divorce anyhow.

"Her big old fat landlady egged her on by saying, 'Honey, you is right! Them womens is out to *ruin* the black race, financially and every which a way. You just wait until another Scottsboro Case comes up. Them white womens will say to their colored husbands, *Don't you-all go to the defense of them boys, daddy. How do you know but what them Negroes are guilty? They ain't in your intelligent position to marry white, so probably they did rape that girl.*' "

"That is a very evil thought," I said.

"Colored womens is evil when it comes to intermarriage. Joyce says there ain't no white man ever asked her if he could marry her," said Simple. "All white mens wants to do is *buy* colored womens, according to Joyce. But colored mens will run after a white woman like a dog—and marry her, too, when they get up in the world, which is a disgrace!"

"Joyce sounds just like a Dixiecrat," I said.

"She is from Dixie," said Simple, "and she is a race-woman, for true.

"Joyce says, 'With all the nice-looking, good-looking, educated young colored girls in the race, I don't see why no black man has to go outside of Harlem to find a wife. We got from dark chocolate to vanilla cream right in our own group. We even got colored blondes.' She looked dead at me.

"I said, 'Baby, I ain't thinking about marrying no blonde. I am thinking about marrying you.'

"Joyce says, 'Actions speak louder than words, Jess Semple, so make me know it! Even if you don't marry me, I better not catch you marrying no white woman. Every time I pick up a paper, another Negro has gone and committed the act—and it is always some big-shot jigaboo making a whole lot of loot who can afford to put diamond rings on lily-white fingers and alligator shoes on her rose-pink toes. I wish I could get hold of some of these big Negroes for just about two minutes. I would put some sense back into their heads,' Joyce says, frowning at me. Why, you would think I was the guilty party—the way she lit into me.

" 'Listen, Joyce, baby,' I says, 'you know I aims to marry *you*. I ain't fixing to marry no white woman.'

"Joyce says, 'I wouldn't put it past you, Jess Semple. You're a man, ain't you? No telling what a man will do, white or colored. But at least, thank God, Jackie Robinson has not taken unto himself a white wife.'

" 'Jackie is already married for years,' I told her.

" 'So was some of them other Negroes,' yells Joyce, 'but that don't stop them! No! The woman that has stuck by them during all their hard struggles when they warn't nobody, they cast aside. When they get up in the world, they marry white. As soon as them big checks start coming in, they cast us aside.'

" 'I have not cast you aside,' I said.

" 'You ain't nobody, neither,' said Joyce.

"Now, that kinder hurt my feelings coming from Joyce. So I guess I said something I am forced to regret."

"What did you say?"

"I said, 'Joyce, maybe white womens are more sympathetic to a man when he is trying to get somewhere.'

"That is all I said, but it made Joyce mad. I should not have said it at dinner time, because she just kept on gnawing the same old bone.

" 'That black king in Africa who was forced to give up his throne on account of marrying some English typist,' Joyce says. 'It's good enough for him! Any black king that wants to marry a white woman ain't got no business with a throne on which to sit. Let him sit on a park bench.' "

"What did you say to that?" I asked.

"Not a word," said Simple. "When Joyce and that big old fat landlady of hers get together on a subject, there's no use of me trying to put a word in edgewise. I did call Joyce's attention to the fact, however, that the Prince of Wales once gave up his throne for the woman he loved.

"Joyce says, 'Yes, but he were white. In fact, both of them were white. They did not give up nothing *but* a throne to marry each other. But this African king gave up his *blackness* to marry that white woman. If I was a man,' says Joyce, 'I would not give up my race for nobody—least of all a white woman. I do not see how that king can expect his subjects to have any respect for what he has done. I do not respect these Negroes here in New York who are marrying white women each and every week—and they ain't even kings.'

"Her big old fat landlady chimes in, 'You right, honey! You is dead right. If any man of mine left me for a white woman, I would fix his little red wagon, I mean, good!'

"Both of them womens looked at me," said Simple. "I do not know why, because I had not said or done a thing. I was just setting there eating chicken and dumplings and keeping my mouth shut. But the way they looked at me made me feel right uncomfortable, so I repeated for the umpteenth time, 'I ain't fixin' to marry nobody but this girl right here. Joyce, I mean you. So I wish you would not cut your eyes at me that way. I am not a king, but if I was, and if I had a throne, wouldn't nobody sit on it but Queen Joyce.'

"That kind of toned her down. Joyce says, 'Baby, will you have some chocolate pudding with whipped cream, or would you rather have some of that tapioca that you liked so well last night?'

"I started to say, 'Tapioca.' Then it occurred to me that tapioca were white, so I said, 'Chocolate pudding.' I did not want to get in bad with Joyce no kind of way. Do you blame me, daddy-o?"

Liberals Need a Mascot

"JUST what is a liberal?" asked Simple.

"Well, as nearly as I can tell, a liberal is a nice man who acts decently toward people, talks democratically, and often is democratic in his personal life, but does not stand up very well in action when some real social issue like Jim Crow comes up."

"Like my boss," said Simple, "who is always telling me he believes in equal rights and I am the most intelligent Negro he ever saw—and I deserve a better job. I say, 'Why don't you give it to me, then?' And he says, 'Unfortunately, I don't have one for you.'

" 'But ever so often you hire new white men that ain't had the experience of me and I have to tell them what to do, though they are over me. How come that?'

" 'Well,' he says, 'the time just ain't ripe.' Is that what a liberal is?" asked Simple.

"That's just about what a liberal is," I said.

"Also a liberal sets back in them nice air-cooled streamlined coaches on the trains down South, while I ride up front in a hot old Jim Crow car," said Simple. "Am I right?"

"You are just about right," I said. "All the liberals I ever heard of ride with white folks when they go down South, not with us, yet they deplore Jim Crow."

"Do liberals have an animal?" asked Simple.

"What do you mean, do liberals have an animal?"

"The Republicans have an elephant, Democrats have a jackass," said Simple. "I mean, what does the liberals have?"

"I do not know," I said, "since they are not a political party. But if they were, what animal do you think they ought to have?"

"An ostrich," said Simple.

"Why an ostrich?" I demanded.

"Ain't you never seen an ostrich?" said Simple. "Old ostrich sticks his head in the sand whenever he don't want to look at anything. But he leaves his hind parts bare for anybody to kick him square in his caboose. An ostrich is just like nice white folks who can smile at me so sweet as long as I am working and sweating and don't ask for nothing. Soon as I want a promotion or a raise in pay, down go their heads in the sand and they cannot see their way clear. 'The time ain't ripe.' And if I insist, they will have the boss man put me dead out in the street so they can't see me. Is that what a liberal is?"

"Could be," I said, "except that an ostrich is a bird that does not sing, and a liberal can sing very sweetly."

"An elephant don't talk," said Simple, "but they are always making him talk in them cartoons where he represents the Republicans. So I do not see why an ostrich can't sing."

"I didn't mean sing literally," I said. "What I really meant was talk, use platitudes, make speeches."

"This ostrich of mine can make speeches," said Simple. "He can pull his head out of the sand and say, 'I see a new day ahead for America! I see the democratic dawn of equal rights for all! I see . . .'

"Whereupon, I will say, 'Can you see me?'

"And that ostrich will say, 'Indeed, my dark friend, democracy cannot overlook you.'

"I will say, 'Then help me get an apartment in that city-built tax-free insurance project where nobody but white folks can live.'

"That ostrich will say, 'Excuse me!' And stick his head right back down in the sand. Then I will haul off and try to kick his daylights out. And Mr. Big Dog will say, 'Shame on you, trying to embarrass a friend of the Negro race.'

"I will say, 'Embarrass nothing! I am trying to break his carcass! Only thing, it is too high up for my foot to reach.' That is another trouble with liberals," said Simple. "They are always too high to reach."

"They're well-to-do, man. That's why liberals don't have to worry about colored folks."

"Then gimme an animal whose hips is closer to the ground," said Simple.

Serious Talk about the Atom Bomb

"I AM tired of talking about race relations," said Simple.

"Me, too," I said. "Let's talk about human relations."

"The only trouble with that," said Simple, "is that we will not have no human relations left when we get through dropping that new atomical bomb on each other. The way it kills people for miles around, all my relations—and me, too—is liable to be wiped out in no time."

"Nobody is dropping that bomb on you," I said. "We are dropping it way over in Asia."

"And what is to keep Asia from dropping it back on us?" asked Simple.

"The Japanese probably do not have any atomic bombs to drop," I said.

"And how come we did not try them atomic bombs out on Germany?" demanded Simple.

"I do not know," I said. "Perhaps they were not perfected before V-E Day."

"Uh-umm! No, buddy-o," said Simple, "you know better than that. They just did not want to use them on white folks. Germans is white. So they wait until the war is all over in Europe to try them out on colored folks. Japs is colored."

"You are thinking evil now," I said. "Besides, it is your government and mine using those atomic bombs, so why do you say 'they'? Why don't you say 'we'? Huh?"

"I did not have nothing to do with them bombs," said Simple. "I see in the *News* where it cost Two Billion Dollars to develop them bombs, and get those atoms so they would split one another. If I had Two Billion Dollars, I would not spend it making something to kill off folks. I would spend it on things to make life better."

"For instance?" I said.

"For instance," said Simple, "I would take half of that Two Billion Dollars and build houses all over the country for poor folks to live in. I would get rid of these slums like Harlem full of cold-water flats and roaches. And I would make a playground in every block for kids to play on. And two bathrooms in every house so you could get in when you are in a hurry. Everywhere houses is old and falling down and too full of people, I would build a housing project with one of them Billion Dollars."

"You are making too much sense now," I said, "so I cannot argue with you."

"It is a wonder you did not bring up some technicality," said Simple, "because I do not see how it is they can spend all that money on warring and killing and in peacetime a man cannot even get Ten Dollars a week on W.P.A., but they can spend ten million times that much to blast somebody down."

"Don't keep on saying 'they,' " I said. "You are a voter, too, and this is your government. That Two Billion Dollars that made those atom bombs came out of your income tax."

"I hereby protest!" said Simple. "And if Adam Powell or Ben Davis or any of these Negroes or white folks either that I voted for last time start running on any Atom Bomb Ticket, they will not get my vote. Them atom bombs make me sick at the stomach! There is plenty we could do with Two Billion Dollars without turning it into double-barreled dynamite."

"What would you do with that other Billion left over after you build all those houses?" I asked.

"With that other One Billion," said Simple, "I would educate racist white folks."

"How?" I said.

"I would take and build schools all over Mississippi and all over the South, for white folks and Negroes, too. Because it is because they are so ignorant down there that they elect racist white folks to *our* Congress. I do not want racist white folks in *my* Congress. (You dig that *my*, don't you? Does my language suit you now, daddy-o?) *We* do not want no segregationist in *our* Congress drawing his salary from *my* income tax—concerning which I cannot vote if I live in Mississippi—and calling Jews and I-talians and me dirty names in the Senate Congress every day. So I would take that other One Billion Dollars and educate segregationist crackers like Bilbo. And my reason is, because if somebody don't educate them, they are liable to get hold of one of them atom bombs themselves—and blow us all off the map! Can you imagine Bilbo with an atom bomb? Then where would Harlem be?"

"Like the bear—nowhere," I said.

"You are being funny, and I am talking serious," said Simple.

Adventure

"ADVENTURE is a great thing," said Simple, "which should be in everybody's life. According to 'The Late Late Show' on TV, in the old days when Americans headed West in covered wagons, they was almost sure to run into adventure—at the very least a battle with the Red Skins. Nowadays, if you want to run into adventure, go to Alabama or Mississippi, where you can battle with the White Skins."

" 'Go West, young man, go West,' is what they used to say," I said. " '*Pioneers! O pioneers!*' cried Whitman."

" 'Go South, young man, go South,' is what I would say today," declared Simple. "If I had a son I wanted to make a man out of, I would send him to Jackson, Mississippi, or Selma, Alabama—and not in a covered wagon, but on a bus. Especially if he was a white boy, I would say, 'Go, son, go, and return to your father's house when you have conquered. The White Skins is on the rampage below the Mason-Dixon Line, defying the government, denying free Americans their rights. Go see what you can do about it. Go face the enemy.' "

"You would send your son into the maelstrom of Dixie to get his head beaten by a white cracker or his legs bitten by police dogs?"

"For freedom's sake—and adventure—I might even go South myself," said Simple, "if I was white. I think it is more important for white folks to have them kind of adventures than it is for colored. Negroes have been fighting one way or another all our lives—but it is somewhat new to whites. Until lately, they did not even know what a COLORED ONLY sign meant. White folks have always thought they could go anywhere in the world they wanted to go. They are just now finding out that they cannot go into a COLORED WAITING ROOM in the Jim Crow South. They cannot even go into a WHITE

WAITING ROOM if they are with colored folks. They never knew before that if you want adventure, all you have to do is cross the color line in the South."

"Then, according to you," I said, "the Wild West can't hold a candle to the Savage South any more."

"Not even on TV," said Simple. "The Savage South has got the Wild West beat a mile. In the old days adventures was beyond the Great Divide. Today they is below the Color Line. Such adventures is much better than 'The Late Late Show' with Hollywood Indians. But in the South, nobody gets scalped. They just get cold-cocked. Of course, them robes the Klan sports around in is not as pretty as the feathers Indians used to wear, but they is more scary. And though a Klan holler is not as loud as a Indian war whoop, the Klan is just as sneaky. In cars, not on horseback, they comes under cover of night. If the young people of the North really want excitement, let them go face the Klan and stand up to it.

" 'That is why the South will make a man of you, my son,' I would say. 'Go South, baby, go South. Let a fiery cross singe the beard off your beatnik chin. Let Mississippi make a man out of you.' "

"Don't you think white adults as well as white youth should be exposed to this thing?" I asked.

"Of course," said Simple. "If the white young folks go as Freedom Riders, let the white old folks go as sight-seers—because no sooner than they got down there, they would be Freedom Riders anyhow. If I owned one of these white travel bureaus arranging sight-seeing tours next summer to Niagara Falls, Yellowstone Park, the Grand Canyon, and Pikes Peak, I would also start advertising sight-seeing tours to Montgomery with the National Guard as guides, to Jackson with leather leggings as protection against police dogs, to the Mississippi Prison Farms with picnic lunches supplied by Howard Johnson's, and to the Governor's Mansion with a magnolia for all the ladies taking the tour—and a night in jail without extra charge.

"Negroes would be guaranteed as passengers on all tours, so that there would be sure adventures for everybody. My ads would read:

SPECIAL RATES FOR A WEEKEND
IN A TYPICAL MISSISSIPPI JAIL

Get arrested now, pay later. Bail money not included. Have the time of your lives living the life of your times among the Dixie White Skins. Excitement guaranteed. For full details contact the Savage South Tours, Inc., Jesse B. Semple, your host, wishing you hell."

Brainwashed

"THAT Minnie has put a touch on me again," said Simple.

"According to you," I said, "your Cousin Minnie has been up North for several years now. Yet every time you tell me about her, she is trying to borrow money from you. Hasn't Minnie got a foothold in the North yet?"

"It is very hard for a Negro to get a toeholt, let alone a footholt," said Simple, leaning on the bar. "I have been in the North longer than Minnie, yet if I was to lose my job tomorrow, I would be right back where I started from—at nothing. Negroes, by and large, do not make enough money to get a footholt. And a handholt I never expect to have."

"That is very pessimistic opinion for a man of your abilities to hold," I said. "How come you never expect to get any farther in life?"

"Because I started behind the eight-ball. Bad schools, half the time no schools, when I was a kid. Jim Crow all the way from Richmond to Washington to Baltimore to New York. High rents in Harlem, low-paid jobs downtown. Advancement for the white man on the job, stay-where-you-are for me. And added to that, I am married to a woman who lives black and thinks white nine times out of ten."

"What do you mean?" I asked. "I thought Joyce was a race-woman."

"She is," said Simple, "in her heart, but sometimes I think her mind has been brainwashed."

"Why do you say that?"

"Joyce reads too many white papers and magazines—and *believes* half of what she reads in them. Me, I believe nothing they say. Joyce is also a fiend for culture. Whose culture? The white man's! Me, I love the blues. But Joyce, every time a Negro plays Show-pan at Town Hall, she wants me to spend $4.40 to go hear it. I just go to sleep on Show-pan."

"Chopin is everybody's music," I said. "It belongs to the world. It is too bad you can't stay awake when Chopin is being played. You have a sensitive wife whom you do not appreciate."

"I love Joyce," said Simple. "But that Atheniannie Art Club my wife belongs to has got me down—especially since they changed their name."

"The Anthenian Arts Club is one of Harlem's leading cultural organizations."

"But they used to be the Negro Art Club," said Simple. "Why did they have to go change their name to Atheniannie? 'It is time to encourage integration,' Joyce come telling me. Well, them women have got a integrated name for that club, but nary a white member as yet. Just like the Colored Golfing Association changed its name to the Associated Golfing Association—but I don't hear tell of no white players associated with them up to now. Them same Negroes are still playing golf with the same other Negroes as before. Suppose I was to change the name of my race from BLACK to BLUE, would I not still be black all over my black carcass? Who is fooling who with all this name changing lately, I want to know?"

"Somebody has to open the way to integration," I said.

"The Polish American Association had a big parade the other day and I did not read where they had changed their name to the Polite American Association. On St. Patrick's Day the Irish have big parades and I never hear tell of the Irish changing their names to anything but Irish. The Jews still celebrate Yom Kippur and close up every store in Harlem. But some Negroes are talking about we ought to change the name of Negro History Week to something *less* colored. Until I get a handholt, I refuse to call my toeholt a footholt because it is not and ain't, North or South, nothing but a *black* holt—of which my Cousin Minnie has less than me."

"Your wife, Joyce, at least, is reaching," I said.

"For Show-pan," yelled Simple.

"While you are reaching for a beer glass," I countered.

"Which now is empty," said Simple. "Set us up."

"I will contribute no further to your already wavering toehold," I said. "Good night."

"Then drop a dime in the juke box before you go," said Simple, "and play my favorite record one more time to liven up this bar."

Wigs for Freedom

"You ought to of heard my Cousin Minnie last night telling about her part in the riots," said Simple, leaning on one of the unbroken bars on Lenox Avenue that summer, beer in hand. "After hearing three rebroadcasts of Mayor Wagner's speech after he flew back home from Europe, Minnie was so mad she wanted to start rioting again. She said old Wagner did not say one constructive thing. Anyhow, Minnie come in the bar with a big patch on the top of her head, otherwise she was O.K., talking about all the big excitement and how she was in the very middle of it.

"Cousin Minnie told me, 'Just as I was about to hit a cop, a bottle from on high hit me.' Then she described what happened to her.

" 'They taken me to Harlem Hospital and stitched up my head, which is O.K. now and thinking better than before,' Minnie said. 'But, you know, them first-aid doctors and nurses or somebody in

Harlem Hospital took my forty-dollar wig and I have not seen it since. I went back to Harlem Hospital after the riots and asked for my wig, an orange-brown chestnut blond for which I paid cash money. But they said it were not in the Lost and Found. They said my wig had blood on it, anyhow, so it got throwed away.

" 'I told them peoples in the Emergency Room, "Not just my wig but my head had blood on it, too. I am glad you did not throw my head away." Whereupon one of them young doctors had the nerve to say, "Don't sass me!" But since he was colored, I did not cuss him out.

" 'I knowed that young doctor had been under a strain—so many busted heads to fix up—so I just let his remarks pass. All I said was "I wish I had back my wig. That were a real-hair wig dyed to match my complexion and styled to compliment my cheekbones." Only thing I regret about them riots is, had it not been for me wanting to get even with white folks, I would still have my wig. My advice to all womens taking part in riots is to leave their wigs at home.'

"I said, 'Miss Minnie, you look good with your natural hair, African style. I did not like you with that blond wig on, nohow. Fact is, I did not hardly know you the first time I run into you on 125th Street under that wig. Now you look natural again.'

" 'The reason I bought that wig is, I do not want to look natural,' said Miss Minnie. 'What woman wants to look her natural self? That is why powder and rouge and wigs is made, to make a woman look like Elizabeth Taylor or Lena Horne—and them stars do not look like natural-born womens at all. I paid forty dollars for my wig just to look *unnatural*. It were *fine* hair, too! All wigs should always be saved in hospitals, bloody or not, and given back to the patients after their heads is sewed up. Since I were unconscious from being hit with a bottle, also grief-stricken from little Jimmy Powell's pistol funeral, when they ambulancetized me and laid me out in the hospital, I did not even know they had taken my wig off.'

" 'Do you reckon you will be left with a scar in the top of your head?' I asked.

" 'If I do,' said Miss Minnie, 'I am proud of it. What is one little scar in the fight for freedom when some people lose their life? Medgar Evers lost his life in Mississippi. All I lost was my wig in Harlem Hospital. And I know that cop did not hit me. He was busy hitting somebody else when I started to hit him; he didn't see me. Some Negro on a roof aimed a bottle at that cop's head—but hit me by accident instead. Bullets, billy clubs, and bottles was flying every whichaway that Sunday night after that Powell boy's funeral. Lenox Avenue were a *sweet* battleground. But I would not have been in action myself had not I seen a cop hit an old man old enough to be his father. He were a young white cop and the man was an old black man who did not do nothing except not move fast enough when that cop spoke. That young cop whaled him. WHAM! WHAM! WHAM! I did not have no weapon with me but my purse, but I was going to wham that cop dead in the face with that—when a bottle whammed me on the head. God saved that cop from being slapped with a pocketbook full of knockout punches from poker chips to a bottle of Evening in Paradise, also a big bunch of keys which might of broke his nose.'

" 'Don't you believe in nonviolence?' I asked.

" 'Yes,' said Miss Minnie, 'when the other parties are nonviolent, too. But when I have just come out of a funeral parlor from looking at a little small black boy shot three times by a full-grown cop, I think it is about time I raised my pocketbook and strike at least one blow for freedom. I come up North ten years ago to find freedom, Jesse B. Semple. I did not come to Harlem to look a white army of white cops in the face and let them tell me I can't be free in my own black neighborhood on my own black street in the very year when the Civil Rights Bill says *you shall be free*. No, I didn't! It is a good thing that bottle struck me down, or I would of tore that cop's head every way but loose.'

" 'Then you might not of been here today,' I said.

" 'That is right,' agreed Miss Minnie, 'but my soul would go marching on. Was I to have gone to the morgue instead of Harlem Hospital, I would go crying, "*Freedom now*," and I would come back to haunt them that struck me low. The ghost of Miss Minnie would walk among white folks till their dying day and keep them scared to death. I would incite to riot every weekend in Harlem. I would lead black mobs—which is what the papers said we is—from Friday night to Monday morning. It would cost New York a million dollars a week to just try to keep us Negroes and *me* quiet. They would wonder downtown what got into Harlem. It would just be my spirit egging us on. I would gladly die for freedom and come back to haunt white folks. Yes, I would! Imagine me floating down Lenox Avenue, a white ghost with a blond wig on!'

" 'I would hate to see you,' I said.

" 'I would hate to see myself,' said Miss Minnie. '*Freedom now!*' She raised her beer glass and I raised mine. Then Miss Minnie said, 'I might not of gave my head to the cause, but I gave my wig.'

"Peoples like to hear Cousin Minnie talk, and sometimes when she gets an audience, she goes to town. It being kind of quiet in the bar last night, folks started listening at Minnie instead of playing the juke box, and Minnie proceeded to expostulate on the subject of riots and white and colored leaders advising Harlem to go slow and be cool. Says Minnie, 'When I was down South picking cotton, didn't a soul tell me to go slow and cool it. "Pick more! Pick more! Can't you pick a bale a day? What's wrong with you?" That's what they said. Did not a soul say, "Wait, don't over-pick yourself." Nobody said slow down in cotton-picking days. So what is this here now? When Negroes are trying to get something for themselves, I must wait, *don't demonstrate*? I'll tell them big shots, "How you sound?"

" 'Be cool?' asked Miss Minnie. 'Didn't a soul say, "Be cool," when I was out in that hot sun down South. I heard not nary a word about "be cool." So who is telling me to be cool now? I have not no air cooler in Harlem where I live, neither air conditioner. And you talking about be cool! How you sound?

" 'Get off the streets! Huh! Never did nobody say, "Get out of the fields," when I was down home picking cotton in them old cotton fields which I have *not* forgotten. In slavery times, I better not get out of no fields if I wanted to save my hide, or save my belly from meeting my backbone from hunger when freedom came. No! I better stay in them fields and work. But now that I got a street to stand on, how do you sound telling me to get off the street? Just because some little old disturbance come up and a few rocks is throwed in a riot, I am supposed to get off of my street in Harlem and leave it to the polices to rule? I am supposed to go home and be cool? Cool what, where, baby? How do you sound?

" ' "My name is Minnie and I lost my forty-dollar wig in the riots, so I am reduced to my natural hair," I'll tell them leaders. But what is one wig more or less to give for freedom? One wig not to go slow. One wig not to be cool. One wig not to get off the streets. When it is a long hot summer, where else but in the streets, fool, can I be cool? Uncontrollable? Who says I was uncontrollable? Huh! I knowed what I was doing. I did not lose my head because when I throwed a bottle, I knowed what I was throwing at. I were throwing at Jim Crow, Mr. K. K. Krow—at which I aimed my throw. How do you sound, telling me not to aim at Jim Crow?

" 'Did not a soul in slavery time tell old bull-whip marster not to aim his whip at me, at me—a woman. Did not a soul tell that mean old overseer not to hit Harriet Tubman (who is famous every Negro History Week), not to hit her in the head with a rock whilst she was a young girl. She were black, and a slave, and her head was made to be hit with a rock by her white overseer. Did not a soul tell that man who shot Medgar Evers in the back with a bullet to be cool. Did not a soul say to them hoodlums what slayed them three white and colored boys in Mississippi to cool it. Now they calling me hoodlums up here in Harlem for wanting to be free. Hoodlums? Me, a hoodlum? Not a soul said "hoodlums" about them night riders who ride through the South burning black churches and lighting white crosses. Not a soul said "hoodlums" when the bombs went off in Birmingham and blasted four little Sunday School girls to death, little black Sunday School girls. Not a soul said "hoodlums" when they tied an auto rim to Emmett Till's feet and throwed him in that Mississippi river, a kid just fourteen years old. But me, I am a hoodlum when I don't cool it, won't cool it, or lose my wig on a riot gig. They burnt down fourteen colored churches in Mississippi in one summer, yet I'm supposed to be cool? Even our colored leaders telling Harlem to be cool! Well, I am my own leader, and I am not cool.

" 'Everywhere they herd my people in jail like cattle, and I am supposed to be cool. I read in one of our colored papers the other day where it has cost Mississippi four million dollars just to keep Negroes in jail. And Savannah, Georgia, spent eighteen thousand in one year feeding black boycotters in jail. One town in North Carolina spent twelve hundred dollars a day on beans for colored students they locked up for marching to be free. One paper said it cost the state of Maryland one hundred thousand dollars a month to send the militia to Cambridge to keep Negroes from getting a cup of coffee in them crumby little old white restaurants which has no decent coffee, nohow, but which everybody ought to have the right to go into on general principles. But me, I can't go in. Yet them that's supposed to be my leaders tell me, "Give up! Don't demonstrate! Wait!" To tell the truth, I believe my own colored leaders is ashamed of me. So how are they going to lead anybody they are ashamed of? Telling me to be cool. Huh! I'm too hot to be cool—so I guess I will just have to lead my own self—which I dead sure will do. I will lead myself.' "

Help, Mayor, Help!

"WELL, if I was mayor of New York," said Simple, "the first thing I would do tomorrow morning would be to get me a Crazy Catcher's Wagon (like the Dogcatcher's Wagon) and go around New York gathering up all the crazy and half-crazy people on the loose from river to river. I would, to tell the truth, have me *two* Crazy Catcher Wagons, a Junior Wagon and a Senior Wagon. The Junior Wagon would be for the kids that cut up subway seats for no reason at all but to be slicing up something. It would also be for them that throws bricks through the windows of trains going up to Westchester when they come from Grand Central out of the underground on Park Avenue and into the Bronx. It would also be for little old young kids who get high on reefers and act wilder than teen-agers who get high on reefers, who in turn act wilder than grown-ups who get stoned. My Junior Crazy Catcher's Wagon would be full all the time from the Bronx to Harlem to Greenwich Village to Brownsville and Bedford-Stuyvesant to Far Rockaway. At Forty-second Street I would add a trailer to my Junior Wagon.

"My Senior Wagon, when it would not be busy being used for crazy-catching, I would use for wino-gathering. I would gather up all the winos drinking wine in public parks all day long and cluttering up the benches so mothers and children cannot set down, and cluttering up the air with bad language, and throwing wine bottles on the sidewalks in the parks so that they cut babies' feet. These old winos I would gather up in my Crazy Catcher's Wagon and take them away so the parks would be free for quiet folks to set down in again and catch a little fresh air whilst relaxing and enjoy the sunshine without hearing the loudest and baddest words in the world in front of children which they ought not hear. Was I the mayor of New York, I would clean the parks of winos, male and female winos, young and old winos. And I would hire me all the boats on the ocean for a month and ship all winos off to some far-off nice warm uninhabited island where they could have the whole island for a park—and drink wine all day to themselves if they wanted to, and have a wino convention and nominate themselves a wino Goldwater and wino Congress and a wino president and inaugurate themselves in wine, and put out a dictionary of bad language so that all wino-talking folks would be hep to the jive should new wino addicts arrive.

"Speaking of addicts, I would also (was I the mayor of New York) have me a Junkie Catcher's Wagon and go around New York gathering up all the junkies and getting them nice pads to cop a nod in—but far away from peoples who do not use junk, in someplace like Mississippi. Junkies would not mind being down in Mississippi because neither Jim Crow nor police dogs nor bombs bother dope addicts at all. A junkie does not care and is not bugged by anything in this world so long as he has his junk. Dear Mayor of New York, put all the junkies in Mississippi and let's clean up our town. Give all the junkies all the junk in Mississippi and put the pushers out of jobs in Harlem, in the Village, and also Times Square. City of New York, get some wagons. Take the junkies on a freedom ride. Free horse, free snow, free heroin, free coke—whatever they want in their new freedom land. Free goofballs and airplane glue to junior junkies. A bonus to all dope addicts who will get in the Junkie Wagon and go to Mississippi—award them an extra reefer, maybe a bag. Dear Mayor, if you do not hurry up and do this soon, you will never get New York cleaned up in time for the second year of the World's Fair, which is 1965. Hurry, Mayor, let's clean up New York.

"Dear Mayor, I would also get me a Hustling Beggars Wagon and collect all the fake beggars sitting in subway entrances with a fake bad leg collecting money. Else stumping through subway trains howling hymns with a cup marked BLIND—when they can see as well as I can. Or panhandling on Broadway claiming they do not have a subway token, so gimme fifteen cents—and making forty dollars a day begging fifteen cents. Get a Beggar Catcher's Wagon, Mayor.

"However, I would not want you to do anything wrong to any of these folks I mentioned, Mayor. Do not hurt them. Just get them out of New York City to where they can run wild in peace, be crazy, take dope, drink acid-raw stinking cheap lye-water wine, play blind in dark glasses and beg from each other to their heart's content. New York is a rich city, so let's maybe buy a reservation somewhere out in the Indian country, Arizona or somewhere like that, and put all teen-age subway seat-slashers, all grown-up dope takers, all middle-aged wino drinkers, all don't-give-a-damn-for-children-in-the-park cussers, all who beg as a profession, not as a need—put them all out West, else settle them in Alaska, else ship them to Puerto Rico and bring all the Puerto Ricans up here where Puerto Ricans want to be, and let them others I mention stop bugging me. Mayor, we now have a Litter Bug Campaign. Why not have a Human Bug Campaign? Put them in nice faraway places—all them that are too crazy to care, too hopped-up to care, too careless to care, or just naturally too mean and evil and nuisance-minded to give a damn. Mayor, let's care about them that don't care about us by giving them a separate state where they can care about each other.

"A Crazy Catcher's Wagon, Mayor, a Junkie Catcher's Wagon, a Professional Beggar Catcher's Wagon, a Wino Wagon, Mayor. Then take over for one week all the buses at the Port of Authority Terminal, and half the trains at Penn Station, and most of the boats in New York Harbor and fill them up with all these people who bug New York and bug themselves and get them all gone somewhere to some new cool wonderful spot out West, or to the Islands of the Sea, up North in Alaska, or anywhere but here. A reservation for the goofy, an island for the winos, a new land for the teen-age subway slashers—palm trees, wide-open spaces, nice happy places —for all the un-nice, upset, disturbed, hopped-up, wine-soaked people who cannot and do not and will not and *won't* act nice of their own accord in New York—and who is driving the rest of us crazy. Help, Mayor! Help! Help! Help!"

Soul Food

"WHERE is that pretty cousin of yours, Lynn Clarisse, these days?" I asked.

"She has moved to the Village," said Simple.

"Deserted Harlem? Gone looking for integration?"

"She wants to see if art is what it's painted," said Simple. "All the artists lives in Greenwich Village, white and colored, and the jazz peoples and the writers. Nobody but us lives in Harlem. If it wasn't for the Atheniannie Arts Club, Joyce says Harlem would be a cultural desert."

"You mean the Anthenian Arts Club," I said.

"I do," said Simple. "But Joyce tells me that thirty years ago Harlem was blooming. Then Duke Ellington and everybody lived here. Books was writ all over the place, pictures painted, lindy hoppers hopping, jitterbugs jumping, a dance hall called the Savoy with fine big bands playing. No more! The only things Harlem is famous for now is Adam Powell, who seldom comes home, and the last riots. So Lynn Clarisse has moved to the Village. But we can always get on the subway and go down and fetch her."

"Or join her," I said.

"Or let her re-join me," said Simple. "Although I am not worried about Lynn Clarisse. She is colleged, like you, and smart, and can take care of herself in the Village—just like my Cousin Minnie can take care of herself in Harlem. Every fish to his own water, I say, and the devil take them that cannot swim. Lynn Clarisse can swim, and Minnie dead sure can float, whereas some folks can only dog-paddle. Now me, my specialty is to walk on water. I been treading on the sea of life all my life, and have not sunk yet. I refuses to sink. In spite of womens, white folks, landlords, landladies, cold waves, and riots, I am still here. Corns, bunions, and bad feet in general do not get me down. I intends to walk the water until dry land is in sight."

"What land?"

"The Promised Land," said Simple, "the land in which I, black as I am without one plea in my country 'tis of thee, can be *me*. American the beautiful come to itself again, where you can see by the dawn's early light what so proudly we hailed as civil rights."

"The very thought makes you wax poetic, heh?"

"It do," said Simple. "But Joyce thinks Lynn Clarisse should have moved to Park West Village, halfway between Harlem and downtown. Joyce thinks Greenwich Village is a fast place where colored are likely to forget race and marry white. My wife is opposed to intermarriage on the grounds of pride. Joyce says she is so proud of her African heritage she don't want nobody to touch it. But do you know what Lynn Clarisse says? She says, 'There is no color line in art.'

"My cousin and my wife was kind of cool to each one another on the surface that day Lynn Clarisse moved out of Harlem. But you know how easy womens get miffed over little things. I don't pay them no mind myself. The only thing that makes me mad is Cousin Minnie wanting to borrow five dollars, which is always once too often. Lynn Clarisse do not borrow. She came to New York with her own money."

"Are her parents well off?"

"Her daddy, my first cousin on my half-brother's side, owns one of the biggest undertaking parlors in Virginia. He makes his money putting Negroes in segregated coffins in segregated graveyards. He sent Lynn Clarisse to college, and now has give her money for 'a cultural visit' to the North. Young Negroes used to have to struggle to get anything or go anywhere. Nowadays some of them have parents who have already struggled for them, so can help them get through college, and get up North, and get more cultured and live in Greenwich Village where rents is higher than they is in Harlem. Thank God, my cousin's daddy is an undertaker."

"Morticians and barbers are almost the only Negro businessmen whose incomes have not yet been affected by integration," I said. "Certainly, restaurants and hotels in Harlem have suffered. Banquets that once were held at the Theresa are now held at the Hilton and the Americana or the New Yorker. And the Urban League's annual Beaux Arts Ball is at the Waldorf. Negro society has taken almost all its functions downtown."

"But as long as white undertakers refuse to bury black bodies, and white barbers will not cut Negro hair, colored folks still have the burying and barbering business in the bag."

"Except that here in New York, I suppose you know, some wealthy Negroes are now being buried from fashionable downtown funeral homes."

"Where the mourners dare not holler out loud like they do at funerals in Harlem," said Simple. "It is not polite to scream and carry on over coffins in front of white folks."

"Integration has its drawbacks," I said.

"It do," confirmed Simple. "You heard, didn't you, about that old colored lady in Washington who went downtown one day to a fine white restaurant to test out integration? Well, this old lady decided to see for herself if what she heard was true about these restaurants, and if white folks were really ready for democracy. So down on Pennsylvania Avenue she went and picked herself out this nice-looking used-to-be-all-white restaurant to go in and order herself a meal."

"Good for her," I said.

"But dig what happened when she set down," said Simple. "No trouble, everybody nice. When the white waiter come up to her table to take her order, the colored old lady says, 'Son, I'll have collard greens and ham hocks, if you please.'

" 'Sorry,' says the waiter. 'We don't have that on the menu.'

" 'Then how about black-eyed peas and pig tails?' says the old lady.

" 'That we don't have on the menu either,' says the white waiter.

" 'Then chitterlings,' says the old lady, 'just plain chitterlings.'

"The waiter said, 'Madam, I never heard of chitterlings.'

" 'Son,' said the old lady, 'ain't you got no kind of soul food at all?'

" 'Soul food? What is that?' asked the puzzled waiter.

" 'I knowed you-all wasn't ready for integration,' sighed the old lady sadly as she rose and headed toward the door. 'I just knowed you white folks wasn't ready.' "

"Most ethnic groups have their own special dishes," I said. "If you want French food, you go to a French restaurant. For Hungarian, you go to Hungarian places, and so on."

"But this was an American place," said Simple, "and they did not have soul food."

"The term 'soul food' is still not generally used in the white world," I said, "and the dishes that fall within its category are seldom found yet in any but colored restaurants, you know that. There's a place where jazzmen eat across from the Metropole that has it, and one or two places down in the Village, but those are the only ones I know in Manhattan outside of Harlem."

"It is too bad white folks deny themselves that pleasure," said Simple, "because there is nothing better than good old-fashioned, down-home, Southern Negro cooking. And there is not too many restaurants in Harlem that has it, or if they do, they spoil everything with steam tables, cooking up their whole menu early in the morning, then letting it steam till it gets soggy all day. But when a Negro fries a pork chop *fresh*, or a chicken *fresh*, or a fish *fresh*, I am telling you, it sure is good. There is a fish joint on Lenox Avenue with two women in it that can sure cook fish. But they is so evil about selling it to you. How come some of these Harlem eating places hire such evil-acting people to wait on customers? Them two ladies in this fish place stand behind the counter and look at you like they dare you to 'boo' or ask for anything. They both look mad no sooner than you enter."

"I'll bet they are two sisters who own the place," I said. "Usually by the time Negroes get enough money to own anything, they are so old they are evil. Those women are probably just mad because at their age they have to wait on anybody."

"Then they should not be in business," said Simple.

"I agree," I said. "But on the other hand, suppose they or their husbands have been skimping and saving for years. At last, at the age of forty or fifty, they get a little business. What do you want them to do? Give it up just because they have got to the crabby age and should be retiring, before they have anything to retire on?"

"Then please don't take out their age on me when I come in to order a piece of fish," said Simple. "Why them two ladies never ask you what you want politely. They don't, in fact, hardly ask you at all. Them womens looks at customers like they want to say, 'Get out of here!' Then maybe one of them will come up to you and stand and look over the counter.

"You say, 'Have you got any catfish?' She will say, 'No!' And will not say what other kind she has or has not got.

"So you say, 'How about buffalo?' She will say, 'We had that yesterday.'

"Then you will say, 'Well, what have you got today?'

"She will say, 'What do you want?' I have already said twice what I wanted that they did not have. So now I say, 'How about butterfish?'

"She says, 'Sandwich or dinner?'

"I say, 'Dinner.'

"She says, 'We don't sell dinners after 10 p.m.' "

" 'Then why did you ask me if I wanted a dinner?' says I.

"She says, 'I was paying no attention to the time.'

"I said, 'You was paying no attention to me neither, lady, and I'm a customer. Gimme two sandwiches.'

" 'I am not here to be bawled out by you,' she says. 'If it's sandwiches you want, just say so, and no side remarks.'

" 'Could I please have a cup of coffee?'

" 'We got Pepsis and Cokes.'

" 'A Pepsi.'

"She rummages in the cooler. 'The Pepsis is out.'

" 'A Coke.'

"She comes up with a bottle that is not cold. Meanwhile the fish is frying, and it smells good, but it takes a while to wait, so I say, 'Gimme a quarter to play the juke box.' Three records for a quarter.

"Don't you know that woman tells me, 'We is all out of quarters tonight.'

"So I say, trying to be friendly, 'I'll put in a dime and play just one, then. What is your favorite record?'

"Old hussy says, 'There's nothing on there do I like, so just play for yourself.'

" 'Excuse me,' says I, 'I will play "Move to the Outskirts of Town," which is where I think you ought to be.'

" 'I wish my husband was here to hear your sass,' she says. 'Is your fish to eat here, or to go?'

" 'To go,' I says, 'because I am going before you bite my head off. What do I owe?'

" 'How much is two sandwiches to go?' she calls back to the other woman in the kitchen.

" 'Prices is gone up,' says the other hussy, 'so charge him eighty cents.'

" 'Eighty cents,' she says, 'and fifteen for the Pepsi.'

" 'I had a Coke,' I says.

" 'The same. You get a nickel change.'

" 'From a five-dollar bill?' I says.

" 'Oh, I did not notice you give me a five. Claybelle, have you got any change back there?'

" 'None.'

" 'Neither is I. Mister, you ought to have something smaller.'

" 'I do not carry small change around on payday,' says I. 'And what kind of restaurant is this, that can't even bust a five-dollar bill, neither change small change into a quarter for the record player? Don't you-all have nothing in the cash register? If you don't, no wonder, the way you treat a customer! Just gimme my five back and keep your fish.'

" 'Lemme look down in my stocking and see what I got there,' she says. And do you know, that woman went down in her stocking and pulled out enough money to buy Harry Belafonte. But she did not have a nickel change.

"So I said, 'Girl, you just keep that nickel for a tip.'

"If that woman owns the place, she ought to sell it. If she just works there, she ought to be fired. If she is the owner's girl friend, was she mine I would beat her behind, else feed her fish until a bone got stuck in her throat. I wonder how come some Harlem places have such evil help, especially in restaurants. Hateful help can spoil even soul food. Dear God, I pray, please change the hearts of hateful help!"

Little Klanny

" 'LISTEN, Little Klanny,' I said, 'in that picture of you in *Ebony* this month at the top of Reverend King's article about *Un-Christian Christians*, you don't look to be no more than five or six years old, standing beside your mama out in this field watching a fiery cross burn, and both of you got hoods and sheets on. At least, you got a part of a sheet on, cut down to your junior size. Little Klanny, your mama ought to be ashamed of herself, bringing you out in the damp of night to a Klan meeting to learn to hate somebody. The head Klansman is up there on a box talking about Negras and Catholics and Jews is no good. Who does he think discovered America? A Catholic—Columbus. And who does he think came next? The Negroes and the Jews. The Negroes is been here in this U.S.A. three hundred years. I don't have no record of the Jews, but I reckon they have been here almost as long. They are a people that get around.

" 'I expect your great-great-grandfather were Jewish, Little Klanny, and your mama don't know it. Or he might have been a big burly Negro. There was lots of mixing back in slavery days. You just happened to get bleached out white in time to join the John Birch Society when you get to be a little older. Little Klanny, you is too small now to know what hate is all about. You is practically a baby, and here your parents got you out there on Stoney Mountain with your robes and regalia flapping in the breeze when you had rather be home watching Donald Duck on TV. White folks must be out of their minds, bringing children to Klan rallies. And I must be out of my mind being present at one myself. But with me, it is all a dream, because I am at home in Harlem in my bed and *Ebony* just fell out of my hand when I dozed off.

" 'I am laying here tossing and turning, Little Klanny, dreaming that I am a reporter for *Time-Life-Ebony-Look* and the *Daily News,* who sent me to report on this rally of the Backwater Klan. I got my helmet on, also my bulletproof vest, and unlaced boots so I can step out of them and run if necessary. No use lying, I am scared. But I got mosquito netting all over my face so the Klansmen won't see how dark I am. Little Klanny, I am one of them folks you are supposed to hate. I am an Afro-American and I do not like nobody calling me *Negra* and worse, like your Kleagle up there on that box is doing. I am a *Negro* and I know, being dark, I have been due in the past to see dark days, but them days is passing. All the fiery crosses in the world is not going to scare me back into where I were before the Harlem riots, Martin Luther King, Adam Powell, and Malcolm X. Also, I might include that lady, Annie Lee Cooper, who hit Sheriff Clark in the eye in Alabama. When a Southern colored woman hits a Southern white sheriff in the eye in a public place like Selma, a new day has come.

" 'Little Klanny, you might as well tell your mammy and your pappy, too, to give up. There is not enough fiery crosses, hoods, and robes in the world to make me turn back now to segregation. The black man, Little Klanny, shall not be moved. I am telling you this because you, being a child, is young enough to understand. Your father and mother is fatheads with bone skulls in which the facts of life cannot penetrate. They don't believe in the United Nations, let alone a united America. They would like to put me back in the cotton fields forever so your daddy could be Old Marster, and you could be Young Marster, and your mammy could set on the veranda and study the beauty cream ads to get her Southern belleness back which were lost in her youthhood due to worrying about how to keep down Negras.

" 'Little Klanny, you know your folks could pronounce the *o* in *Negro* if they wanted to, and not say *Negra* all the time, which sounds too much like that other way of spelling it, with two *g*'s. Anyway, Little Klanny, you better not try to use neither one of them words. You might get your tongue twisted. You are only five years old now, I think, so just go home and learn your Mother Goose and don't bother with race problems until you get to be six. Seven or eight years is an even better age to take up the problem of Afro-Americans. At seven, study how we Negroes got here. At eight, study how we managed to stay here in America. And at nine, try to solve the problem of what are you-all going to do with us now. Or maybe the other way around. What is we going to do with you? Since you-all is, as *Ebony* says, *The White Problem*.

" 'When that problem is solved, Little Klanny, you can use your hood and robe for a play suit, and you can play with little colored children and have some fun, go next door to their house and eat soul food, beat the drums in the neighborhood combo with the hip cats, set up in Sunday School at the Sanctified Church, sing gospel songs, and in general have a good time. In fact, Little Klanny, you can be integrated into my race, the black race, without disgrace. Little Klanny, the day of American youthhood is coming when your parents can no more hold back young folks than they can hold back Negroes. Old Negroes and young white folks is going to own the world! Amen! And march together. I will be a preacher and a teacher going about the South teaching *old* white folks how to behave in the *new* age, since the color line is broke down.

" 'Little Klanny, I am dreaming up a breeze, ain't I, out here on Stoney Mountain? Rockaby, baby, on the tree top! When the wind blows, your cradle will rock. When the bough breaks, your cradle will fall, and down will come baby, cradle, and all. BAM! What's the matter with this dream? Am I falling, too? Me? Is my dream done turned into a nightmare? Has that Kleagle hit me in the head with a rock? Somebody just knocked me out of bed! Or did I fall out myself? I better stop dreaming, Little Klanny. But my last words to you is, "Pay your pappy and mammy in them white sheets no mind. Good night, baby! I'm gone." ' "

Simple's Psychosis

"I WONDER why the human race won't behave itself?" I said.

"Because they don't want to," said Simple. "You are always wondering something foolish like that. You must be simple!"

"Whatever do you mean?" I said.

"Well, for instance," said Simple, "the other day I heard you say you wonder why white folks don't act right to Negroes."

"Why don't they?" I said.

"Because they don't want to," said Simple.

"That fails to explain their behavior," I said. "Why is it they don't want to? Why do American white folks fail to see it is to their own advantage to treat Negroes better?"

"Maybe they don't want that advantage," yawned Simple.

"Yes, they do! They want decent relations with the rest of the world, no more war, and all that. But if they don't change their attitude toward colored folks, they won't have a decent world," I said.

"Maybe they had rather have their attitude," said Simple.

"Well, I contend it will bring them to rack and ruin," I said.

"So what?" asked Simple.

"That would be too bad for them—and us, too," I said.

"How do you figger?" asked Simple.

"America would go to the dogs!" I said. "And if America went to the dogs, so would we."

"I had rather go to the dogs than to be a dog," said Simple. "And that is what I am now—as far as white folks are concerned—a dog!"

"You are only a dog if you think you are one," I said, "or if you let outside forces make you one."

"Then outside forces are hell," said Simple, "especially if they is white."

"You have got a white-complex," I said, "also a dog-psychosis. You need to be psychoanalyzed."

"For why?" said Simple.

"To change your mind," I said.

"It is not *my* mind that needs to be changed," said Simple. "It is them white folks."

"You are obsessed with the subject," I said. "You need to get it off your mind, else it will get you down. You have a white-folks fear-complex which psychoanalysis could remove."

"It is the white folks who are afraid of me," said Simple. "I sure ain't scared of them."

"You talk about them all the time," I said.

"Not as much as they talk about me," said Simple. "Besides, what is this psychoplexis you are talking about?"

"Well, it has to do with releasing your inner tensions," I said.

"Huh?" said Simple.

"In other words, it takes the weights of conflict off your mind," I explained.

"I have no waits, neither conflicts, in my mind," said Simple.

"Oh, but you have," I said. "White folks is one. You think about them night and day."

"I tell you it is them that thinks about me!" said Simple. "What I mainly thinks about is the good times I have had, not the bad—white folks or no white folks."

"You do seem to enjoy yourself," I said.

"I sure do enjoy myself," said Simple. "And when I get as old as Methuselah, I am going to get me a rocking chair. Every time I rock I am going to smile, I am going to remember the good times I have had—in spite of the white folks!"

"Then I guess you do not need to be psychoanalyzed," I said. "That is only for people who are not having a good time out of life."

"It must be for white folks," said Simple, "because they always talk like they are worried. Sometimes you talk like white folks yourself."

"Only when I am talking with you," I said. "Some of these arguments you hand out worry me. I have got to stop taking you seriously or else I will have complexes."

"Then let's us have a beer," said Simple. "That is very good for a man's complexions. Lend me a quarter and I will set you up. I am always kinder broke towards the end of the week."

"I am broke, too," I said.

"Then we will not have no beer," said Simple. "We will just keep on having complexions."

Part Three

AFRICA AND BLACK PRIDE

The Necessaries

THE television was going full flicker in Paddy's, but since there were no fights on that night, few were watching. Its racket only interfered with conversation. Everybody shouted at everybody else. But Simple seemed slightly subdued.

"One sure thing, you can't have your beer and drink it, too," he said, gazing at his empty glass. "To think I have come to this—another winter gone and not a penny. Now it's spring—and I am ragged as a jaybird."

"I sympathize with you," I said, "but sympathy is *all* I can do. I am not thirsty myself." I made no effort to order beers, being slightly out of pocket. Simple fell silent and turned away from me to examine the bar. He was trying to judge the financial status of those nearby.

"You see that fellow over there, Watermelon Joe?" he asked. "He still owes me a quarter from last year. If he don't pay me soon, I'll sure as hell take it out in melons this summer. When he starts pushing his cart, I will demand my slice."

"By now he owes you interest on that Twenty-five Cents," I said.

"He can keep the interest. In fact, anybody who is as ugly as Watermelon Joe, I really should give him a quarter. That man is homely! Do you see his head? Bootsie has nothing on him. Do you dig his feet? His feet are so big they look like animals starting to breathe. His nose is the size of Uncle Wambo's. That is one messed-up man!"

"You should talk, Apollo Belvedere," I said.

"Don't 'dearie' me," objected Simple. "I ain't no woman. I might not be handsome, but one thing sure—out of eight million people in New York, I'm the *only* one who looks like me."

"A unique distinction, but the same could be said for Watermelon Joe!"

"You can beg my apology if you put me in a class with Joe. I may look like Zip, but I do not look like Joe. Anyhow, the womens love me."

"I don't see any women taking care of you," I said.

"I'm independent. I would not let a woman take care of me unless I was married to her. All I want from a woman is love. As I told Joyce the other night:

"A *preacher's heart is food.*
A *woman's heart is kindness.*
A *young man's heart is money—*
But my heart is love.

"Joyce said, 'That is so beautiful! Jess, say it again.'

"So I repeated myself. Facts, if I had another beer, I could repeat some more toasts. I got a new one for you."

"As entertaining as I find your toasts," I said, "I cannot afford to let *all* my money flow over the bar tonight."

"Do you mean to say a beer would take your last dime?"

"Almost," I said, relenting. "But here goes. My final quarter."

"Two beers for two steers! Bartender, I don't mean water. Now I will say you a toast:

"*If you want a good reason for drinking,*
A great one just entered my head—
If a man don't drink when he's living,
How can he drink when he's dead?

That's one I learned in Dallas, from a Negro who were so well-off he not only changed clothes every day, he changed diamonds. It were Prohibition times, too, when they were selling around-the-corner hooch."

"What is around-the-corner hooch?" I asked.

"Take one drink, walk around the corner—and die! That's how bad it were. But I survived. I have survived a great many things. Now, if I can just get Watermelon Joe to return my quarter! I believe I will approach him. I see him down at the end of the bar sporting 'em up. Protect my stool until I come back. If Watermelon gives me a quarter, the next beer is on me."

"I accept with pleasure," I said.

"Don't be too pleased," said Simple, "because if what you expect don't happen, then what don't happen is what to expect. Is that clear? I will now request my quarter."

A couple of comedians were getting yocks from the television audience, but none from the barflies. Nobody paid the TV screen the least mind. Shortly Simple returned to his stool grinning. He had gotten the quarter and promptly proceeded to spend it. Two beers and a nickel in the juke box. Broke again! So he started talking.

"I went window-shopping tonight with no money," said Simple. "All up and down 125th Street—Howard's, Crawford's, Wolfe's, Hollywood Al's. I thought to myself, broke as I was, look at all those clothes a Harlem Negro is expected to wear! Last night at the Victoria, Joyce and me saw a picture about Africa and the only thing the man had on there was a lion-cloth. All the ladies wore was a sarongish little wrap-around which didn't pay no attention to the upper-round. Think how much money they save! Also how much time they save getting up in the morning—just slipping on one piece. And they don't have to remember what sizes they wear, because everything is the same size. I never remember what size my hat is, how long my shirtsleeves is supposed to be, or if I wear a eight or a twelve shoe. And right now I am ragged from tip to toe. I really ought to be halfway sharp to take Joyce out. But do you know how much money it would take to dress me up this spring? Do you know how many pieces of clothes I have to buy to look brand-new? I figured it out last night and it is *some* figure."

"How many, and how much?" I asked.

"Starting at the bottom," said Simple, "which is basic, No. 1, shoes. The kind I want costs $18.50. Next, sox, three pairs, $1.00

each, which is \$3.00. After that, garters, \$1.50. Next, to cover my modesty, drawers, \$1.50. Undershirt, \$1.00. Now getting to what the public sees—the *main* thing, suit, \$58.00—\$60.00 at a pinch. A sweater if the suit ain't warm enough, \$6.85. Shirt, white, \$4.95. Tie, \$2.00. Overcoat, not less than \$60.00 if it's warm. Skypiece, \$8.00. Pocket handkerchief, 60¢. One to blow my nose, 25¢. Muffler to keep from catching cold, \$2.00. Gloves, \$2.50. Belt, \$2.50. Suspenders, \$1.50. Oh, yes, a tie-clasp. And pajamas when I take everything else off, for night wear, to keep from being bare, \$3.00. These are the twenty-two necessaries a man must have to be dressed up in the U.S.A. Not counting the pennies, they comes to One Hundred and Seventy-eight Dollars."

"When do you start shopping?" I asked.

"Man, it would take me one hundred and seventy-eight years to get *all* them items at once. Each and every time I buy a suit, my shoes is wore out. Before I can get new shoes, the suit is old. I get a muffler in the fall. Before I can purchase a topcoat, I lose the muffler. I buy a pair of shorts. Before I've got a undershirt to go with them, the shorts have split. I am telling you, man, Africans have sense! They just grab one rag, put it on, and are dressed. Daddy-o, I would not care if I were an African."

"You *are* an African, just born out of place and out of time."

"Out of money, too," said Simple, "and yet I need all them necessaries."

That Word *Black*

"THIS evening," said Simple, "I feel like talking about the word *black*."

"Nobody's stopping you, so go ahead. But what you really ought to have is a soap-box out on the corner of 126th and Lenox where the rest of the orators hang out."

"They expresses some good ideas on that corner," said Simple, "but for my ideas I do not need a crowd. Now, as I were saying, the word *black*, white folks have done used that word to mean something bad so often until now when the N.A.A.C.P. asks for civil rights for the black man, they think they must be bad. Looking back into history, I reckon it all started with a *black* cat meaning bad luck. Don't let one cross your path!

"Next, somebody got up a *blacklist* on which you get if you don't vote right. Then when lodges come into being, the folks they didn't want in them got *blackballed*. If you kept a skeleton in your closet, you might get *blackmailed*. And everything bad was *black*. When it came down to the unlucky ball on the pool table, the eight-rock, they made it the *black* ball. So no wonder there ain't no equal rights for the *black* man."

"All you say is true about the odium attached to the word *black*," I said. "You've even forgotten a few. For example, during the war if you bought something under the table, illegally, they said you were trading on the *black* market. In Chicago, if you're a gangster, the *Black Hand Society* may take you for a ride. And certainly if you don't behave yourself, your family will say you're a *black* sheep. Then, if your mama burns a *black* candle to change the family luck, they call it *black* magic."

"My mama never did believe in voodoo, so she did not burn no black candles," said Simple.

"If she had, that would have been a *black* mark against her."

"Stop talking about my mama. What I want to know is, where do white folks get off calling everything bad *black*? If it is a dark night, they say it's *black* as hell. If you are mean and evil, they say you got a *black* heart. I would like to change all that around and say that the people who Jim Crow me have got a *white* heart. People who sell dope to children have got a *white* mark against them. And all the white gamblers who were behind the basketball fix are the *white* sheep of the sports world. God knows there was few, if any,

Negroes selling stuff on the black market during the war, so why didn't they call it the *white* market? No, they got to take me and my color and turn it into everything *bad*. According to white folks, black is bad.

"Wait till my day comes! In my language, bad will be *white*. Blackmail will be *white*mail. Black cats will be good luck, and *white* cats will be bad. If a white cat crosses your path, look out! I will take the black ball for the cue ball and let the *white* ball be the unlucky eight-rock. And on my blacklist—which will be a *white*list then—I will put everybody who ever Jim Crowed me from Rankin to Hitler, Talmadge to Malan, South Carolina to South Africa.

"I am black. When I look in the mirror, I see myself, daddy-o, but I am not ashamed. God made me. He also made F.D., dark as he is. He did not make us no badder than the rest of the folks. The earth is black and all kinds of good things comes out of the earth. Everything that grows comes up out of the earth. Trees and flowers and fruit and sweet potatoes and corn and all that keeps mens alive comes right up out of the earth—good old black earth. Coal is black and it warms your house and cooks your food. The night is black, which has a moon, and a million stars, and is beautiful. Sleep is black, which gives you rest, so you wake up feeling good. I am black. I feel very good this evening.

"What is wrong with black?"

Colleges and Color

"You remember my dark-black young cousin F.D.? Cousin Mattie Mae's son that adopted me when he wished himself a train ticket to New York?" Simple greeted me with questions.

"Well, good evening to you, too!" I said, to remind him of his manners. "And, yes, I remember F.D. As I recall, you borrowed a book or two from me because F.D. wanted to read. Why do you bring him up this evening?"

"That young cousin of mine, Franklin D. Roosevelt Brown, told me that his girl friend Gloria wants him to go to college. Ain't that something? And they aim to go this fall. Let's play something on the juke box to celebrate! Dinah Washington, Johnny Ray, Billy Eckstine, Mel Tormé . . ." Simple pondered his choices.

"Has F.D. begun the application process?" I asked.

"Says he already wrote and got the application forms. Now he says he got to write home to his high school and get his basketball transcript, his football record, and his grades. I had to remind that boy that he told me he played baseball, too, in school. I didn't want him to forget nothing important," explained Simple.

"Look here," I interrupted, "would F.D. be going to college to *play*—or to study?"

"Both," said Simple. "So if I live and nothing happens—and I get straight—I am going to send him the money for his first pair of football shoes."

"Well, if F.D. goes to college, what you should think about helping him buy is not football shoes but books. Men go to college to study, not to play football."

"Footballing is all I ever read about them doing," said Simple. "Since I do not know any college boys, I thought they went there to play."

"Of course, the ones who play football get their names in the papers," I said. "But there are thousands of other students who graduate with honors and never even see a football game. What sort of college is F.D. planning to go to, may I ask? A white college? Or a colored college?"

"I hope to a colored college," said Simple.

"Why?" I inquired.

"So he can get a rest from white folks."

"A student doesn't go to college to get a rest from anything. He goes to gain knowledge."

"At a colored school he can dance with the girls, and not be no wallflower."

"A *man* is hardly likely to be a wallflower," I said. "But I see what you mean. At a colored college he can be among his own race and have a well-rounded social life. Still, I insist, you don't go to college to dance. You go to get educated."

"If I was going to college," said Simple, "I might not get educated—but I would come out with a educated wife."

"Football, dancing, marriage, are all side issues. A college is for the propagation of knowledge—not fun or sex."

"I don't see how you are going to keep sex out of a boy's life, nor fun, neither. If F.D. was a son of mine, not just my cousin, I would say, 'F.D., son, go have yourself a good time whilst you are learning, because in due time you will be married like Carlyle and cannot enjoy yourself like you can in school. Also, go to a colored college where you will get to know better your own folks—because when you come out of college, if you don't work with colored folks, you are going to have to work *for* white folks. And the jobs white folks give educated colored mens are few and far between. If you get to be a doctor, you will have to doctor *me*. I am black. How can you doctor me good if you don't know me?' That is what I would say to my son."

"You have a point there," I said, "but I still insist the prime purpose of college is education."

"Do you mean book-learning?" asked Simple.

"Approximately that."

"Then you are approximately wrong," said Simple. "I do not care what you know out of a book, you also have to know a lots out of life. Life is hard for a colored boy in the manhood stage to learn from white folks. If F.D. does learn it around white folks, he is going to learn it the hard way. That might make him mad, or else sad. If he gets mad, he is going to be bad. If he's sad, he is going to just give up and not get nowheres. No, I will tell F.D. tonight not to go to no white school and be snubbed when he asks a girl for a dance, and barred out of all the hotels where his football team stays. That would hurt that boy to his heart. Facts is, I cares more about F.D.'s heart, anyhow, than I do his head."

"I admit there has to be a balance," I said. "And certainly there are good Negro colleges like Lincoln, Howard, or Fisk, where a boy can learn a great deal, and have fun, too. But the way you talk, fun is first and foremost. You imply that there is no fun to be had around white folks."

"I never had none," said Simple.

"You have a color complex."

"A colored complexion," said Simple.

"I said *complex*, not complexion."

"I added the *shun* myself," said Simple. "I'm colored, and being around white folks makes me feel *more* colored—since most of them shun Negroes. F.D. is not white. He's not even light, so F.D. would show up very dark in a white college."

"That would make him outstanding," I said.

"*Standing out—all by himself*, you mean," said Simple, "and that is just where the 'shun' comes in."

"You are confusing the issue," I said.

"I had rather confuse the issue than confuse F.D.," said Simple.

Whiter than Snow

"UM-HUMM-MM-M! This morning there is snow. Must not be long on the ground because it is still white. Nothing stays white in Harlem except the mens that own the stores—and they was born that way. Um-hummm-m-m—snow! Good enough to eat, clean enough to advertise a laundry, cool enough to calm a hangover. I wonder where is my galoshes?

"Yes, daddy-o, I woke up this morning and I saw all that snow down in the areaway and I thought to myself, 'My ancestors in

Ethiopia was never so lucky as to be this unlucky because, beautiful as it is, I never really did like snow.' The best thing about winter is staying in a nice warm house, if you didn't have to go to work. Or better still, a nice warm bar full of people, with plenty of friends inside to set a man up to a drink, and Zarita to once in a while rub her cheek up against yours. Then I feel warm inside and out. Otherwise, winter is not for me."

"That's your African blood," I said.

"Ethiopian," replied Simple. "Anyhow, as soon as it starts getting cold, I start turning ashy. In the summer, I am a dark brown. But in the winter I am a light ash. I also have goose pimples when I go out in the street. Also my feets get wet."

"I gather you do not like winter," I said. "But I hate to think where the colored race would be if it were not for cold weather. Cold weather makes you get up and go, gives you life, vim, vigor, vitality."

"It does not give me anything but a cold," said Simple.

"You're an exception," I said. "It's a well-known fact that Northern races have more aggressiveness than Southern races, also that civilization has taken its greatest strides in the North. Look at Mother England on whose Empire the sun never sets."

"There's a mother for you!" said Simple. "It's setting now."

"Well, then look at Sweden," I said, "one of the happiest states in the world. Norway, one of the healthiest. Also France, modern culture's cradle. They are all cold countries."

"Which has what to do with me?" asked Simple.

"The American Negro, product of a cold climate, is leading the Negroes of the world in attainment," I said. "You are an American Negro."

"But I ain't nowhere myself," said Simple.

"I still say *you're* an exception. Take Joe Black, for example. What other country has a ballplayer like Joe Black? Has Africa? Has Jamaica? Has Brazil? No! Those countries have millions of Negroes. But have they a Lena Horne? No! A Marian Anderson? No! A Dr. Percy Julian? No! They are all hot countries. But here in the U.S.A.

where it drops to zero in December, a Negro has to jump and go, do something, be somebody."

"Do you reckon I could jump up next December and be Rockefeller?"

"You're reaching for the moon."

"I ain't. I'm just reaching for a million," said Simple. "My grandma always told me to hitch my wagon to a star. She did not say no colored star. Besides, I want enough money to go to them warm countries when it gets cold up here. I told you I don't like cold weather."

"Ah, but it puts ambition into you," I said. "Suppose Paul Robeson had been born in a hot country like Brazil. Do you think he would be raising so much sand? Cold weather makes a man vociferous, aggressive, dynamic, ambitious. Take Joe Louis. After those cold Detroit winds off Lake Erie hit him in the face as a boy, he became the world's greatest heavyweight champion. Do you think he would have been as great, had he stayed down in nice warm Alabama?"

"You know Joe couldn't fight no white boys in Alabama," said Simple, "so how could he be the champion? But I ain't built like Joe. And cold weather just drives me to drink."

"You're trifling," I said.

"Then don't trifle with me when I'm cold," said Simple. "Winter makes me evil. I do not love winter. I do not like snow. And I don't feel good when it is cold. I cannot keep my feet warm."

"Perhaps you have low blood pressure. Have you seen a doctor lately?"

"I have not seen a doctor for five years, and then only because Joyce drug me off to the hospital when I had pneumonia, like I told you, and them nurses would not let me get out. I believe they liked me. But I have been cold ever since I was born, except in the summertime, so it has nothing to do with my blood pressure. I do not think I was meant for winter, nor winter for me."

"There could be something in what you say," I said. "Perhaps we are just not the right color for winter, being dark-complexioned.

In nature, you know, animals have protective coloration to go with their environment. Desert snakes are sand-colored. Tree lizards are green. Certain fur-bearing animals have coats the color of the environment in which they live so you can hardly tell them from the foliage or the forest leaves. Ermine, for example, is the color of the snow country in which it originates."

"Maybe that is why white folks is white, to go with the snow, since they come from the North. Which accounts for me not having no business wading around in snow, because it and my color do not match. I am only two shades lighter than dark. Saint Peter will have a hard time washing me white as snow."

"Now you are getting things of the body and things of the spirit mixed up," I said. "When you go to heaven that will be a spiritual change, not a physical one."

"I will have wings, won't I?"

"Wings of the spirit," I said.

"According to the song, they will be snow-white. But if I remain black, my wings will not match me—which must be why I am due to be washed whiter than snow. I never did see a Sunday School card with no dark angels with white wings on it."

"You know why, don't you? Sunday School cards are made by white folks."

"They have them in colored churches," said Simple. "Why don't the colored religions print some colored cards of their own? Every time I went to Sunday School when I was a little boy, they come handing me a card with white angels and a white Moses and white Adams and white Eves on it. I thought everybody in heaven was white. And we was always singing, 'You shall be whiter than snow.' I used to wonder about that—because I would not know my own mother if I went to heaven and she come running to meet me *white*. I would be forced to say, 'Mama, you certainly have changed!' "

"I keep telling you that you are looking at things with physical eyes, not spiritual ones. There are no colors in the other world. 'White' means purity. And being washed 'whiter than snow' refers to the shedding of your sins, not your color."

"I do not want no parts of snow," said Simple. "As I told you, I hate anything cold. And I sure would hate to be turned into a snowman, God forbid!"

"Have no fear," I said. "You are not likely to go to heaven anyhow. You are certainly no model of virtue on earth."

"I *could* turn over a new leaf just before I die," said Simple.

"Your end might come without warning, then there wouldn't be time."

"True. In which case, I reckon I'd be in the Devil's rotisserie," said Simple. "But, at any rate, I would be warm."

Big Round World

"THE other day a white man asked where is my home," said Simple. "I said, 'What do you mean, where is my home—as big and round as the world is? Do you mean where I live now? Or where I *did* live? Or where I was born?'

" 'I mean, where you *did* live,' the white man said.

" 'I did live every-which-a-where,' I told him.

" 'I mean, where was you born—North or South?' the white man said.

" 'I knowed that's what you mean,' I said, 'so why didn't you say so? I were born where you was born.'

" 'No, you weren't,' he declared, 'because I was born in Germany.'

" 'Some Negroes was born as far away as Africa,' I said.

" 'You weren't, were you?' he asked.

" 'Do I look like a Mau Mau?' I said.

" 'You look African, but you speak our language,' that white man told me.

" '*Your* language,' I hollered, 'and you was born in Germany! You are speaking *my* language.'

" 'Then you are an American?'

" 'I are,' I said.

" 'From what parts?' he kept on.

" 'All parts,' I said.

" 'North or South?' he asked me.

" 'I knowed you'd get down to that again,' I said. 'Why?'

" 'Curiosity,' he says.

" 'If I told you I was born in the South,' I said, 'you would believe me. But if I told you I was born in the North, you wouldn't. So I ain't going to say where I was born. I was just borned, that's all, and my middle name is Harlem.' That is what I told that white man. And that is all he found out about where I was borned," said Simple.

"Why did you make it so hard on him?" I asked. "I see no reason why you should not tell the man you were born in Virginia."

"Why should I tell him that? White folks think all Negroes should be born in the South," said Simple.

"There is nothing to be ashamed of about being born down South," I said.

"Neither about eating watermelon or singing spirituals," said Simple. "I like watermelon and I love 'Go Down, Moses,' but I do not like no white man to ask me do I like watermelon or can I sing spirituals."

"I would say you are racially supersensitive," I said. "I am not ashamed of where I was born."

"Where was you borned?" asked Simple.

"Out West," I said.

"West of Georgia?" asked Simple.

"No," I said, "west of the Mississippi."

"I knowed there was something Southern about it," said Simple.

"You are just like that white man," I said. "Just because I am colored, too, do I *have* to be born down South?"

"I expect you was," said Simple. "And even if you wasn't, if that white man was to see you, he would think you was. They think all of us are from down in 'Bam."

"So what? Why are you so sensitive about the place of your birth certificate?"

"What old birth certificate? Where I was born they didn't even have no birth certificates."

"Then you could claim any nationality," I said. "East Indian, West Indian, Egyptian, German."

"I could even claim to be French," said Simple.

"Yes," I said, "or Swiss."

"No, no!" said Simple. "Not Swiss! Somebody might put *chitterling* in front of it. And I am not from Chitterling-Swiss! No, I am not from Georgia! And I have not traveled much, but I have been a few places. And one thing I do know is that if you go around the world, in the end you get right back to where you started from—which is really going around in circles. I wish the world was flat so a man could travel straight on forever to different places and not come back to the same place."

"In that case it would have to stretch to infinity," I said, "since nothing is endless except eternity. There the spirit lives and grows forever."

"Suppose man was like the spirit," said Simple, "and not only lived forever but kept on growing, too. How long do you suppose my hair would get?"

"Don't ask foolish questions," I said.

"Negroes who claim to have Indian grandmas always swear their grandma's hair was so long she could set on it. My grandma did not have so much hair in this world. But, no doubt, in the spirit world, that is changed, also her complexion, since they say that up there we shall be whiter than snow."

"That, I think, refers to the *spirit*, not the body. You change and grow in holiness, not in flesh."

"I would also like to grow in the flesh," said Simple. "I would like to be bigger than Joe Louis in the spirit world. In fact, I would like to be a giant, a great big black giant, so I could look down on

Dixie and say, 'Don't you dare talk back to me!' I would like to have hands so big I could pick up Georgia in one and Mississippi in the other, and butt them together, bam! And say, 'Now you-all get rid of this prejudice stuff.' I would also like to slap Alabama on the backsides just once, and shake Florida so bad until her teeth would rattle and she would abolish separate schools.

"As I grew taller, I would look over the edge of the big round world and grab England and shake her till she turns the Mau Maus free, and any other black parts of the world in her possession. I would also reach down in South Africa and grab that man Malan and roll him in mulberry juice until he is as dark as me. Then I would say, 'Now see how *you* like to be segregated your own self. Apart your own hide!'

"As I keep on growing bigger and taller, I'll lean over the earth and blow my breath on Australia and turn them all Chinese-yellow and Japanese-brown, so they won't have a lily-white Australia any more. Then some of them other folks from Asia can get in there where there is plenty of room and settle down, too. Right now I hear Australia is like Levittown—NO COLORED ADMITTED. I would not harm a hair of Australian heads. I would just maybe kink their hair up a little like mine. Oh, if I was a giant in the spirit world, I would really play around!"

"You have an imagination *par excellence*," I said, "which is French for *great*."

"Great is right," said Simple. "I would be the coolest, craziest, maddest, baddest giant in the universe. I would sneeze—and blow the Ku Klux Klan plumb out of Dixie. I would clap my hands—and mash Jim Crow like a mosquito. I would go to Washington and rename the town—the same name—but after Booker T., not after George, because by that time segregation would be plumb and completely gone in the capital of the U.S.A. and Sarah Vaughan would be singing like a bird in Constitution Hall. With me the great American giant, a few changes would be made. Of course, there would be some folks who would not like me, but they would be so small I would shake them off my shoe tops like ants. I would take one step and be in California, another step to Honolulu, and one more to Japan, shaking a few ants off into the ocean each time I stepped. And wherever there was fighting and war, I would say, 'I don't care who started this battle, stop! But right now! Be at peace, so folks can settle down and plant something to eat again, particularly greens.' Then I would step on a little further to wherever else they are fighting and do the same. And anybody in this world who looked like they wanted to fight or drop atom bombs, I would snatch them up by their collars and say, 'Behave yourselves! Talk things out. Buy yourselves a glass of beer and argue. But he who fights will have *me* to lick!' Which I bet would calm them down, because I would be a real giant, the champeen, the Joe Louis of the universe, the cool kid of all time. This world would just be a marble in my pocket, that's all. I would not let nobody nick my marble with shells, bombs, nor rifle fire. I would say, 'Pay some attention to your religion, peoples, also to Father Divine, and shake hands. If you has no slogan of your own, take Father's, *Peace! It's truly wonderful!*' "

Roots and Trees

"MY wife is an intellect," said Simple, "and that club she belongs to is always pursuiting culture. Nothing wrong, except that it takes so much time. Joyce was setting up in the library all last Saturday reading up on that old problem of how to solve the question of 'you can take a Negro out of the country but you can't take the country out of the Negro'—which I say is a lie. Harlem has certainly taken the country out of me. When I first come to the Big Apple, I did not know beans from bull foot. But look at me today—hip, slick, cool, and no fool."

"You manage to hold your own in New York," I said.

"A foothold is all I need," said Simple, "and my hands will hang on. I been hanging on in New York for a right smart while, and intend to stay. I will not return to the country, North or South. No backwoods for me. I am a big-city man myself. My roots is here."

"In other words, urbanized."

"That's a word I heard Joyce use," said Simple. "What her club is studying is how to make the un-urbanized Negro do right and stop throwing garbage out the window, sweeping trash in the street, fussing on the stoop, and cussing on the corner. Joyce says her club is making that a project. To which I said, 'Joyce, I think you all have bit off more than a ladies' club can chew.'

"To which Joyce answers, 'Well, you men are doing little or nothing about it. What club do you belong to, Jesse B. Semple, that is trying to remedy the disgraceful conditions of adult delinquency here in Harlem? I am not talking about children but grown delinquent men.'

"I said, 'Baby, do not look at me in that tone of voice. You know I carries myself right, drunk or sober.'

"To which Joyce says, 'To act right yourself is not enough. You must also help others to act right. We are all our brother's keeper —and cousin's, too.'

"I knowed Joyce was referring to my Cousin Minnie, who sometimes do not act like a lady. But I ignored Joyce's last remark. I said, 'Darling, you know I belong to the N.A.A.C.P., and I would join the Elks if my budget would let me.'

" 'Our club,' says Joyce, 'is an auxiliary of the Urban League, and our president, Mrs. Sadie Maxwell-Reeves, is an officer in the Harlem branch of the League, which has done much to help transpose the rural Negro to big-city ways, the Southern customs to Northern manners.'

" 'Then that is where I should send my Cousin Minnie,' says I, 'to your club—to see if you-all can't take some of that down-home loudness out of her mouth. Minnie would be a right nice woman if she were not so loud.'

" 'Minnie also needs a job adjustment,' said Joyce.

" 'A job—period!' says I. 'But the kind of job where she does not have to go on time.'

" 'There are no such jobs in an urban community,' says Joyce. 'In the city, folks work by clocks, not by how they feel when they get up in the morning.'

" 'That I learned early,' I agreed. 'Before I married you and sobered up, Joyce, I learned to go to work on time, hangover or no hangover, else be fired. Northern white folks is harder on a late Negro than they are down South.'

" 'That is because the whole South runs late,' said Joyce. 'But up here in the free North—'

" 'A man ain't free to be late,' I said, cutting her off.

"But once Joyce latches onto a subject, there is no cutting her off. Joyce said, 'Jesse B., I want you to help me form a Block Club.'

" 'A what?' says I.

" 'A club to keep this block clean.'

" 'Baby,' I said, 'it would take more than a club. It would take artillery, tanks, and the state militia.'

" 'I am not joking,' said Joyce. 'Just theory and no action gets society nowhere, so Sadie Maxwell-Reeves said in her talk at the All-State Women's Convention last month, where she were the only colored woman to appear at the windup session. The message she brought back to us here in Harlem was, *action and more action*. Jess Semple, we women are marching into action. And you men are going to help us.'

" 'Joyce, baby,' I knowed I had better ask, 'what do you want me to do?'

" 'Help us take away their country ways and prepare them for big-city days.'

" 'In plain words,' I said, 'to live in the city, get with the nitty-gritty, wise up and be witty.'

"Joyce did not even smile. All she said was 'Jess, don't be silly.' So I pulled a long face, too. Now, you know I got to try to do what Joyce wants me to do. Next thing you know, Joyce will be president of our Block Club, and *I* am going to help her."

"Amen!" I said.

"Joyce says Harlem has got to let down our roots where we are," said Simple, "and let our trees grow tall. I wonder where is the tallest tree in the world, anyhow?"

"I have seen some pretty tall trees among the redwoods in California," I said, "and some very tall palms in Africa."

"But there has to be some tree on earth somewhere that is taller than any other tree anywhere," said Simple, "maybe just a tiny smidgen taller, say a quarter of an inch, or maybe only an eighth of an inch, but that little tiny bit extra of a fraction of an inch would make it the tallest tree, taller than any other tree in the world. And it could be proud. I wonder where that tree is? Probably in Africa—and, if so, the black race can be proud of having the tallest tree in the world."

"Nonsense," I said. "How can any race be proud of something it did not create? You know that song that so many singers moo and croon and bawl over about 'only God can make a tree'? How can a man be proud of a tree that just grew?"

"Well, at least he did not cut it down," said Simple. "Say, what do you think it would be like to be married to the tallest woman in the world? A little short woman is hard enough to keep in harness. And even a medium-size woman like my wife, Joyce, I am sometimes afraid to tackle. But the tallest woman in the world, unless she was married to one of the Globe Trotters, would be something for a man to handle. It is funny how God lets some folks grow so tall like Wilt Chamberlain, and others grow so short like Sammy Davis, and me so in-between with neither shortness nor tallness. Nobody makes admiration over me no kind of way—except my wife. Sharp-tempered as she can be sometimes, there is other times when Joyce says to me, 'Baby, you are the sweetest man on earth!' And she looks at me with them sweet, wonderful admiring eyes of hers; then I feel like the tallest tree in the world—that tree that is maybe just one little one-eighth of an inch taller than any other tree anywhere in the world. Me, I am that tree. Oh, friend, the power of a sweet kind word to keep you tall."

Pictures

"SINCE I saw them pictures a while back on the front page of *The New York Times* of that police dog in Birmingham biting a young black student in the stomach, I have ceased to like white folks," said Simple.

"As bad as Birmingham is," I said, "surely you do not blame white people in New York or Detroit or San Francisco for that Alabama dog."

"I do," said Simple, "because white folks is in the majority everywhere. They control the government in Washington, and if they let such doings go on in this American country, such as has been going on in Alabama and Mississippi, I blame them all. If white folks was bit by police dogs and prodded with electric rods, you can bet your bottom dollar something would be done about it—and quick—before you could say *Jackie Robinson*."

"You are no doubt right," I said, "but as long as they themselves are not bitten by dogs and prodded by electric rods and denied the right to march or to vote, most white folks in the North will do very little to help Southern Negroes."

"And I will do very little toward loving them," said Simple. "I am not Martin Luther King. Neither am I a young student or a child. I am a man, and I believe a man has a right to defend his self."

"Passive resistance is a technique designed as defense for the defenseless," I said, "a weapon for the poor and unarmed. I would like to see you standing up effectively to police dogs, clubs, and mobs. Except passively, how would you or could you compete?"

"I might die," said Simple, "but I would die fighting back."

"Then why do you not go down South and die? You are safe here in Harlem, New York City, talking so bravely now. Go South and see what happens to you, friend."

"I will not," said Simple. "That is why I left the South and come North when I was a young man, so I would not blow my top, get mad, fight, get beat, and die. I paid my own good fare to come up North. I figure the rest of those Negroes down South could do the same. What does anybody want to stay in Alabama, Mississippi, or Georgia for, as long as buses, trains, planes, or kiddy cars run and tickets are sold to get away? The Irish left Ireland when the going got rough. The Jews left Germany when Hitler turned on the gas ovens. The Hungarians run toward the Statue of Liberty some years back instead of staying in Hungary hungry. A lot of the white Cubans left Cuba when Castro let his beard grow. Why should not every black chick and child able to scrape up the fare *not* light out from there and say, 'Farewell, Mississippi! Farewell, Alabama! Farewell!' "

"I admit I do not know what makes anyone choose to stay in so unfriendly a land as the South seems to be," I said. "But I also am forced to admire—and *greatly* admire—those black men and women who do stay there and pray and march and demonstrate to make the South a better land."

"Which to happen, we will have to fight."

"What have Negroes got to fight white folks with?"

"God," said Simple.

"So you are going to drag God into the race problem," I protested.

"His eye is on the sparrow," said Simple, "so I know He watches white folks."

"And what means will God use to accomplish Civil Rights?" I asked.

"God works in a mysterious way," said Simple. "Maybe one of their own atom bombs will misfire, fall back to earth on Mississippi, and make cracker gravy out of every cracker down there. Maybe a moon rocket will circle the moon and drop on Birmingham and scare the Klansmen so bad they will tear their britches. Maybe the gold standard will drop out from under white folks and they will land in hell. Who knows what means God will take to straighten out this wicked world? But He will fix it."

"I did not know you are a man of faith," I said.

"Some days I am," said Simple. "Anyhow, God helps them that helps themselves. Ignited we stand, divided we fall."

"Meaning by that, what?"

"Meaning we of the colored race have got to stick together. In fact, I should say all the colored races of the world, including Africa, and elect either Adam Powell or Nkrumah leader."

"Your usual platform," I said. "Black Nationalism."

"Pure black," said Simple, "from Africa to Harlem. Ignited we stand!"

"You are ignited tonight," I said, "six beers—but I reckon you are speaking your sober mind."

"Sober as I can be in my mind," said Simple, "and my mind is most in generally clear. Besides, who can get high on just a little beer? And no matter how high I get, I am still colored, and still me, and still right here in Harlem by night, and working for white folks downtown by day. Dark night, white day—but without white folks no pay. Harlem is run by white folks. And it has done got so a colored man cannot even write a few numbers and stay out of jail. And if he do write numbers, he sends the money downtown to the big white number bankers. It is them that controls us. Undertakers and barber shops is about the only businesses Negroes can own and control any more. And I even hear tell it is getting fashionable now for rich Negroes to have white undertakers. Do you reckon I will live to see the day when we have white barbers?"

"No telling what integration will bring," I said. "But I think it will be quite a while before white barbers take over Harlem shops, if ever. But surely, if you believe in democracy, you would not draw the color line on white barbers, would you?"

"So long as they did not draw their combs too hard through my head," said Simple.

Simple Arithmetic

"NEXT week is Negro History Week," said Simple. "And how much Negro history do you know?"

"Why should I know *Negro* history?" I replied. "I am an American."

"But you are also a black man," said Simple, "and you did not come over on the *Mayflower*—at least, not the same *Mayflower* as the rest."

"What rest?" I asked.

"The rest who make up the most," said Simple, "then write the history books and leave *us* out, or else put in the books nothing but prize fighters and ballplayers. Some folks think Negro history begins and ends with Jackie Robinson."

"Not quite," I said.

"Not quite is right," said Simple. "Before Jackie there was Du Bois and before him there was Booker T. Washington, and before him was Frederick Douglass and before Douglass the original Freedom Walker, Harriet Tubman, who were a lady. Before her was them great Freedom Fighters who started rebellions in the South long before the Civil War. By name they was Gabriel and Nat Turner and Denmark Vesey."

"When, how, and where did you get all that information at once?" I asked.

"From my wife, Joyce," said Simple. "Joyce is a fiend for history. She belongs to the Association for the Study of Negro Life and History. Also Joyce went to school down South. There colored teachers teach children about *our* history. It is not like up North where almost no teachers teach children anything about themselves and who they is and where they come from out of our great black past which were Africa in the old days."

"The days of Ashanti and Benin and the great trade routes in the Middle Ages, the great cities and great kings."

"Amen!" said Simple. "It might have been long ago, but we had black kings. It is from one of them kings that I am descended."

"You?" I exclaimed. "How so? After five hundred years it hardly seems possible that you can trace your ancestry back to an African king."

"Oh, but I can," said Simple. "It is only just a matter of simple arithmetic. Suppose great old King Ashanti in his middle ages had one son. And that one son had two sons. And them two sons each had three sons—and so on down the line, each bigger set of sons having bigger sets of children themselves. Why, the way them sons of kings and kings' sons multiplied, after five hundred years, every black man in the U.S.A. must be the son of one of them African king's grandsons' sons—including me. A matter of simple arithmetic—I am descended from a king."

"It is a good thing to think, anyhow," I said.

"Furthermore, I am descended from the people who built the pyramids, created the alphabets, first wrote words on stones, and first added up two and two."

"Who said all those wise men were colored?"

"Joyce, my wife—and I never doubts her word. She has been going to the Schomburg Collection all week reading books which she cannot take out and carry home because they is too valuable to the Negro people, so must be read in the library. In some places in Harlem a rat might chaw one of them books which is so old and so valuable nobody could put it back in the library. My wife says the Schomburg in Harlem is one of the greatest places in the world to find out about Negro history. Joyce tried to drag me there one day, but I said I had rather get my history from her after she has got it from what she calls the archives. Friend, what is an archive?"

"A place of recorded records, books, files, the materials in which history is preserved."

"They got a million archives in the Schomburg library," said Simple.

"By no stretch of the imagination could there be that many."

"Yes there is," said Simple. "Every word in there is an archive to the Negro people, and to me. I want to know about my kings, my past, my Africa, my history years that make me proud. I want to go back to the days when I did not have to knock and bang and beg at doors for the chance to do things like I do now. I want to go back to the days of my blackness and greatness when I were in my own land and were king and I invented arithmetic."

"The way you can multiply kings and produce yourself as a least common denominator, maybe you did invent arithmetic," I said.

"Maybe I did," said Simple.

Africa's Daughters

"YOU know," said Simple, "my wife kind of shook me up when she come telling me this morning, 'Us women is meeting in Africa next spring.' "

" 'What women?' I said.

" 'Colored women,' said Joyce. 'Us, Africa's daughters.'

" 'For what?'

" 'To discuss our problems,' says Joyce.

" 'What problems have colored womens got that mens have not?'

" 'Colored men,' said Joyce, 'are our problem.'

" 'No kidding,' I kidded.

" 'Jobs,' said Joyce. 'One of our problems also is jobs. All over the world, what kind of jobs are there for colored women? The world must think we are all cooks, servants, baby-sitters. Lots of white folks never heard of a colored stenographer, clerk, bookkeeper, woman doctor, scientist.'

" 'Then they don't read *Ebony*,' I said.

" 'One of our problems is to teach white people to know,' said Joyce.

" 'Know what?'

" 'Who we are,' said Joyce.

" 'But why meet in Africa to do that?'

" 'Africa is the fountainhead,' said Joyce. 'Africa is the new day. Africa will lead the way. Ethiopia shall stretch forth her hand.'

" 'And not draw back a nub,' I said. 'Anyhow, I agree with you, Joyce: Africa is up and coming, humming, done stopped drumming. But, Joyce, exactly what is you talking about, however?'

" 'I am talking about going to Africa,' said Joyce. 'If my club does not send me, I might not be able to go—in the flesh. But I will be there in spirit. An African conference of women, black, Jesse B., like me! From all over the world where there are black women—which is the U.S.A., also Cuba, Haiti, Jamaica, and Trinidad. Also Brazil, where they are black and beautiful like in that movie *Black Orpheus*, and all the West Indies, not to speak of Africa, full of beautiful black women! From everywhere the sisters of Africa are coming together next spring to meet to discuss how to get a good education for every child of every black woman. Also how to be sure husbands and fathers make a decent living anywhere in the world. Also that no woman has to be beholding to any man, white or black, for her living. And no woman needs to make her body a part of her job, like too many women have had to do in the past. I BELONG TO ME is the new slogan for black women. I SHALL BE FREE! the new slogan for black women. EQUAL JOBS AND EQUAL RIGHTS FOR MEN AND WOMEN, BLACK OR WHITE is our new slogan.'

" 'I am glad you include equal rights for mens, too.' I grinned.

" 'Keep on laughing,' said Joyce, 'but she who laughs last is always a woman.'

"I wiped that grin off my face, because I could see that Joyce was getting serious."

African Names

"MONEY is so hard for Negroes to make," complained Simple. "That is why we come North, to better ourselves. In recent years, so many Negroes have left Mississippi and Alabama that there is a shortage of labor in the cotton fields. So I hear that the white folks have proposed to bring in monkeys from Africa to help pick cotton. But they tell me one old Southern Senator is dead set against it. Do you know why? He says, 'Would you want your daughter to marry a monkey?' "

"Absurd," I said.

"Right," said Simple, "because how would he know if monkeys would be interested in them poor white Southern girls? On paydays the monkeys might head right straight for the colored parts of town. In Africa, monkeys is used to black faces. In America, white faces might scare them monkeys to death. I once heard about a pair of monkeys they brought from Africa for the Bronx Park Zoo that never would come out of their cages until they peeked through a hole and saw some colored folks standing in the crowd. Then they would come out and say, 'Howdy!' "

"You can really make up some far-out tales," I said.

"Animals have got plenty of sense. Them monkeys in that zoo knew that not a Negro in the U.S.A. would send way over to Africa for a pair of monkeys to put in a cage. Colored folks have neither the time nor the money for monkeys."

"Baw!" I said.

"Baw is right," said Simple. "That is what one sheep said to the other sheep one day: 'Baa!'

" 'Baa!' the second sheep replied.

" 'Whereupon, the first sheep answered, 'Moo!'

" 'Moo?' asked the second sheep. 'What does *moo* mean?'

" '*Baa* in a foreign language,' said the first sheep."

"I guess that sheep was majoring in French in school," I said.

"No," said Simple, "he were majoring in *bull*."

"Sometimes I think you must have majored in that yourself."

"You know I did not go far in school."

"Well, you can certainly tell some mighty tall tales," I said.

"Believe it or not," declared Simple, "my great-grandpa was so strong he could pull a plow without a mule. Fact is, his old white master sold his mule and kept Grandpa, and the plowing went on just the same. Just imagine, if Grandpa had of been plowing for his self, how rich we would have been today. The white Semples is a wealthy Virginia family what got rich off of plantations and slavery, but all they gave us Negroes was their name, *Semple*. And that I do not want. I would give Semple up for an African Mohammedan Ali Baba name any day."

"A black man with an African name would be colored in America just the same," I said.

"You has no race pride," stated Simple. "If I ever have a son, I am going to give him an African name."

"Roland Hayes has a daughter named Africa," I said.

"More power to him," said Simple. "Indian names is nice, too, but I do not know what my grandmother's great-grandpa's name were, otherwise I might take it, long as it were not Black Foot."

"Maybe it was Red Wing," I said.

"Nice name," said Simple. "I wonder how my wife would like to be called Joyce Red Wing. I am going to ask her."

"Sitting Bull was also a famous Indian name," I said.

"No Bull," said Simple. "I do not think Joyce would like being Mrs. Bull."

"There was once a beautiful dancer named Maria Tallchief," I said.

"And a colored blues singer named Pine Top," added Simple.

"But I reckon he was only part Indian, like me. If I was to find out my Indian name and add it to my African name in front of my Mohammedan name, nobody would ever know I had been Jesse B. Semple before. I could put on my Social Security card a name out of this world. And when folks asked me my race, I could say, 'Just try to trace.'

"Suppose my name were Buffalo Horn Yusef Ali Congo, would it not have a noble sound? When Mr. and Mrs. Congo went out together, we would be solid gone. In there, like the bear! Me with my beard and Joyce with her Ashanti robe. And me, I would have on one of them fez caps like Dizzie Gillespie brought back from North Africa. And was I to run into Sammy Davis, who is Jewish, I would say, 'Shalom!' And Sammy would answer, 'Mazel tov!' "

"And what would Joyce say?" I inquired, getting quite intrigued with Simple's fantasy exchange.

"Joyce would say, 'Hallelujah!' " said Simple, "because it would be hard for her to get over her Baptist training."

Harems and Robes

"ONE nice thing about dogs," said Simple, "is that they are usually not stuck up. No matter how much pedigree a dog has got, it would just as leave belong to me as to Harry Belafonte. To a dog, a master by any other name smells just as sweet. Dogs is democratic. I love dogs."

"You're an old dog yourself," I said.

"I used to think about becoming a Mohammedan," declared Simple.

"A Mohammedan?" I said. "Why?"

"So I can stop being the least and look toward the East," said

Simple, "grow a beard on my chin and give up gin, because you know Mohammedans do not drink. They think."

"An admirable ambition," I said, "if it would work with you. How about beer?"

"Have no fear. Were I to go on the Mohammedan side, I would abide by their laws and hymns. What I do, I do whole hog, once I *do* do. I been listening to the Muslims speak and I thirst for what they seek—to step beyond the *N* to the *M*."

"Meaning by that, what?" I asked.

"*N* stands for *Negro*, but *M* stands for *Man*. Also for Muslims. Muslims is colored, so I would just be joining hands with more colored, were I to become a Muslim. But my only drawback is Joyce. My wife is Baptist. Were I to come home one day renamed Alim, Joyce probably would holler out loud, demand that I shave off my chin whiskers, and drag me off to baptism. But I hear tell that Muslims can have four wives, so I could always hold a harem over her head."

"Four wives in Mohammedan countries, perhaps," I said, "but you live in the U.S.A., where the civil law prohibits plural marriages. In New York you can have only one wife. Besides, Joyce would hardly share you with *one* woman, let alone three. Also, how would you take care of *four* wives on your salary? Where would you put four wives in a Harlem kitchenette?"

"I would manage," said Simple. "Only thing that would worry me would be, how would I ever win an argument with four wives? But there is nothing in the Muslim religion that says a man *has* to marry four wives. I could just stay three-fourths single like I is. I would keep Joyce—and let the other three go. But I might buy myself a Muslim robe just so as to look different. With so many people in my neighborhood wearing robes, it is hard these days to tell real Africans from Harlem Africans. Folks are letting their hair go natural, jazz bands are playing African music, men are wearing Sékou Touré caps, womens are in Nigerian robes. I met a girl in a beautiful robe at a party on Lenox Avenue Saturday night.

"I said, 'Miss, what part of Africa are you from?'

"She said, 'Alabama.'

"I said, 'I reckon you can get served in a bus station down in Alabama, then.'

"She said, 'That is one reason I wear these robes. They help—even in New York—if you are black. Another reason I wear these African robes is because I am proud to be descended from Africa, proud of my ancestry, proud of my people, and proud of their robes.'

" 'Good,' I says. 'Sister, I am proud of you. Meet your brother.'

"On that we shook. But when I asked her for a dance, she said no, she was with her boy friend and he was six feet tall. So I went back to dancing with my wife.

"I said to my wife whilst dancing, 'Joyce, honey, let's get ourselves some African robes and see if they help us get our rights quicker.'

"Joyce said, 'Not I. Just as I would not pass for white, so I will not pass for African. I want my rights in the U.S.A. just as I am, black, without one plea.'

" 'Baby,' I said, 'you have to plea more than once with American white folks to get what rightfully is your rights. If a robe and turban help, why not?'

" 'I will stand up for my rights without a robe,' says Joyce. 'The black women of America have as much right to all rights as white women have, without putting on any foreign robes to get them. I love Africa, but I was born in Florida, U.S.A., America. Of my African blood I am proud, but I want American rights. Of my black face I have no shame, therefore I have the right to want the right to show my face anyplace in America any other folks show their face. I say, no more segregation in the U.S.A. for Africans with robes or Negroes without robes. Rights should not depend on a robe.'

" 'Neither on a turban,' I said. 'But you remember how a Negro newspaper man few years ago put on a turban and went down South and got served from here to yonder and the Carolinas to Texas. Them stupid Southerners thought he was an A-rab.'

" 'An air-rab,' says Joyce.

" 'Some kind of foreigner, anyhow,' I said. 'So with a turban he was not Jim Crowed—yet he was black as me. Which goes to show there is no reason for prejudice. It do not make sense. Dress like me—segregated. Dress like a foreigner, take a foreign name, speak Spanish, and wear a turban—integrated. I see no harm in fooling white folks, myself.'

" 'It is so undignified to have to lie,' said Joyce. 'So undignified not to be *able* to be yourself, whoever you be. I want to be *me*—Mrs. Jesse B. Semple.'

" 'Good for you, Joyce,' I says.

" 'My Afro-American angel,' cooed Joyce, dancing with her head on my shoulder.

" 'Congo cutie,' I whispered in her ear.

" 'Lenox Avenue lion,' she purred to me.

" 'Whrrr-rr-er!' I roared. 'You're *mine*!' "

Part Four

PARTING LINES

Nothing but Roomers

AUTUMN in New York. No burning leaves, no woodsmoke in the air. But skyscrapers at dusk burst into a kind of golden glare. There's coolness, then coldness, then maybe snowflakes in the air. Bang on the radiator—if you've got the nerve—and try to get some heat. The law says they got to turn the heat on by October 15. Simple's old landlady says, "The law? What law? I am the law in here!"

"Well, anyhow, madam, if you don't care nothing about me—my name being Jesse B. Semple—nor about Mr. Ezra Boyd, nor none of the other tenements in your house, remember there's babies upstairs—Carlyle's baby and that little girl-baby down underneath me. It ain't them babies' faults they're nothing but roomers."

"It ain't my fault they're babies. I told *everybody* when they moved in here, 'No children in this house.' And then them gals had to come up pregnant! I had nothing to do with it. Now, with all the gas they are using heating milk, washing diapers, burning the light all night with the colic, I don't make a cent out of this house. The law says to turn on the heat October 15th, so you say. Well, this is still Indian summer."

"I am part Indian, madam, and it do not feel like summer to me."

"You are all run down, that is what is the matter with you, also run out. At your young age, you got no business being cold-natured, Mr. Semple. Now, you take my husband, who is a settled man, he is not cold. Neither am I. But I keeps heat on downstairs for Trixie, that is the reason. She is old and her hair is thin."

"Them babies is young and ain't got no hair a-tall yet. How about them?"

"Can I help it if babies are hairless? Who is running my

business—you or me? Just because you been living here seven years, don't think you nor any other roomer can take over, Jesse B. Semple. This is still a private house, a home, and I runs this house like a home. You are my guests. But you are not in charge. I intend to send some heat upstairs as soon as them radiators get drained. That is why there is no heat—I do not want to flood this place. So just hold your horses before you come running down here accusing me of being the kind of woman who freezes babies, I don't care whose they are—even if they were bred by accident."

"Madam, there's no telling how many of us was accidents."

"I'll have you know *my* father and *my* mother was married two years before I was born. I was their third child."

"Three children in two years? Two was twins?"

"No twins—one girl—one boy—then me—a year apart, stair-steps."

"Then that first step must have been a misstep."

"What?"

"I mean three babies in two years is going pretty fast, isn't it, unless somebody got a head start somewhere?"

"I will thank you to leave my presence and stop reflecting on my parents—and on me. The facts are, I must have disremembered. They were really married *three* years when I were born—which, I know now, is what I meant to say. Us stair-steps was three years apart."

"Excuse me, madam, for catching you up. I always was good at mathematics."

"You can't seem to figure out how to keep ahead on your rent. You are almost always behind. Explain me that, if you are so good at figures."

"If I was always on time, would you give me a bonus, a discount for cash on the line?"

"Why don't you try getting ahead sometime and see? One thing I will do, if you showed your appreciation for me by paying promptly every week *absolutely on time*, I would hang you some new winter drapes that would make your room more presentable. You seems to take no interest at all in decoration yourself. Nothing up on your walls but them nude calendars, and they are blondes. I'll bet you, you would not have them white naked nudes up on your walls down South. As race-minded as you pretend to be, I wouldn't have them up on my walls here. Don't your licker store nor bar have no colored girls on their calendars?"

"They do, but they all got clothes on."

"Naturally, no colored woman would have her picture taken with each and every point bared to the breeze. We are more modest. Never would I pose in a meadow for nobody without my clothes on."

"I hope not, madam."

"*Meaning* by that . . . ?"

"Meaning you have such a beautiful character you do not have to show your figure. Your soul does it, madam. There is sweetness in your face. F.D. loved you like a mother."

"I thank you. Have you heard from F.D.?"

"That boy's done got on the freshman football team. He sure is a kicker. And he sends you his regards."

"Thanksgiving I'll send that F.D. a fruitcake. You have a smart young cousin, Mr. Semple. I am one who likes to see young people get ahead in this world. Were I young again, I would go to college myself."

"Where did you get your education, madam?"

"The hard way. I was working in a tobacco barn when I was fourteen. I first married when I was sixteen and started buying a house. This man is my third husband. This house is my fourth house. And this house I swear I am gonna keep. Neither husbands nor mortgages is gonna take this house from me. I handles this business myself now. This property is in my own name—and all the papers. Losing husbands and losing houses is what has been my education. Now I say, 'To hell with husbands—I am going to hang on to this house!' I'll tell any woman, a roof over your head is better than a husband in your bed! A good woman can always get a man, but a house costs money.

"Set down, Mr. Semple. If you're interested in my education, I'll tell you. Me and my No. 1 husband—that Calvin were as young as Carlyle when I married him—we mortgaged our house to start a barbecue restaurant in Charlotte in *his* name, with a juke box. Don't you know that Negro put all his profits in the piccolo, playing records, entertaining every chippie that come in, trucking, sanding, dancing our dimes away, lindy-hopping all day long, rainbow lights just flashing in the vendor. The concession what owned that tune box come every week with twelve new records, and lugged off twelve tons of nickels out of it, mostly what Calvin had put in. That's where our profits went. Husband lost the business, I lost the roof over my head.

"Husband No. 2, I said we'll put the house and the business in *both* our names. We did. Started buying a nice little cottage, too, in Durham, with a yard. Opened up a nice little soda-pop, newspaper, shoeshine stand. Instead of selling soda pop, Renfroe started selling moonshine—without fixing the cops up in front. You can't fool no cop when he sees a man set down at a soda fountain sober and get up drunk. Renfroe went to jail. Lawyers, bails, fines, a little present of some folding money for the judge to let him off light. Shoeshine and soda-fountain stand padlocked. Me worried out of my mind. Lost the house again. I divorced that Negro.

"This man I got now, I make him work for himself. I owns this house *myself*. I runs it. My home and my investment is all in one so I can stay home and keep an eye on my business, too: ROOMS FOR RENTS. No man is mixed up in my finances no more. From now on, a husband might share my bed, but not my bankbook. Oh, no! I have learned my lessons. When a woman wants to get ahead, she cannot tie a millstone to her feet. Most men is millstones."

"I am sorry, madam, you have such a low opinion of mens, but it looks like all your experiences have been disfavorable. You should have met *me* in your young life."

"God forbid! Joyce can have you. But I hope you and Joyce have laid your plans to buy a nice little home when you get married, which she will put in *her* name. Y'all certainly can't live here. Your room ain't big enough for two, neither is it a kitchenette. Besides, I do not want no couples—and no more babies. That is a *single* room."

"Don't worry, madam, me and Joyce do not plan to room with nobody. Facts are, we intends to buy a house and keep roomers ourselves. But only roomers with recommendations, Joyce says."

"It's a good thing you will be *married* to her, then, otherwise you couldn't live in that house yourself."

"You wouldn't give me a recommendation, was I to need one?"

"What have you ever gave me except a frown when I remind you your rent is due?"

"I have walked your dog—which is a favor for any man to be seen with."

"I am beginning to understand that you just don't have a nature for dogs, you mentions that so frequent. I will not ask you to walk Trixie again. I hope, however, you will never be crippled up with rheumatism yourself and need somebody to walk a dog for you."

"I will turn my dog loose in the back yard and let him run around in circles."

"Then your dog will be just a plain old cur, I reckon, that can get his exercise by chasing his own tail."

"Which would be good exercise right on. His hind feet would never catch up with his front ones, nor his front feet with his hind."

"Just like you never catch up with your rent."

"If you keep harping on that, madam, you will make me hot."

"Good—because you sure ain't gonna get no heat upstairs this evening."

"Good night, madam."

"Good night."

"*Damn* good night!"

"What did you say?"

"*Good night!*"

Simple Santa

"CARLYLE'S wife is pregnant again," said Simple. "What do you reckon they are going to do with two babies in one room?"

"I imagine your landlady is worried about that, too."

"She is," said Simple. "She done swore she won't rent to no more *young* married couples. From now on, they have to be settled folks that works hard—too tired and settled to raise a family in her house."

"Is your landlady really as hardhearted as that toward children?" I asked.

"No," said Simple. "But she has her rules. Still and yet, she is really crazy about both them little old babies in the house, spite of the fact she objected to them being born. Every time she boils some beef for Trixie, she sends them babies up a cup of hot broth. And if one of them gets the colic, she is more worried than their mamas. Only thing she does not worry about is giving them heat. She says babies is due to stay wrapped up in blankets with bootsies on their feets. And if a house is too hot, they get overheated. So I asked her to give me an extra blanket since I do not have bootsies. Do you think she did?"

"Ha! Ha!" I said.

"She come giving me some kind of spiel about what makes men so cold-natured when women, she says, go around in zero weather in open-work shoes on the streets, yet do not catch pneumonia and die. Neither do they freeze. Which is true, I have never heard of a woman having chilblains yet. But if a man went out in his sox-feet in the winter, me for instant, I would be so full of cold the next day I could not draw a decent breath. Women can go low-necked and bare-footed in the snow in party shoes and do not even sneeze. In this New York zero weather, if men dressed like women we would develop galloping consumption and go into decline. Then where would the human race be without mens? For instant, without your father, you would not be here today."

"The same goes for your mother," I said.

"Cut it out," yelled Simple. "I'm not playing the dozens. Listen, I want to borrow a dollar."

"For what?"

"To give a kid."

"What kid?"

"Not my kid, 'cause I ain't got none," said Simple. "But if you was to go across the street with me, you would see what kid. It is a kid who wants to buy his grandma a present for Christmas."

"Do you know his grandma?"

"No. Neither do I know the kid. But he made a mistake. He saw a present a week ago in the West Indian store window, and the sign was written wrong. It said, 'One—twenty-nine cents.' But it was written like this—see: O-N-E—and a dash—and a twenty-nine-cent sign. 1–29¢. The kid thought it meant one for twenty-nine cents. But what it really meant was One Dollar *and* Twenty-nine Cents."

"For one what?" I asked.

"Dustpan," said Simple.

"What in the world does a kid want to give his grandmother a dustpan for?"

"Because that is what she wants for Christmas," said Simple. "So this kid had been saving up his pennies till he got twenty-nine cents. Now the man wants a *Dollar and Twenty-nine Cents* for that dustpan."

"I never heard of such a price!" I said. "A Dollar and Twenty-nine Cents for an ordinary dustpan?"

"It is made of genu-wine metal," said Simple, "and painted red with a white handle. It is a *fine* dustpan! So I want to borrow a dollar off of you to give that kid. He has got his heart set on giving his grandma that dustpan, so he is standing over there crying. See?

"He is only eight-nine years old—and he read that sign wrong. Some people do not know how to paint a sign. Besides, I remember when I was a little kid, I did not ever have any money but a nickel now and then, and I always wanted to buy something that costs more than I had. I have got no kids myself, but if I did have, I would want him to be happy on Christmas and give presents—so I am going to give that kid a dollar to get that there dustpan."

"You are a very sentimental Santa Claus," I said. "You haven't got a dollar and you do not even know the lad."

"No, I do not know that kid," said Simple, "but I know for a kid to save up Twenty-nine Cents sometimes is hard. When he wants to give it away in a present to his grandma instead of eating it up in candy or going to see Humphrey Bogart, I admire that kid. Lend me a dollar!"

"Here! Pay me back Fifty Cents. I will also invest in an unseen dustpan for an unknown boy and his unknown grandmother."

"You are making fun of me and that kid," said Simple.

"I am not," I said. "It just strikes me as funny—a dustpan for a Christmas present! But hurry up across the street and give the youngster the dollar before he is gone."

"If he's gone, I'll be coming back—and we'll drink this dollar up."

"Oh, no!" I cried. "Either give it to the child, or give my money back to me."

"Then I will be broke," said Simple, "and I want to wish you a Merry Christmas ahead of time. How else can I wish you a Merry Christmas except to buy you a drink?"

"With my money?" I said.

"Don't be technical!" said Simple.

When he came back into the bar, he was grinning.

"That kid thinks I'm Santa Claus," he said. "Right now I wish I was Santa Claus for just one day so I could open some of that mail he gets up yonder at the North Pole. I would particularly like to latch onto that mail from children down in Alabama, Mississippi, and Florida. I would answer them white kids down there in a way they would never forget."

"Race again, I'll bet! Those kids," I said, "have nothing to do with Jim Crow, and it would be a shame to intrude the race problem into their Christmas thoughts."

"A shame, nothing!" said Simple. "They are growing up to be a problem. And if I was a Santa Claus, being my color, I would teach them a lesson before they got too far gone. Suppose I was to open a letter from some little Johnnie Dixiecrat in Mississippi asking me to bring him a hunting rifle, for instant. I would dip my pen in ink and reply:

North Pole, Santa Claus Land
December the so-and-so
Year Now

Johnnie:

I would call you "Dear Johnnie," but I am a colored Santa Claus, so I am afraid you might be insulted, because I fears as a white child in the South you have been reared wrong in regards to race. You say you are seven years old. Well, I hope you do not want that rifle you wrote me about to lend your cousin Talbot to shoot a Negro—because where you live lynchings is frequent, although they do not call them by that name now. I read in the paper the other day where eight white mens riddled one black man with bullets. Johnnie, the grown mens in your place do not act right. If you don't, I will not bring you a thing after you grow up. I will bring you this hunting rifle now, little as you are, because I believe you are still good.

But listen, Johnnie! When you get up in your teens, don't let me catch you getting on the bus in front of some crippled old colored lady just because you are white and she is black. And don't let me catch you calling her by her first name, Sarah, and she is old enough to be your grandma, when you ought to be calling her Mrs. Whatever-Her-Name-Is. If you do such, I will not bring you that bicycle you gonna want to ride to high school. And you sure won't get that television set if you go around using bad words about colored folks. As long as Santa Claus stays black, I will not stand for that!

Also, Johnnie Dixiecrat, sir, if you gets to be a salesman or a in-

surance man or a bill collector in Meridian or Jackson, Mississippi, show your manners and take off your hat when you go in a colored woman's house. If you don't, I will not put nothing in your sox on Christmas Eve, not a doggone thing! And if you get big enough to vote, see to it that colored folks can vote, too. If you don't, I'm liable to drop down your chimney a present you don't want—a copy of the United States Constitution. See how that would be for your constitution—since it says everybody is free and equal.

I am signing off now, dear Johnnie, since I have got one million letters more to answer from Alabama and Georgia, so I cannot take up too much time with you in Mississippi. If you see me on Christmas Eve, you will know me by my white beard and black face. Up North the F.E.P.C. has given a Negro the Santa Claus job this year. Dark as I am, though, I intend to treat you equal.

MERRY CHRISTMAS! The rifle I will bring when I come. Don't be rowdy. *Cheerio!*

JESS SIMPLE SANTA CLAUS"

Empty Houses

"ONCE when I was a wee small child in Virginia," said Simple, "I was walking down the street one real hot day when a white man patted me on the head and give me a dime.

"He said, 'Looks like you could stand an ice-cream cone,' to which I said, 'Yes, sir.'

"That cone I bought sure was good. I were staying with some of my mother's distant kinsfolks at the time, and when I went home and told them I had bought an ice-cream cone they said, 'Where did you get the money?'

"I said, 'A white man give me a dime.'

"They said, 'What was you doing out in the street begging for a dime?'

"I explained to them that I had not begged, but they said, 'Don't lie to me, boy. Nobody is gonna walk up to you and just give you a dime without you asking for it.' So I got a whipping for lying.

"They could not understand that there is some few people in the world who do good without being asked. It were a hot day, I were a little boy, and ice-cream cones are always good. And that man just looked at me and thought I would like one—which I did. That is one reason why I do not hate all white folks today because some white folks will do good without being asked or hauled up before the Supreme Court to have a law promulgated against them.

"Not everybody has to be begged to do good, or subpeanoed into it. Why, a cat in the bar the other night I hardly knowed offered me a beer, and when I said, 'Man, I'm sorry, but I am kinder short tonight and cannot buy you one back,' he said, 'Aw, forget it!' He bought me the beer anyway.

"Some folks think that everything in life has to balance up, turn out equal. If you buy a man a drink, he has to buy you one back. If you get invited to a party, then you have to give a party, too, and invite whoever invited you. My wife, Joyce, is like that—which makes folks end up having to give parties they do not want to give, and going to a lot of parties to which they do not want to go. Tit for tat—I give you this, you give me that. But me, I am not that way. If I was to give somebody I liked a million dollars, I would not expect them to give me a million dollars back. I would give a million like it warn't nothing. But even if you give a million and don't give it free-hearted, it is like nothing. Do you get what I am trying to say?"

"You are dealing in very high figures," I said, "so it sounds complicated. Nevertheless, since you have been standing at this bar for the last half hour with an empty glass, I will give you a beer."

"I accept," said Simple. "Thank you."

"Don't mention it," I said. "It's nothing."

"Nothing is everything," said Simple, "when it comes from the heart. But even a glass of beer when it don't come from the heart tastes like nothing. You know, I told you before, I were a passed-around child, so I know when something tastes like nothing. Even a Sunday dinner can taste like nothing, and if you are a little small child, you wonder why.

"One Sunday when I was little down in Virginia, even before they nicknamed me Simple, I went looking in the rain that dusk-like evening for something I did not know what, somewhere I did not know where. Seems like I was looking for somebody, I did not know who, because I had just come out of a house full of peoples but they was lonesome to me, and I was lonesome to them. Nobody put me out of no house that day, and they had give me plenty to eat, but I just went off in the rain by myself walking down the street looking. I went down a street with big rich fine houses setting on lawns under trees where poor folks did not live, nor colored. And I thought nobody lonesome like me ever lived there, which maybe was wrong. I were only a little small child and I did not know then that rich folks sometimes might be lonesome, too, in a house full of loneliness even when their big fine house is full of peoples.

"Sundays my aunt sent me to Sunday School, and I looked at Jesus, who were white, on a Sunday School card, and at Moses, who were white, and Mary Mother of God, also white, and I were lonesome in that colored Baptist church in Virginia with Sunday School cards that were white—and me not the color of nobody I knew with white relatives. Jesus was the color of the white folks that black folks worked for in our town. Jesus had long straight hair that hung down to the neck of His robes, and I wondered what kind of drawers Jesus wore under His robes. All the men on them Sunday School cards had on robes, and I wondered if they wore underneath pants or what. I also wondered why Bible peoples wore their hair so long. Also, how did an angel with such long wings ever set down? On the Sunday School cards the angels were always standing up, else flying. These such thoughts I thought, setting in Sunday School, until the old lady teacher said, 'Now let's all sing, "Jesus loves me, that I know, because the Bible tells me so." ' We also sang 'Jesus Wants Me for a Sunbeam.' Then she said, 'Let us pray.'

"I pictured in my mind a white God listening to me praying. And

I wondered if He cared anything about a little colored boy's prayers, or did He just listen to the peoples in the big fine houses with the porches and lawns and trees and the pretty lamps with big shades in their windows at night? Did He listen to me setting in Sunday School wondering what kind of drawers Jesus wore? Anyway, I was walking that day in the rain. And I was thinking about my old aunt who was not really my aunt, but who was my father's stepfather's sister and who took me in and took care of me while my mother was away somewhere. I were a passed-around child. While my mother was not there and my father was not there and they was separated, I were left with whoever would take care of me when they was not there.

"Nobody was mean to me, and I do not know why I had that left-out feeling, but I did, I guess because nobody ever said, 'You're mine,' and I did not really belong to nobody. When I got big and grown-up, I took for my theme song in my early manhood years that old record of Billie Holiday's which says, 'God bless the child that's got his own.' If I had a child, be he or she girl or boy, I would make sure I kept that child with me and it were my own and I were its own. I would make sure it did not want to go back home, even when it came dinnertime and you was hungry.

"Since I married my second wife, Joyce, I do not have that left-lonesome feeling so much any more. But it took me a long time to find somebody you want to come home to where the house does not feel empty even with somebody in it. It is bad for a full-grown man to come home to somebody who is not there, even if they have got dinner ready. For a little small child, it is worse—that nobody-home-that-belongs-to-you feeling. Even if the house is full of peoples, it is not enough for them to just be there.

"If they do not have a little love for whoever lives in the house with them, it is a empty house. If you have somebody else living in the house with you, be it man, woman, or child, relative or friend, adopted or just taken in, even if it is just a roomer paying rent—even if you give them no money nor a piece of bread and not anything—if you got a little love for whoever it is, it will *not* be a empty house. But if nobody cares, it is an empty house. I have lived in so many empty houses full of peoples, I do not want to live in a crowded empty house no more."

God's Other Side

"SOME Negroes think that all one has to do to solve the problems in this world is to be white," I said, "but I never understood how they can feel that way. There are white unemployed, just as there are black unemployed. There are white illiterates, just as there are blacks who can hardly read or write. The mere absence of color would hardly make this world a paradise. Whites get sick the same as Negroes. Whites grow old. Whites go crazy."

"Some of us in Harlem do not have sense enough to go crazy," said Simple. "Some Negroes do not worry about a thing. But me, well, Jim Crow bugs me."

"Bigotry disturbs me, too," I said, "but prejudice and segregation alone do not constitute the root of *all* evil. There are many nonracial elements common to humanity as a whole that create problems from the cradle to the grave regardless of race, creed, color, or previous condition of servitude."

"But when you add a black face to all that," said Simple, "you have problem's mammy. White folks may be unemployed in this American country, but they get the first chance at the first jobs that open up. Besides, they get seniority. Maybe some white folks cannot read or write, but if they want to go to Ole Miss to learn to read or write, they can go without the President calling up the United States Army to protect them. Sure, white folks gets sick, but they don't have to creep in the back door of the hospital down South for treatment like we does. And when they get old, white folks have got more well-off sons and daughters to take care of them than colored folks have. Most old white folks when they get sick can suffer in comfort, and when they die they can get buried without going in debt. Colored folks, most in generally, do not have it so easy. I know because I am one."

"You let yourself be unduly disturbed by your skin," I said. "Sometimes I think you are marked by color—just as some children are born with birthmarks."

"My birthmark is all over me," said Simple.

"Then your only salvation is to be born again."

"And washed whiter than snow," declared Simple. "Imagine all my relatives setting up in heaven washed whiter than snow. I wonder would I know my grandpa were I to see him in paradise? Grandpa Semple crowned in Glory with white wings, white robe, white skin, and golden slippers on his feet! Oh, Grandpa, when the chariot swings low to carry me up to the Golden Gate, Grandpa, as I enter will you identify yourself—just in case I do not know you, white and winged in your golden shoes? I might be sort of turned around in heaven, Grandpa."

"What on earth makes you think you are going to heaven?" I asked.

"Because I have already been in Harlem," said Simple.

"How often do you go to church?" I asked.

"As often as my wife drags me," said Simple. "The last two times I was there the minister preached from the text 'And I shall sit on the right hand of the Son of God.' Me, half-asleep, I heard that much from the sermon. And it set me to wondering why it is nobody ever wants to set on the *left*-hand side of God? All my life, from a little small child in Virginia right on up to Harlem, in church I have been hearing of people setting on the right-hand side of God, never on the left. Now, why is that?"

"When a guest comes to dine, you always seat him or her on your right—that is, the main guest sits there," I said. "The right-hand side is the place of honor, granted always to the lady, or the oldest, or the most distinguished person present. The right side is the place of honor."

"I would be glad to set on any old side," said Simple, "were I lucky enough to get into the Kingdom. Besides, if everybody is setting on the right-hand side of God that says they are going to set there, that right-hand side of God would be really crowded. One million Negroes and two million white folks must be setting already on the right. How is there going to be room on that side for anybody else?"

"In the Kingdom there is infinite room, whichever side is chosen," I said.

"No matter how much room there is," said Simple, "that right side of the Throne is crowded by now. I see no harm in setting on the left. God must turn His head that way once in a while, too."

"I suppose He does," I said. "But if you have your choice, why not sit on the right?"

"Just because everybody else is setting there," said Simple. "I would like to be different, and set on the left-hand side all by myself. I expect I would get a little more of God's attention that way—because when He turned around toward me, nobody would be there but me. On His right-hand side, like I said, would be setting untold millions. And all of them folks would be asking for something. God's right ear must be so full of prayers He can hardly hear Himself think. Now me, on the left-hand side, I would not ask for nothing much, were I to get to heaven. And if I did ask for anything, I would whisper soft-like, 'Lord, here is me.'

"Were the Lord to grant me an answer, and say, 'Negro, what do you want?' I would say, 'Nothing much, Lord. And if you be's too busy on your right-hand side to attend to me now, I can wait. I tried to leave my business on earth pretty well attended to—but just in case my wife, Joyce, needs anything, look after her, Lord. I love that girl. Also my Cousin Minnie—protect her from too much harm in them Lenox Avenue bars which she do love beyond the call of duty. Also my young cousin, F.D., that I helped to raise when he first come to Harlem in his teens, who is out of the Army and married now, show F.D. how to get along with his wife and be a good young man, and not pattern himself too much after me, who were frail as to being an example for anybody.

" 'The peoples that I love, Lord, is the only ones I whispers into Your left ear about. If I was on Your right side, which is crowded with all the saints who ever got to Glory, me, who ain't much, might have to holler from afar off for You to hear me at all. Me, who never was nobody, am glad just to be setting on Your left side, Lord—me, Jesse B. Semple, on the left-hand side of the Son of God! And I wants to whisper just *one* thing to You, God—I hope You loves the ones I love, too.' "

Dog Days

"ADDED to all the other worriations she has in her life," said Simple, "my Cousin Minnie has now got another dog here in Harlem."

"What kind of dog?" I asked.

"A French poodle," said Simple.

"How on earth did Minnie get a French poodle?"

"From some old white lady for whom Minnie did some day's work. That old lady's poodle had poodles, and one of them puppy poodles became so attached to Minnie that the old lady asked Minnie if she had anywhere to keep a dog—if so, she could have it.

"Minnie said, 'I got a six-room apartment,' which were the biggest lie ever told, because Minnie has hardly got a six-foot room. Anyhow, the lady gave her the dog, and Minnie brought it home, all clipped and shaved with neck ruffs and leg ruffs like French poodles has when they is barbered right. But now that its hair is growing out again, that poodle looks like any other dirty white rag-ball of a dog to me."

"A French poodle is an aristocratic kind of dog," I said, "which needs to be taken care of in high style, washed weekly, and clipped by experts. I doubt if Minnie has the time or money to give that dog the kind of care it needs to show off its pedigree properly."

"You may doubt it, but I *know* it, she hasn't," said Simple. "Minnie has already sung that dog its theme song, 'I Can't Give You Anything but Love.' She is fond of that dog, God knows, but my cousin has no business with a animal. There are too many dogs in Harlem as it is. She should have left that dog out on Long Island where it could run and romp with its own kind. A French poodle has no more business in a furnished room than a polar bear has in hell. Minnie cannot even afford to buy it dog food, let alone keep it trimmed and clipped. Why, that dog was even perfumed when she got it."

"What does Minnie feed it?" I asked.

"Scraps," said Simple, "on which it seems to thrive. Fact is, it is getting fat."

"French poodles are not supposed to get fat. They should be dieted so as to keep their figures long, slim, and trim."

"This poodle will soon be big as Minnie, I expect," said Simple, "also as dark, if she do not give it a bath soon."

"Poor thing!" I said. "What did Minnie name the dog?"

"Jane," said Simple.

"Why?" I asked.

"Because when Minnie first got it, it being a female, Minnie was always saying, 'That Jane sure is cute.' So she just named her Jane. Now, me, myself, I would not like to have no dog have a person's name. I would have called it Little Bits or Fluff or Snowball or Frenchie or Snoodles, something like that. How many dogs do you reckon there is in Harlem?"

"Certainly thousands," I said, "all over the place."

"I thought Harlem was going to the dogs," said Simple. "Anyhow, there are more dogs in the United States than there are Negroes."

"I did not know that," I said. "Where did you get hold of such a piece of information?"

"From the World Almanac which my wife buys every year," said

Simple. "There are only about twenty million Negroes in America. But the World Almanac states there are twenty-two million dogs. Do you believe they count dogs more careful than they count Negroes?"

"It is easier to keep track of dogs because each dog has to have a license," I said. "Therefore most of them are registered."

"Negroes do not have to have a license," said Simple, "so it is not so easy to count us. Neither do we belong to anybody. But I'll bet back in slavery time every Negro was counted, and if one head was missing, the bloodhounds were sent after him. I would hate to be a slave chased by a bloodhound. In fact, I read somewhere once where in them days a good bloodhound was worth more than a good Negro, because a bloodhound were trained to keep the Negroes in line. If a bloodhound bit a Negro, nothing were done to the dog. In fact, Negroes were supposed to be bit."

"You can come up with the strangest information," I said.

"White folks do the strangest things," said Simple. "Imagine training a dog to chase Negroes! The kind of dog I would like to get acquainted with, me, myself, is that kind that walks around with a licker flask tied under his chin over there in them Swiss mountains, and if you need it, he will give you a drink."

"Saint Bernards," I said.

"Them dogs are saints," said Simple, "bearing drinks. I would like to have me a big dog like that, a dog that would not yip-yap-yip, but bark, BARK, BARK—I mean a real bass bark. I would like a dog-dog, not a play-dog, you know, a boxer, or a collie, or a nice old flop-eared hound. Not no poodle nor nothing like that. Neither no Doberman pinscher, which is too nervous a dog for me. And my dog would not have to own no pedigree. I do not want no dog finer than myself. But I sure would have me a dog if Joyce would let me."

"Your wife doesn't care for dogs?" I asked.

"She do, but not in a New York apartment," said Simple. "Joyce claims a dog should have a yard to run in and romp in, and also she has no time to be taking a dog out to walk on no lease mornings before she goes to work and evenings when it is time to cook dinner. Joyce says she knows I would not get up in time to do so, and when I come in from work I would be too tired, which is right. I reckon the real place for a dog is in the country where he could find a dogwood tree, and not have to depend on no fireplug. And speaking of dogwood trees, it were beneath one that I first found love in dog days in Virginia one August when the church had a picnic and that girl's grandma let me eat out of her picnic basket—since she thought I was hanging around because I wanted chicken. But what I really wanted was that girl, so we snuck off to the edge of the ravine and I kissed her beneath a dogwood tree."

"Why do you bring that up?" I asked.

"To revive my remembrance," said Simple. "Dog days and dogwood—doggone! And the chicken were good, too!"

Weight in Gold

"LIKE Billy Eckstine and Frank Sinatra's son, I wish I was rich enough to be kidnapped," said Simple, "because if I was, I would have done spent all my money before the kidnapping happened. I would never let them hold me for ransom, because the ransom money would be gone. I would just say, 'Boys, you have come too late. My pockets and my bank account is both now turned inside out. I have run through my million. Better to have had and spent than never to have had at all.' "

"My dear fellow," I countered, "if you ever possessed a great deal of money, say a million or so, you would find it next to impossible to spend it all. Besides, if you were sensible, you would invest the principal and live on the interest, like most rich people do."

"I would not be sensible," said Simple. "If I had money, I would go stark-raving mad and spend it! I could not stand being rich. There is so much I have wanted in past days, and so much I still want now—I would just spend it all, yes. And what I did not spend, I would give away to peoples I love. I would give Joyce, my wife, One Hundred Thousand Dollars. I would look up Zarita, that old gal of mine, and, for old times' sake, I would give her Fifty Thousand Dollars. To you, Boyd, my old beer buddy, I would give Twenty-five Thousand, and to my Cousin Minnie, Ten, so she would not have to borrow from me any more. Also, I would present Minnie with a brand-new wig, since she lost hers in the riots. And for every neighbor kid I know, I would buy a bicycle, because I think every boy—and girl, too, if they wants—should have a bicycle while young."

"In this New York traffic, as heavy as it is, you would give kids bicycles?"

"They can always ride in Central Park," said Simple. "When I were a kid, I always wanted a bicycle, and nobody ever bought me one. To tell the truth, if I was rich I would buy myself a bicycle right now. Then next month I would buy me a motorcycle. I always wanted one of them to make noise on. Then after riding around on my motorcycle for a couple of weeks, I would buy me a small car, just big enough for me and Joyce. After which I would buy a *big* car, then a Town and Country, then a station wagon. After that I would get a foreign sports car. I would do this gradual, not letting the world know all at once that I am rich. Also, I would not like to be kidnapped until *all* the money were spent. I would like to have my fun first, then be kidnapped with my name in the papers. 'JESSE B. SEMPLE NABBED BY MOB. *Held for Ransom. Harlem Shaken by the News.*' "

"You would be missed in this bar," I said.

"If I was rich, I would own this bar," said Simple. "I would buy up all the bars in Harlem and keep the present white proprietors employed as managers. I would not draw no color line. Of course, if the white mens quit and did not want to work under me, black, I would go to HARYOU and ask them to send me some bright young colored managers."

"HARYOU?" I said. "HARYOU hardly supplies bartenders, does it?"

"I would not request bartenders," said Simple. "I would be employing colored *managers*. They tell me HARYOU is set up to give young Negroes a chance."

"Why, tell me, please, if you had money," I asked, "would you buy only bars? Why not restaurants, grocery stores, clothing shops, wiggeries?"

"Because bars has the quickest turnover," said Simple. "Besides, if I owned all the Harlem bars, I would have credit in each and every one of them. I would never have to ask anybody to buy me a beer. In fact, I would treat *you* every time we met. Oh, if I was rich, daddy-o, I would be a generous son-of-a-gun, specially with everybody I like. I not only like you, Boyd, but I admire you. You are colleged. You know, if I had money, I would send every young man and young woman in Harlem to college, that wanted to go. I would set up one of these offices that gives out money for education."

"You mean a Foundation for Fellowships," I said.

"And Girlships, too," declared Simple. "Womens and mens from Harlem would all be colleged by the time 1970 came. It do not take but four years to get colleged, do it?"

"That's right," I said, "depending on your application."

"I would tell all the boys and girls in Harlem to make their applications now," said Simple, "and I would see that they got through. White folks downtown would have no excuse any more to say we was not educated uptown, because I would pay for it."

"In other words, you would be Harlem's Ford Foundation," I said, "on a really big scale."

"Yes," said Simple, "because on my scales, every kid in Harlem is worth his weight in gold."

Sympathy

"SOME people do not have no scars on their faces," said Simple, "but they has scars on their hearts. Some people have never been beat up, teeth knocked out, nose broke, shot, cut, not even so much as scratched in the face. But they have had their hearts broke, brains disturbed, their minds torn up, and the behinds of their souls kicked by the ones they love. It is not always your wife, husband, sweetheart, boy friend or girl friend, common-law mate—no, it might be your mother that kicks your soul around like a football. It might be your best friend that squeezes your heart dry like a lemon. It might be some ungrateful child you have looked forward to making something out of when it got grown, but who goes to the dogs and bites you on the way there. Oh, friend, your heart can be scarred in so many different ways it is not funny," said Simple.

"Why do you bring up such unpleasant subjects on a pleasant evening?" I asked. "We have got two nice cold glasses of beer sitting up here in front of us at the bar, and we could be talking about President Johnson and his budget problems."

"Or about Adam Powell and the lady they say he called an old bag-woman," said Simple.

"Or about who kidnapped Billy Eckstine and took the ransom out of his own pocket," I added.

"Else why Cassius Clay stuck by Elijah Muhammad instead of Malcolm X."

"Or why Malcolm X changed his name to Malik El-Shabazz."

"Or how come, if you are a Black Muslim, a man can change his name any time he wants to," said Simple.

"We could even be talking about the weather," I said.

"Or the price of eggs," agreed Simple. "But I am talking about how a man's heart or a woman's is *not* an egg, and, broken though your heart may be, it is seldom busted. It is a good thing folks cannot crack the heart and drop the insides in a frying pan like an egg. It is a good thing a man cannot make an omelette out of your trouble. Your ticker may be battered, mistreat it as you might, but that old heart keeps on beating until you die *d-e-a-d* dead."

"Who did what to your heart, old man, that you keep on harping on the same subject this evening? Did your wife look at you cross-eyed when you came home from work tonight? Is Joyce on the rampage?"

"No," said Simple. "My subject has nothing to do with myself. I am standing here thinking about Cousin Minnie. In spite of her faults, Minnie is a good woman, although somewhat overweight, and inclined to borrow money from her relatives when she ought to get out and earn it herself. Last year, you know, Cousin Minnie thought she had found a good man who would neither beat her nor cheat her, kick or mistreat her, and would never go upside her head. This man did not do such heavy-handed things. But he did worse. Hainsworth lived a lie in Minnie's presence. He kept another woman around the corner with who he spent half the night. When Hainsworth come home to Minnie, it were almost time to get up and go to work. But this was not so bad. He told this other woman things on Minnie that a man should not tell God. He talked about Minnie like a dog outside the home, and this is what hurted Minnie the most—that this other woman should know more about her than she knowed about herself—and from Hainsworth."

"How did Minnie find out all this?" I asked.

"At the beauty shop," said Simple, "which is where womens exchange news, regardless of who is listening over the partitions. In Harlem the beauty shop booths is so close together, anybody is liable to hear anything. And Minnie overheard it from the horse's mouth—the other woman's—direct, herself—even as to what kind of skin lightener Minnie uses before she goes to bed. Also that Minnie has a strawberry birthmark on her left-hand thigh—which nobody could know to tell anybody except Hainsworth."

"I'll be dogged!" I said.

"Yes," said Simple, "that is what broke Minnie's heart."

"Temporarily, I hope."

"Minnie will recover," said Simple.

"Such little things," I said, "should hardly break a woman's heart."

"A small pin can puncture a big balloon," stated Simple. "Minnie's pride were like a big balloon and her love for Hainsworth were great—until she found out he had told this other woman all them things. She said to the whole beauty shop that Minnie could not even boil rice proper, neither fry fish crisp, that she made soggy biscuits and bitter coffee, and also Minnie looked like a pig in a poke when she come to bed."

"Great day!" I exclaimed. "What did Minnie say to Hainsworth?"

"She hit him in the head with a small hammer," said Simple.

"What? Where is he now?"

"In Harlem Hospital with a knot on his noggin like a hen's egg, also a split over his left eye which dead sure will leave a scar. But Minnie has a scar on her heart—which is worse," said Simple. "Also Minnie has lost her faith in men, plus losing her meal ticket. Hainsworth were a good provider. Only trouble was, he were feeding two womens. Now both of them will suffer with him off the job. Had not that other girl blabbed so much in that beauty shop, both of them womens could have had a good dinner tonight."

"That's a shame," I said.

"Yes, it is a shame," said Simple. "To have a scar on your heart is bad enough, but to have nothing in your stomach is worse."

"That's bad," I agreed.

"Yes," affirmed Simple. "That *is* bad, especially since lately Minnie has not been feeling well. Do you know what she told me last night? Out of the clear blue sky in this bar Minnie said, 'Jess, the doctors say I have a tumor, and when they say that, you are liable to have cancer,' said Miss Minnie. 'I am going to the hospital on Monday, Jess Semple. Goodbye.'

" 'Just like that, you say goodbye tonight? And you are going home this early?'

" 'Yes,' said Miss Minnie. 'I did not tell you I was sick before, I do not tell you I am sick now. But I am. Monday I go to be prepared for the operation. Maybe it might not take, like vaccination. If it do not take, I am gone to Glory. If I go to Glory, maybe you will remember me who set beside you once on this bar stool. And if not, or if so, anyhow, goodbye.'

" 'Cousin, are you sure enough really sick? Are you telling me straight?'

" 'Yes, straight—and it's late. Goodbye.'

" 'Late what?'

" 'Just late, that's all. Goodbye.' And she left."

"She left?"

"Yes."

"Just like that?"

"Just like that. Minnie did not even tell me what hospital she would be in—Harlem, Bellevue, Medical Center, or where. She just left. Minnie would borrow money from me at the drop of a hat. Yes, she would. But I guess she don't want to borrow sympathy."

"No?"

"No," said Simple, "I guess she don't. She just up and left."

Money and Mice

"NOW, you take my boss," said Simple. "I come to work earlier than he do, I work longer, and I leave later. But that white man makes one hundred times more money than I do. Why is that?"

"That is because he uses his brains, he can do what you can't do, and he knows more than you ever know," I said.

"That is no reason why he should get all *that much more* money—because if it wasn't for what I do, there wouldn't be no results coming from what he know. I turn out what he thinks out.

Who does the work in the plant? Me, and mens like me. Old boss comes to work at 10 a.m. and before you can turn around, he has gone out to lunch again. He comes back from lunch at 3 p.m. and goes home at four-thirty before the traffic gets heavy, also so he can stop for a drink at the club. He takes a looo-oo-ong weekend, leaves the office of the plant on Thursday afternoon and don't come back no more until Tuesday morning. Yet I am there working all day long, each and every day during the week. But he gets the most pay, for the *least* hours, for doing the least."

"You have to realize, old man, that what your boss does, he does in his head."

"Yes, but what I do, I do on the job, and with hard labor at that. What he sells, I help to make. My boss can't turn out nothing just from his head that anybody can see and feel and buy. His head can't turn out no products."

"No, but his products start in his head," I said.

"But they end in my hands," said Simple. "So ain't my hands worth as much as his head?"

"Unfortunately, no," I said. "Smart heads are rare—but handy hands are common. Almost anybody can drive a nail or use a lathe. But not everybody can think up new furniture styles, for example. Your boss is an industrial designer, a planner, and a merchandiser."

"But I make the merchandise," insisted Simple. "I make it. I do not care who thinks it up—I MAKE it."

"But if somebody didn't think it up, what would you have to make?"

"I'd make something else," said Simple. "And I figure that MAKING is as important as THINKING. Besides, anybody can think quicker than they can do. I can think of all kinds of things in a minute that it would take me days to make. For one minute's thought, should I get ten days' pay?"

"If you think wisely and well enough, in a single minute, it is conceivable that you might merit more than ten days' pay. What a creative mind can conceive in a short time might be worth more than what many hands can do in a long time. For example, take

Edison—when he thought up the electric light bulb, imagine what a gift of light he gave humanity. But the concept of a bulb, the original design, had to first come out of Edison's mind. Did he not deserve great monetary awards for thinking up such a boon to mankind as the electric light?"

"Edison might could think up one light, and make one light. But to make all the millions of bulbs used today, it takes factories full of men working all day long, and with their hands, like I work, and at machines, to make all them bulbs. And them mens deserves their awards, too. If they never think thoughts, their hands make things that thoughts have already thought up. And thoughts without hands would not account to a thing. All I am trying to say is, let me who makes the things get some of the money, too, and some of the short hours, too, and the long weekends, too. And don't let the man with the mind make a hundred times more a day than the man with the hands. I am the man with the hands."

"Friend," I said, "I have never heard you discuss any one subject so long before without bringing in race and color. When are you going to bring it all around to race?"

"I am not thinking about race today," said Simple. "What I am thinking about is how we is all caught in a trap, and how prices has gone up so high that a man, no matter what his race and color, needs to make more money to live. I am thinking about money, which is green, neither black nor white—money, which do not care who spends it; money, which don't feel as good to me in somebody else's pocket as it does in mine. Friend, I am thinking about money—which goes beyond race. If all the Negroes in the world had money, the color problem would be solved in the morning. In this American country, money makes a man a MAN, otherwise he is nothing but a mouse. To be men or miceses, that is the problem. And I sure would hate to be a mice."

"You would hate to be a mouse," I corrected.

"I mean a mouse," said Simple, "because I see in the papers where doctors and laboratories and such used up twenty million mice in the U.S.A. last year testing out new medicines and needles and things on them. I would hate to belong to any part of the mice family, white or otherwise, and be snatched up and vaccinated with some kind of needle to see if I am going to catch whatever it is they are testing for. I pity them poor animals—born to die with fevers and things before their time."

"Don't you think it is better mice serve some useful purpose than just getting caught in a trap baited with cheese and having their necks broken in the corner of somebody's kitchen? At least in the laboratory a mouse has a function. New drugs that cannot be tried out on human beings may be tested on mice, and their effects noted. Also diseases, by inoculating mice. Thus they serve the cause of science."

"If I was a mouse, I would hate to have my life cut short for science or anybody else," said Simple. "I had rather take my chances on the trap and the cheese. Let me pick my own trap and fall in it. Life ain't nothing but a trap, nohow, and inside the big trap is all kinds of little traps. But I don't want nobody to up and throw me in no trap just to see how I will react. That paper said the reactions of the mouses were being studied as to how they reacted when they are injected. A mice in a trap do not have to react, because his neck is broke. He is dead. I had rather be dead than stuck with a needle to see how I will react. And you would, too, wouldn't you?"

"I would hate to be a guinea pig," I agreed, "or a mouse in a laboratory. But then I would hate to be a mouse anyway."

"I would hate to be a man were I not already one," said Simple. "I have never heard of animals sticking another one with a needle to see how it would react, or putting him to sleep just to see if he will wake up again. Animals do not do no such things to each other. Only mens do such to animals."

"Your holier-than-thou attitude toward science is surprising," I said. "You eat pork chops, but a pig has to be killed to get those chops for you. You eat beefsteak, veal, lamb, chicken, and in all cases some animal has to face his end to feed your belly. So why this sudden compassion for mice—just because you happen to read a little article on medical research in the papers today?"

"Sometimes it do not take much to start me to thinking," said Simple. "Twenty million is an awful lot of mice. And now you have started me to thinking more. Every time I eat a piece of meat, some animal has died so that I might eat and live. You are right! Lord, come to think of it, when I die the worms will eat me. Chickens will eat the worms. Folks will eat the chickens. Then where will I be? What kind of trap is we all caught in, I ask you? And me with no money, neither!"

Population Explosion

"NOW that winter has come and it is getting real cold on Lenox Avenue," said Simple, "some nights I just stay home and read the papers, in which I see a lots these days about the population explosion and how we ought to be doing something about it."

"What *we*?" I asked.

"We white folks," said Simple. "Did you not see in the papers last week where a blue-ribbon citizens' committee has propositioned to the White House that our American nation spend One Hundred Million Dollars on birth control? If that be so, we intends to go hog-wild. It looks like to me not One Hundred Million but just one *single* million would be enough to subsidize every drug store in the United States and buy ten times enough birth-control things for every man, woman, and child in the country."

"What things exactly do you mean?" I asked.

"I hear it is against the law to tell anybody what them things' names is because that would be birth control—which is only to be *did*—not spoken about. You know that?"

"I am afraid I am not an authority on birth control," I said, "not being a married man."

"You should be *authority the most*," said Simple, "also the most careful. The way many a unmarried man has got hooked is by *not* being an authority. But I suppose you can learn, since a great deal of that One Hundred Million, the newspaper states, might be spent on education."

"Certainly a lot of people are unfamiliar with birth-control devices," I said.

"They should not be if they is over ten years old," declared Simple. "But a lot of education would have to be translated, anyhow."

"Translated?" I inquired.

"Yes," affirmed Simple, "for colored—into jive talk for Harlem, into Indian for Indians, Gypsy for Gypsies, and Chinese for China."

"Why are you naming just colored folks?" I inquired.

"Because that is who the white folks is aiming birth control at, is it not?" asked Simple. "They always talking about there is nine hundred million people in India and in another ten years there will be ten hundred million. And in China there is seven hundred million, which will be ten hundred million by 1992. Africa has got so many million Africans that white folks do not even count them, and many is too dark to see. Every so often our white folks hints at Harlem, too, but they do not dare come right out and say we has a population explosion on Lenox Avenue. They just say 90 percent of the free maternity wards in Manhattan is occupied by colored."

"I see in today's paper where the American Medical Association indicates favor of birth control, even of sterilization and abortion when advisable."

"They got all kinds of Health Wagons going up and down the streets of Harlem now, free X rays, free vaccine shots and things. But nobody has to take them. Suppose, though, they passed a birth-control law and the Supreme Court upheld the right of the city to cut down by law on the uptown population explosion and they sent a Sterilization Wagon to Harlem. Naturally, like they did with HAR-YOU-ACT, they would try it out on colored folks first, calling themselves being helpful to 'poor underprivileged Harlem,' curbing the population explosion. But you know and I know, Harlem do not want to be stopped from exploding. They better send that Sterilization Wagon to Vietnam, where they can gas the people into being caught and made prisoners and sterilized. Suppose we fought the whole war with Sterilization Wagons? That would be one way to wipe out all future Vietcongs for generations to come."

"But suppose the Vietcong captured a lot of our Sterilization Wagons and then used them against American troops," I said.

"Negotiations for peace would begin at once," said Simple. "White folks are not thinking about being sterilized, neither in war nor in peace. It is India, China, Africa, and Harlem they is considering—One Hundred Million Dollars' worth of birth control for us! You know, I really do believe white folks always got something up their sleeve for colored folks. Yes, they has!"

Youthhood

"I WONDER where," said Simple, "did I leave my youthhood?"

"And why such wonderment?" I asked.

"When I go upstairs now, I pants," said Simple, "out of breath."

"You go upstairs too fast," I said.

"I used to go upstairs and I did not pant," said Simple, "so I must be getting ageable."

"I trust nothing worse is happening to you than shortness of breath."

"Not yet," said Simple. "I still has all my functions—and hope to have until I get to my second childhood."

"I trust you are not one of these people who want to go back to their childhood: 'Oh, to be a child again just for tonight.' "

"Not I," said Simple. "I do not want to be no child again, especially at night. Nighttime is when I were the most lonesome, when I were a child. And I would be lonesome now was it not for Joyce. As for going back to my youthhood, not me! No, never! In my youthhood I did not have nothing I wanted, and it looked like I did not even know what I was looking for. No, I do not want to be young again, not me."

"I am glad to hear you say that," I said, "because it always seems sort of silly to me hearing grown-up folks say they would like to be children again—to avoid cares and responsibilities, I suppose. But it is such a futile wish."

"I say again, not me," said Simple. "I had more cares and responsibilities when I were a child than I have now. Grown-up peoples were a worriation to me. Every time I got attached to somebody I was living with, I got shifted to somebody else. I were a passed-around child. The only relative that really wanted me, and loved me, were my old Aunt Lucy. And to tell the truth, she were nothing but a step-aunt. But Aunt Lucy tried to raise me right. She whipped me almost every day. She tried to rid me of my badness, but the only way she knowed was prayers and whippings. But I tried to do better, and I did better, and I growed up to be a man, all on account of Aunt Lucy. I give that old lady credit. But I would not want to be no child again. 'Spare the rod and spoil the child' was the motto in them days—and my behind is still sore.

"Were I to have a child, I do not believe I would lay nothing heavier on it than the palm of my hand, and I would go light on that. I would use psychology on a child—unless I lost my patience. In which case I would spank it just enough to make it scared. I might lose my patience again, but I would hate to really get mad and whip it. Grown-up peoples should not get mad with a child, even when they aggravate you. We is too much bigger and too much older than children to get mad at them. Children has nowhere else to live except with grown peoples, and when you get mad with children, you make them feel like you do not want them any more.

"A little small child cannot take care of his self, neither can a teen-ager who has no experience in the world. So the worst thing you can do to a child or a teen-ager is to make him feel like you do not want him around. All them relatives of mine that made me feel that way in my youthhood is a stone in my heart right now. But Aunt Lucy never did make me feel like she did not want me around. Even when she whipped me, I knowed she loved me. Which makes all the difference in the world. But if I had a child, I do not believe I would ever even whip it."

"You would probably spoil it," I said. "You know, the psychologists say there is such a thing as too much love."

"I do not believe there ever is," said Simple.

Hail and Farewell

"I AM practically gone," said Simple.

"Gone home tonight, you mean?" I asked.

"Further than home," declared Simple, "and longer than tonight."

"To Glory?" I said. "Or Vietnam?"

"Worse," said Simple. "I am going to the suburbans."

"To the suburbs? How come? Listen, what's happening, huh?"

"Joyce has saved enough money to make a down payment on a house, that's what's happening. You know my wife always wanted a house. She is now going to make a down payment," said Simple. "The first week of the first of the year 1966, my Joyce—who controls the budget and our Carver Savings Bank book—which is *not* a *joint* account—is having the cashier make out a certified check to this real estate agent who has done sold my wife a house so far away from Harlem you have to get off the train at the dead end of the subway, then take a bus to get to our street, then walk three blocks after that to reach this house which my wife is making me buy. I will be shoveling snow, stoking the furnace, and putting washers in sinks for the rest of my natural life."

Simple took a long drink from his beer glass; in fact, he drained it, then signaled the bartender for another.

"You don't sound too happy about it," I said.

"I am not," moaned Simple. "I had rather have a kitchenette in Harlem than a mansion on Long Island or a palace in Westchester. A lawn with grass to mow and leaves to rake is the *last* thing I want. And God knows I do not like to shovel snow. No, I do not like shoveling snow! *No!*"

"Maybe you can pay the little boy next door to shovel snow," I said.

"Suppose there is not a little boy next door," said Simple. "Or suppose he is white."

"Are not you-all moving into an integrated neighborhood?" I asked.

"Joyce says we will be the first Negroes in the block," said Simple. "That will also be a drag. I likes to be around my people. But Joyce says it is our duty to show white folks we can keep a house up as well as anybody else. I know Joyce will work me to death keeping that house spick-and-span inside and out, just to show white people Negroes are not tramps. Colored folks have always got to be worried about what white folks thinks. Joyce says they do not meet enough representative Negroes—whatever kind that is—so when we move we are going to show our neighbors a neighborhood do not run down just because colored peoples move in."

"Suppose your neighbors object to your presence, start throwing stones at your windows and things like that, then what?"

"They say our neighborhood is integrated, but the block is not. It is still an all-white block this week, but FOR SALE signs are up everywhere. It will be an all-colored block before you can say *Jackie Robinson*. Joyce and me will be breaking the ice in January—then the real estate agents will do the rest—selling houses to Negroes at twice the price. Me and Joyce will be 999 years paying off our mortgage—and I will be still sending back payments from the Golden Gates. To me there is not a suburb in the world worth the price they is charging us for our house. But Joyce always did say she wanted a house with trees and a big back yard, and a picture window in the front room. I told Joyce we liable to look out the window someday and see the Ku Klux Klan in hoods and robes standing there. I asked her is there any Deacons for Defense amongst our colored neighbors in the next block. But Joyce says the real estate man assured her there is not trouble in the offing. Just pay our money down and move in, he says. But, Boyd, I do not want to move out of Harlem. I will miss Harlem, Seventh Avenue, Lenox, the Apollo, and the Palms, also this little old bar in which I am now drinking. I will also miss my friends—and you."

"I'll come over some Sunday and pay you a call," I said. "In fact, I will come to your housewarming—if it is not in the wintertime."

"I do not blame you for not wanting to wade through snow from the end of the bus line," said Simple. "But if you really be's my friend, you will come over once in a while just to cheer me up. I will need it, way out yonder by my lonesome, without a juke box nowhere in earshot. And unless we build a playroom in our basement, there will not be a bar in sight—only a carton of beer from the supermarket, which I will have to fetch myself in case Joyce will break our budget to raise my beer allowance. Joyce will have to do something to keep me happy in the suburbans, I'm telling you. I been a Harlemite too long to be a suburbanite, even if I am getting a bit ageable. Joyce states we are old enough to settle down now, stop paying rent to landlords, and live like decent folks in our prime. What does she mean by *prime*?"

"Prime," I said, "means the time in life when the experiences of youth and the wisdom of maturity meet to give you a balanced viewpoint on living—the time when a man is really ready to live."

"If that be true, then," said Simple, "why leave the place where life is—to go live with the birds, the bees, and caterpillars and bats? Life to me is where *peoples* is at—not nature and snow and trees with falling leaves to rake all by yourself, and furnaces to stoke, and no landlords in earshot to holler at downstairs to keep the heat up, and no next-door neighbors on your floor to raise a ruckus Saturday nights, and no bad children drawing pictures on the walls in the halls, and nobody to drink a beer with at the corner bar—because that corner in the suburbans has nothing on it but a dim old lonesome street light on a cold old lonesome pole. And to get to Harlem from where you live you have to walk to a bus line, then ride to a subway line, then change at Times Square for the A train to Harlem. Friend, when I move to the suburbans, I am gone. So bye-bye-bye-bye! Goodbye! Yes, Jesse B. Semple is gone."

Sources of Stories

Simple Speaks His Mind (1950)
Ways and Means; The Law; After Hours; When a Man Sees Red; Nickel for the Phone; Possum, Race, and Face

Simple Takes a Wife (1953)
Better than a Pillow; Explain That to Me; Baltimore Womens; Less than a Damn; Never No More; Simply Heavenly; Staggering Figures; Joyce Objects; The Necessaries; That Word *Black*; Colleges and Color; Whiter than Snow; Nothing but Roomers; Simple Santa

Simple Stakes a Claim (1957)
Big Round World

The Langston Hughes Reader (1958)
That Word *Black*

Simple's Uncle Sam (1965)
The Moon; Domesticated; Self-protection; Ladyhood; Lynn Clarisse; American Dilemma; Coffee Break; Adventure; Wigs for Freedom; Soul Food; Roots and Trees; Empty Houses; God's Other Side; Dog Days; Weight in Gold; Sympathy

Langston Hughes Manuscripts, James Weldon Johnson Collection, The Beinecke Library, Yale University
Remembrances; Wigs, Women, and Falsies; Hairdos; Cousin Minnie Wins; Riddles; Color of the Law; Everybody's Difference; Intermarriage; Brainwashed; Help, Mayor, Help!; Pictures; Simple Arithmetic; Africa's Daughters; African Names; Harems and Robes; Money and Mice; Youthhood

Chicago Defender newspaper columns

On Women Who Drink You Up (June 24, 1944); Simple and the High Prices (April 19, 1947); Liberals Need a Mascot (May 21, 1949); Serious Talk about the Atom Bomb (August 18, 1945); Simple's Psychosis (May 18, 1946)

New York Post newspaper columns

Little Klanny (August 14, 1965); Population Explosion (December 10, 1965); Hail and Farewell (December 31, 1965)

Printed in the United States
59814LVS00002B/247-252